SAMUEL

THUNDER IN PARADISE

OTHER BOOKS AND AUDIO BOOKS
BY CLAIR M. POULSON:

Blind Side

Conflict of Interest

Cover Up

I'll Find You

Lost and Found

Mirror Image

Relentless

Runaway

Evidence

SAMUEL

THUNDER IN PARADISE

A NOVEL

CLAIR M. POULSON

Covenant Communications, Inc.

Cover art by Nathan Pinnock

Cover design copyrighted 1996 by Covenant Communications, Inc.

Published by Covenant Communications, Inc.
American Fork, Utah

This is a work of fiction. The characters, names, incidents, places, and dialogue are products of the
author's imagination, and are not to be construed as real.

Printed in Canada
First Printing: July 1996

12 11 10 09 08   11 10 9 8 7 6 5 4 3

ISBN 13: 978-1-59811-382-2
ISBN 10: 1-59811-382-8

To my son Wade for the tremendous ideas that he shared with me.
They contributed so much to this work.

CHAPTER 1

"Father! Father! I'm afraid!"

Samuel rolled groggily onto his side, away from his wife, and sat up at the edge of their soft grass mat. "Maribel," he called. "It's all right. It's just another storm."

"No, Father . . ." the little girl screamed, but the rest of her words were smothered by another loud crack of thunder. Then she found her father's arms, and Samuel swept her to his breast.

"What is the matter with Maribel, dear?" Ophera asked sleepily as she stirred beside them.

"The storm, Ophera. It has frightened Maribel."

Thunder cracked again, and a jagged streak of lightning lit the swaying palm trees outside the window. Samuel held his nine-year-old daughter tightly. Her small forehead lay against his cheek, and it felt clammy and cool. Ophera's arms encircled them both, and her long blond hair hung across Samuel's chest and brushed the little girl's cheeks. Between thunderclaps, she said tenderly, "It will soon be over, Maribel. You may lie here with us until morning. There is nothing to be afraid of."

Indeed, during the ten years that Samuel and his family had lived on this temperate island, there had been little to fear. Storms such as this one had come and gone many times. They occasionally left the landscape marred. But always, within a few short weeks, lush vegetation had grown back, covering the scars with a rich new layer of flowering green.

Samuel thought of this island haven as his paradise, and he smiled as he lay beside his pretty wife and daughter, listening to the fury of the storm. The thunder soon ceased, the wind abated, and rain fell in rhythmic torrents.

Until God had brought Samuel, his friends, his family, and a few others to this secluded section of the earth, Samuel had battled evil men. Here he occasionally fought the elements, and defeats, when they came, were unimportant and short-lived.

The island was filled with wild animals and birds. A variety of sweet fruits, coconuts, and wild roots were always available to supplement the crops and gardens the dozen families on the island so carefully cultivated. Samuel and Ophera had truly come to love their peaceful life on this island paradise.

"Father, is he gone?" Maribel asked, surprising Samuel in his peaceful thoughts. He had thought she was asleep in his arms.

"Is who gone?" he asked, reaching for one of her little hands. It was moist and trembling.

"The ugly man at my window," Maribel said, and a sob of fear brought her head against Samuel's chin.

"Maribel, it is just a storm," he began soothingly. "You must have seen a shadow or . . ."

"There was a man there, Father," Maribel interrupted with conviction in her voice.

Lying still beside her husband and daughter, Ophera asked quietly, "Was your brother teasing you?"

"It wasn't Jath! It was an ugly face, and his nose was bent," Maribel said earnestly.

"That doesn't sound like any of the men on the island," Ophera said lightly. "I'm sure you were having a bad dream, Maribel."

"I was awake, Mother," Maribel retorted with disgust. "I know when I've been dreaming."

"But no one would be out on a stormy night like this," Ophera reasoned calmly.

"He was looking in my window. I saw his face when the lightning made it shine," Maribel said. "He was grinning an awful grin, and he didn't even have all his teeth. His beard and hair were wet."

"What color was his hair?" Samuel asked, though still not convinced that his daughter had really seen someone.

"Black, and it was long and stringy. His beard was black, too, and so were his eyebrows. They were big," Maribel said earnestly.

This caught Samuel's attention. "His eyebrows?" he asked. "You noticed his eyebrows?"

"Yes, Father. They were like huge, black fuzzy caterpillars, and his eyes were like tiny black beads. They were staring right at me!" she went on, and Samuel felt still another tremor of fear rack her slender body.

Samuel's hand groped for Ophera's in the darkness, and he said softly, more to himself than to her, "Long black hair and beard, small black eyes, big eyebrows, and a crooked nose." His mind instantly reverted back to an enemy he had known and fought in his youth.

Antium!

He shook his head in confusion. But Antium was dead, killed by a monstrous snake in front of Samuel's own eyes. With his bare hands and the help of his Lamanite friend Gadoni, Samuel had buried the evil man's half-eaten carcass beside a river. He shuddered at the memory. Old Antium had been a terrible foe.

"Samuel, what is it?" Ophera took his hand. "Surely you don't believe Maribel actually saw someone, do you?"

Samuel detected a quiver of doubt in her voice, and he squeezed her hand. "I don't know," he said, trying to shake off the spell that the memory of his evil old enemy had cast upon him. "But Maribel seems very sure. I'll check around. You stay here with her."

Maribel went willingly to her mother's arms. A moment later, Samuel stood in his daughter's small room and stared at her window. It was lit now by only occasional flashes of distant lightning. He tried to envision the face of Antium in the window, but he could not. It was just too ridiculous. Antium was dead these many years, and there could not be another like him.

He turned and stepped lightly to the room across the hall where his son Jath, a strapping youth of seventeen, lay sleeping. He reached to touch him, then drew back. Jath's breaths were light and even, and Samuel thought it foolish to awaken him. Instead, he turned to the door.

"Father, is that you?" his son's voice asked groggily.

Samuel turned back sheepishly. "Yes, son. I'm sorry I disturbed you. Go back to sleep."

"What is it, Father? It's not like you to wander about the house in the middle of the night. Is something wrong?"

Samuel smiled into the inky darkness at the barely discernable form of his son. How he loved this young man. So strong, so handsome, but most importantly, so very good. Samuel could never see the resemblance, but Ophera often stated that Jath was an exact replica of his father at that age. Oh, he did have the same strong build and brown hair, and his eyes were even the same shade of blue as his father's, but to Samuel he was more like his mother: softer features, tender feelings, and full of love and concern for others. *A bit of a tease, too, but what boys aren't?* he thought.

"Father?" Jath inquired again.

"Something frightened Maribel. I was just looking about."

"The storm, Father," Jath said with a chuckle. "It was rather fierce for a while."

"That's what your mother and I thought, too, but Maribel insists that she saw a man's face at her window."

Jath came to his feet with a bound, nearly colliding with Samuel. "I heard her scream, Father! Who could she have seen?"

Jath did tease her a lot, but he loved his little sister, and Samuel knew it. Samuel's heart quickened at the intensity of Jath's words. His son seemed to have no doubt that if Maribel said she saw a face, that indeed she had.

"I don't know who it could have been, Jath. It doesn't make sense," Samuel said uncertainly.

"Did she describe him?" Jath asked intently.

"Yes," Samuel answered, and he repeated her words to his son.

"A stranger, Father. An invader!" the young man said with conviction as he grabbed his father's arm. "Come, Father, let us light torches."

Minutes later, Samuel and Jath stood in a misty rain and stared in horror at a set of huge sandal tracks in the mud outside Maribel's window. A moment later, they were staring at the same tracks, only this time they were outside Jath's window. They moved apprehensively around the house in silence, but they found no further sign of the invader's large footprints except where they led past the drenched vegetable garden and into the dripping palms a hundred paces from the house.

"We must follow him, Father," Jath declared. "Maribel could be in danger."

"No, it would be too dangerous at night, Jath. We are not even armed. Anyway, we cannot leave your mother and sister alone."

"We have swords and bows in the house. I will arm myself and follow him," Jath declared stubbornly. "You stay and guard the house in case he returns."

Another of his mother's traits, Samuel thought grimly. He knew Jath would not be dissuaded, so he said, "You cannot go alone. Awaken—"

"Uri," Jath injected quickly.

Uri, a half-brother to Samuel, was now twenty, and he had recently built a small house a few hundred paces up the beach from Samuel. A very independent young man, he had insisted on not being a burden to Samuel and Ophera when he was capable of taking care of himself. Not that he intended to be alone forever, for he had his eye on one of the young women of the island.

Samuel and Ophera had raised him as their own from the time he was nine, following the death of his parents, who had been murdered by the Gadianton robbers. They had taken him with them into the wilderness when they fled the pursuit of those evil men.

Samuel was still reluctant to allow Jath, even with the able assistance of Uri, to chase off after an unknown enemy in the storm-racked night. The years of peace he had known after leaving the land of Zarahemla, a land where he had fought Lamanites, traitorous Nephites such as Antium, and the deadly Gadianton robbers, had left him with no desire for conflict.

"Jath, this is crazy. Someone must be joking with us," Samuel said in desperation. "There are no evil men on this island."

"Invaders, Father. We found this island and so could others."

"We were driven in a terrible storm to this island," Samuel corrected him.

"So we were, but we have traveled to other islands. Who is to say that someone could not do as we have done?" Jath reasoned.

His reasoning was sound. Under the able leadership of Captain Baronihah, the captain of the ship that had brought them in the fierce storm to this beautiful place ten years ago, they had often followed the stars, the currents, and the prevailing winds to uninhabited islands both north and south. But Samuel had never feared being discovered by others. Maybe it was because he hoped no one would ever come to disturb the serenity of the few who lived here. But doubts assailed him now as he stared down at the ground at the grim evidence of an evil and unwanted presence.

"Father, I must hurry," Jath said decisively, and Samuel followed him to the house, where they both retrieved their weapons from a deep closet. Then Samuel stood at the open door and watched with a heavy heart as Jath strode purposefully into the darkness with his glowing yellow torch.

"Sam?" Ophera called from over his shoulder. "Where is Jath going? And why are you both armed?" Samuel heard a hint of fear in her voice as she stepped beside him and slipped her slender hand into his larger one.

"There was someone out there, Ophera. Jath believes our island has been invaded."

Those words invoked a sharp intake of breath from his wife.

"He is going after Uri," Samuel continued. "They will follow the tracks if they can."

"But, Sam, they don't have your experience, and it is dark. Their torches will give them away," she said with more than a little concern.

"They have tracked much game, Ophera, and they have played at tracking one another. They are very bright and will be cautious," he said hopefully. "And remember, your brother, Josh, has taught them well. He is the best tracker I have ever known."

"But it is so dangerous. What if there really is a stranger . . . ?" she began, but a sob filled her throat and a small hand flew to her mouth in anguish.

Samuel glanced at her upturned face in the dancing light of his torch, and his heart filled his throat. How happy he and this beautiful woman had been on this rich and peaceful island. The threat of an evil man—or men, he thought with trepidation—could mar or even destroy the peace they had known. Jath was right. Invaders, if there truly were some on the island, must be destroyed or driven away at once. To Ophera he said, "Jath and Uri will try to locate whomever was here. Then, my dear, if they are an enemy, they must be quickly defeated. We cannot—will not—allow our peace to be destroyed."

"Oh, Sam," Ophera sighed as she clung tightly to Samuel.

"Is Maribel sleeping?"

"Yes, and quite soundly at last. Samuel, she had a bad fright."

"Yes, indeed she did. But we will wipe out the threat," he said with the determination he had always exhibited when confronted with evil. "The Lord led us here, and He will preserve us."

"Sam, let's pray," Ophera suggested earnestly.

* * *

As Samuel offered a sincere and powerful plea to the God he knew and loved and served, Jath and Uri hurried into the thick palm forest. They were not long in rediscovering, on the drenched ground, the large tracks of the very sandals that had supported a silent and sinister spy at Maribel's window. To their chagrin, those tracks were soon joined by another set of tracks, and then by a third!

"What if they see our torches?" Uri cautioned as they slowly trudged along through the trees.

"They are heading in the direction of Captain Baronihah's place," Jath said. "Let's extinguish our torches and go there. It will soon be dawn anyway, and we can go on in the daylight."

Both young men quickly put out the yellow flames and were mildly surprised that, through the thick clouds above, a touch of dim grey light was already breaking the long night's strangle-hold of darkness and gloom.

As they neared the sturdy house of the wise old shipbuilder and mariner and his family, Jath heard sobs. He glanced at Uri and knew at once that he, too, heard the soft crying. Uri leaned toward him and whispered, "Go softly, Jath. Something has happened here."

Jath nodded, and with a sudden fear in his heart, he followed Uri's lead and dropped to the wet ground. On their hands and knees, they crept forward through the shrubs and thick foliage that bordered the captain's house. A few paces from the door, the foliage gave way to coarse grass, short and matted. Something large and dark lay near the door.

Jath's heart suddenly felt cold as he recognized in the dim light the white of Captain Baronihah's hair and long beard. Dara, his wife, was folded over him sobbing, but she sat up and looked in their direction. Upon recognizing them, she dropped the weapon she still held in her hand, then rose and rushed, her arms outspread, toward the two young men. She embraced them both at once, crying softly.

Jath feared the worst as he stared over her shoulder at the still form of their beloved captain and friend. Baronihah, in his mid-fifties, was the oldest person on the island, and he was trusted and loved by all. He was ten years the senior of his good wife but had always been robust and in good health.

"Can we help?" Uri asked in a choked voice.

"Please," she said, breaking the embrace and leading them back to her husband, where she knelt once more. "Some men were here," she said in a low voice. "It was just a short while ago. Their voices were not familiar, and they were laughing in a coarse sort of way. My husband grabbed his sword and rushed out before I could stop him. There was a fight. I threw a knife. One of the men screamed, so I know I injured someone. Then they ran off, but by then the captain was . . ." She stopped, unable to go on.

"Is he . . . ?" Jath began apprehensively.

"He is still alive, but I fear that he may be near death," Dara uttered fearfully. "I stopped the bleeding, but he is so large I cannot move him."

"We'll help," Uri said at once.

It took only a few minutes for the two strong young men to carry Baronihah into the house while Dara lit a torch. They laid him gently on a soft mat, and Dara hung the torch in a wooden holder on the wall and began to gently stroke her husband's clammy brow and wet hair.

"Are your children okay?" Uri asked helplessly. Dara and Baronihah had two young children, a boy of nine and a little girl of seven.

"Yes," she responded, "and they're sleeping. They awoke during the worst of the storm, but went right back to sleep when the thunder ceased."

Relieved that they had slept through the violence, the first ever on this island paradise, Jath said, "Can we get someone to help you?"

She looked at him hopefully. "Do you think Samuel and Ophera would come?"

"Of course. I'll go—" Jath began, then broke off at the look of puzzlement that Dara suddenly cast his way.

"What . . . I mean, why are you boys out so early?" she asked with sudden concern. "And you are both armed? Have your folks had trouble, too?"

"One of the men frightened Maribel, but she is all right. He left. We were tracking him . . . them, actually," he explained. "We believe they have invaded the island."

Uri spoke up. "I'll stay with Dara, Jath. You get your parents. If we are to save the life of Baronihah, then we must be quick about it."

Jath spun obediently to the door and hurried back through the forest. He found his folks awake and huddled near the door. "Where is Uri?" Ophera cried in alarm as Jath rushed in alone.

"With Dara," Jath blurted. "There has been trouble. The invaders have injured the captain. He may be near death, and Dara asked me to—"

Ophera cut him off. "Sam, get Maribel. We must go at once," she said decisively.

"That is what she wanted," Jath said as Samuel grabbed his bow and arrows, then left the room and returned a moment later with Maribel held gently in his powerful arms. The little family then trudged with heavy hearts over the forested ridge toward the home of their beloved captain.

They found Dara still working furiously on her husband's numerous wounds. She looked up as they entered her home. "He seems a little better," she announced as Ophera knelt beside her. "Sam, will you bless him?"

Samuel did as he was bidden. He, as well as Baronihah, held the priesthood. Samuel had been ordained under the hands of the prophet Helaman before departing from the village of Gilead during the uprising of the Gadianton robbers and the invasion of the Lamanites more than ten years earlier.

When he had finished with his blessing, he stood and said, "I believe he will live, but he will be a sick man for a long time. He will need a lot of care."

"And he will receive it," Dara said firmly. Her eyes were moist, but her face showed clearly the relief that Samuel's words of faith had instilled in her heart.

Samuel turned to Jath and Uri. "You two must alert the other families. Forget the pursuit of the invaders for now. We must all assemble and plan our strategy to save our lives and the peace of this island."

Jath and Uri nodded obediently. "Go swiftly," Samuel went on. "I hope there are no more injured ones. Have everyone assemble here."

The twelve families who inhabited the island were scattered far around the northern portion of the island and included Samuel's brother Oreb and his wife, Kapilla. They had three young children. Her twin brothers, Kim and Kib, sturdy men of twenty-three, also lived with them. Beyond them, Gadoni and his family had settled. Still farther was the home of Nemti and Samuel's sister, Nonita, and their four little ones. Ophera's brother, Josh, and his wife, Eva, lived beyond Gadoni with their young son.

Scattered for several more miles were still other families who had chosen to inhabit this island while others, who had also been on the ship when it wrecked here ten years ago, had elected to go on in a newly built craft. Those who had not stayed had hoped to find the place where Hagoth, the famous shipbuilder, Helaman's brother, Corianton, and other Nephites dwelt.

As the young men ran swiftly on their assigned task, they talked breathlessly. "I hope that the others are all right," Uri said. "We are so vulnerable all scattered out like we are."

"But who could have ever known that evil men would find us here?" Jath countered gloomily.

"We will find and destroy them," Uri said fiercely.

"We must," Jath agreed.

It was now quite light, but a gentle drizzle persisted as they approached Oreb's house. They were relieved to find the family sleeping peacefully after the tumultuous night. Jath called through the door, "Oreb, wake up. There is trouble on the island."

Oreb stumbled sleepily to the door, followed by Kim and Kib. "What are you two up to?" he asked with a characteristic grin. "There couldn't be trouble. The storm wasn't that bad." Then his eyes took in their weapons, and the grin fled from his broad face. "Why the weapons?" he asked.

"The island has been invaded. Baronihah is seriously injured," Jath explained.

Oreb's face turned dark as the young men went on to tell him of the night's events and of Samuel's desire for them to gather for safety. He quickly assembled his family and strapped on his own weapons as the twins did the same. They rushed back toward the captain's house as Jath and Uri continued toward Gadoni's home.

It was midday before all the families had been alerted and early evening before all were assembled safely in the vicinity of the captain's place.

"Baronihah is much stronger. He is out of danger now," Samuel told Jath and Uri as the two exhausted, wet, and muddy young men returned behind the last of the island's families. "We will camp here and post a strong guard. In the morning, we will pursue the invaders if they are still on the island. We will not allow them to destroy our peace.

Jath and Uri were too tired to protest. They had spent a long and strenuous day gathering the people together. The general atmosphere among the people of the island was one of both exhaustion and fear. The storm had passed, but the threat of evil men hung over them like a black cloud. The children played, but they were subdued, even though the idea of evil men was new to them. They had never known anyone who was wicked, and they did not comprehend the full extent of the danger that now surrounded them.

Samuel and Gadoni spoke words of cheer to all, but even after ten years of peace, those who had known terror in the land of Zarahemla remained upset and fearful.

Fear had taken hold of this island paradise with an icy grip.

CHAPTER 2

In a tiny alcove rimmed with green trees, shrubs, and vines, a large double canoe had been pulled from the sea and hidden beneath the foliage. The band of men who had brought it here from a far distant island were also hidden from view, and they talked in low, conspiring voices.

"How many people inhabit this place?" one man asked.

"Unless there are more on the far side of the island, and we could see no evidence of it when we sailed around there, then there are not more than ten or twelve families," another reported.

"It will not take long to rid ourselves of them. They have so foolishly scattered themselves around that we can finish them off before they even know we are here," a third said from his bed on the ground. All eyes turned on him, their wounded leader.

"Then we will take over this island?" a short, stocky man of about twenty asked with a questioning smile on his dark, Lamanite face.

"Of course, Migroni," said the leader from his place on the ground. "It has everything we need: houses, food, and women. We shall keep the young women for ourselves when we destroy the people, and then we shall inhabit this place." He shifted himself uncomfortably and gingerly touched his wounded face.

"Whoever threw that knife at you sure knew what he was doing, Antium," said a lanky, black-haired man known as Zermanah.

"I think it was a woman," laughed one of the men who had been with the man they called Antium.

"Woman? Do their women fight in this place?" Migroni asked contemptuously.

"This one did. She throws a knife with considerable skill," Antium admitted painfully. "But she will not be a threat for long. I killed her husband, and I shall do the same to her."

"When your face heals," a small, wiry man with reddish hair and a scrubby beard chuckled.

"This wound is not so serious," Antium snapped. "I'll be fine in a day or two."

"Only if we put a fresh poultice compress on it to aid in the healing," the wiry one said.

"Oh, all right, Shecum, you old woman," Antium snarled as he shifted himself so that Shecum could more easily attend to the deep wound in his right cheek.

"You're lucky you didn't lose your eye," Migroni said as he watched Shecum remove the bloody bandage from the wound.

"It did come within a finger's width of one eye," Shecum observed wryly.

"He'd have looked exactly like his father did if she had destroyed his eye," a man known as Pagros taunted. Next to Antium, Pagros was the largest man in this wild band of twenty renegade mariners. At nearly forty, he was also the oldest, and the only one besides Antium who had known their leader's infamous father.

"My father, Antium the Elder, was a mighty warrior," the wounded leader of the renegades responded with pride. Sometimes referred to as Antium the Younger, this large man of thirty resembled his father in almost every way.

He was an exceedingly large man with dirty, long black hair, bushy eyebrows, dark beady eyes, and a great hook nose. When this wound he had acquired from the knife of Dara healed, he would have a bold scar from his chin to the top of his cheekbone. Antium was certainly not a handsome man, and even more repulsive than his physical appearance was his nasty disposition. Antium the Younger was a surly, selfish, and bloodthirsty man.

Antium's men had heard him brag often of Antium the Elder, and never did he speak of his father without cursing the two young men he believed responsible for his father's disappearance. Antium the Elder was mostly an absent idol to his young son. Although the cruel man was not badly missed by his abused wife, he was mimicked in every particular by his little son. During those few times he appeared at the run-down house in Zarahemla where little Antium and his mother lived, he spent much of his time cursing a young Nephite he called Samuel and his Lamanite friend, Gadoni.

Toward the end of a long war between the Nephites and Lamanites, Antium the Elder had served as a traitorous captain in the Lamanite army. Young Antium and his mother had expected him to return when the fighting ended, but he did not, and they never saw him again. Each year since then, Antium the Younger had cursed Samuel and Gadoni, although he had never met either. Whether or not they had had anything to do with his father's death, he did not care. His father, Antium the Elder, had been an indestructible warrior, and only murder could have prevented him from returning to the son who idolized him.

When he was fifteen, Antium the Younger and his mother were persuaded to accompany her righteous brother on one of the departing ships of the famous mariner, Hagoth. His hatred of Samuel and Gadoni never wavered, and despite the persistent ministrations of his uncle, Antium did very little that was not evil.

Several years after settling with the other Nephites and a few righteous Lamanites on a distant island, a ship arrived from still another island. The immigrants on that last ship told a story of a shipwreck, the building of a new ship, and the subsequent voyage. They also told of several families who had stayed behind to inhabit the luxurious island they had left. Antium had shown little interest in the tale of the new settlers until the day he had heard the names of two of those who had stayed behind.

Samuel and Gadoni!

That had been nine years ago, and during that time Antium had dreamed of nothing but revenge. His expulsion from Hagoth's island just the year before, along with his small band of cut-throat rebels, had been the stimulus that set him on his determined course to find that distant island and avenge the death of his father.

When Shecum had finished bandaging the wound on Antium's cheek, the renegade mariner sat upright and spoke solemnly to his band of men. "This is the island we have spent the past year searching these vast uncharted waters for."

"How can you be so sure?" someone asked.

"The man I killed last night was Captain Baronihah. You should remember the stories told of him. He was the ship's captain who stayed with Samuel and Gadoni when the new ship sailed," he answered curtly.

"How do you know it was him?" Shecum asked. "You've never seen him before, have you?"

"No, but I saw the white hair and beard he was said to have!" Antium thundered. "And I heard a woman scream his name." Seeing his men nod in agreement, Antium smiled painfully and continued, "Yes, we must be patient, my friends. We will avenge the death of my father and have our own island as a bonus. Here there will be no one to tell us how to live. If any ever dare to mention the Nephite God, he will be put to death!"

In those thunderous words, Antium reconfirmed his hatred for all that was righteous and good. His soul had been cankered early by his traitorous father, and the years had only made him even more bitter. Never had a more evil man lived on the isles of the sea than Antium the Younger.

Thunder cracked, and for the second night in a row, a fierce storm eroded the peace of the island.

* * *

The night was a long and miserable one. The people of Samuel crowded into hastily made shelters of palm fronds and long, wide blade grass. But the rain came in more readily than it did through the steep, thatched roofs of their homes, and everyone was wet. Throughout the long night, the men took turns standing guard, three and four at a time.

It was during the darkest hour before dawn that Jath, somewhat rested, awakened. He hoisted his quiver of obsidian-tipped arrows, strapped on his sword, and slung his bow over his shoulder. Then he walked into the dripping trees that surrounded the home of Captain Baronihah. There he listened for any suspicious sound that might penetrate the falling rain and moaning wind.

After a tense half-hour of pacing back and forth, Jath became convinced that danger from any invaders was not likely at that hour. He met and conversed briefly with Kim, who shared his feelings. Then the two parted, and Jath wandered back the way he had just come.

Rain flowed gently down his face, and Jath closed his eyes and wiped the water from them. When he opened his eyes again, his heart turned to stone! A shadowy figure, barely discernable, moved toward him in the darkness. Jath awkwardly jerked the sword from its sheath, not sure whether to run and alert the others or stand and fight.

Unused to facing danger, Jath's legs, which suddenly resembled a jellyfish, made his decision for him. He could not make them move. The figure glided closer, and Jath's voice succeeded where his legs were failing. "Stop right there!" he called out hoarsely, "or I'll cut you in a thousand pieces."

His bold warning failed to bring the response of instant surrender and submission he had expected. The reaction was more dramatic. With a cry of fear, the figure collapsed at his feet.

Jath was so surprised that he involuntarily took a step backward. For a moment he simply stood and stared while his racing heart slowed to a more functional pace. Finally, holding his trembling sword with its sharp point toward the fallen figure, he coaxed his legs into action and moved forward.

"You there," he said in a commanding voice as he poked tentatively with his sword. "Throw down your weapons and sit up. You are my prisoner."

The figure stirred, and Jath braced himself, wiping at the water that kept blurring his vision.

"Please, sir, don't hurt me," a small voice whispered. "I have no weapons."

Jath's mouth gaped open in astonishment.

The voice went on. "Please. I'm lost. I didn't mean to offend you."

Jath hastily sheathed his sword and sheepishly knelt beside the figure. "I'm sorry," he said. "I didn't know you were a girl."

He had recognized the voice as one belonging to the pretty daughter of the widower, Ontius, whose home had been among the last he had warned of the invasion the day before.

"Who are you?" the frightened girl asked as she slowly pushed herself from the soggy ground.

"I'm sorry, Lariah," he said as he reached to help her to her feet. "It is just me, Jath, the son of Samuel. I was at your home yesterday. Remember?"

"Don't touch me!" she cried, and Jath jerked his hand back as if he'd been bitten.

"I was just going to help you stand up," he said hotly.

"Father says I am to let no one touch me," Lariah said firmly as she rose to her feet unaided.

Though it was dark and all Jath could see of the girl was a shadowy figure, he certainly had no trouble picturing her delicate features. Lariah was a beautiful, shy girl, somewhat younger than Jath. She was slender and of slight build with hair as black as the sea at night and skin as white as the meat of the coconut.

She was something of a mystery to Jath and the other young men of the island, for they seldom saw her. But when one of them caught a glimpse of her, it was as a vision in the night. To behold Lariah was a treat beyond belief.

When she told Jath not to touch her, he obeyed, for he knew her father, Ontius, was a strange and brooding man. He was not much younger than Jath's father, Samuel. Ontius had been a happy, hard-working person when he and his wife and two daughters had first inhabited this island with Samuel and the others. Then an unexplained illness had robbed him of his fair wife and Lariah's younger sister only a couple of years after settling here. From that day, a subtle change had come over Ontius, and the people of the island avoided him.

He brought Lariah to Sabbath services only occasionally, and when he did, he spoke to no one. He lived with his daughter in virtual seclusion most of the time. Samuel had spoken of him to his family frequently, but the strange behavior of Ontius and his unnaturally long mourning was cause for most of what little gossip occurred among the people of Samuel.

Thus it was that even though Lariah was known, she was not known well. None of the young men had dared risk offending her father, so they avoided both Ontius and his fair daughter.

"Jath?" the sweet voice of Lariah inquired, bringing him from his reverie.

"What?" he asked coldly.

"Were you really going to cut me into a thousand pieces?" she asked, her eyes sparkling with mirth.

"Lariah," Jath said in frustration, "I thought you were one of the invaders. You shouldn't be out here alone where you might get hurt. Why aren't you with your father?"

"He is out here somewhere, taking his turn at guard like you are. I was alone and afraid, so I went in search of him and got lost," she explained. "Father will be terribly angry if he finds out." To Jath's frustration, her eyes had lost their sparkle and she seemed on the verge of tears.

"I'll show you the way back," Jath said quickly, and instinctively he reached a hand to comfort her, then suddenly pulled back.

"I will follow you, Jath," she said, and the way she spoke his name made his spine tingle. "And please, don't tell Father that I was lost."

As they walked Jath wondered at this strange girl he had felt so quickly drawn to. He wondered even more about her father. What kind of man was he? Did the people of Samuel really know Ontius? He shivered at the thought of this strange man and the way his mourning was affecting this beautiful but mysterious girl.

Jath also wondered about how the two of them lived, and as he did, he felt a strange tugging at his breast. He felt the urge to touch her soft arm again, but he dared not, so he walked slowly as she stumbled along behind him. After he had left her in the camp, he returned to stand guard, and for the rest of his watch he could not drive thoughts of her from his mind.

* * *

Daylight saw no letup in the steady downpour of warm rain. Samuel ordered a couple of tentative patrols to search for any sign of their enemies, but he did not allow them to go far or be gone long, for he feared attack.

For three days, the bad weather persisted, and for three days there was no further sign of the elusive invaders. Were it not for the constant vigil over a still critically injured Baronihah, it would have been easy to believe that no danger had ever been present.

Unrest prevailed, and grumbling was eventually heard. Ontius grew sullen and morose. On the evening of the third day, as the storm grew quiet, he approached Samuel. "I'm taking my daughter home," he announced.

"I think it would be best if we all stayed together until we wipe out the danger," Samuel responded. "The weather is clearing, and we will find the invaders soon now."

"Surely they have gone—if they were ever here," Ontius said with a frown.

"Maybe. But we must be sure if we are to ever live in peace and feel safe again," Samuel argued.

Ontius' face grew hard and his frown turned to a scowl. His dark green eyes glowered at Samuel. Samuel glanced at Lariah, who stood like a small statue at his side. He marveled at her exquisite features, but he worried over her troubled and sad face and the fear in her pretty eyes.

Ontius spoke again. "You fear for my daughter?"

"I do, and for all the children."

"Fear for the others if you choose, Samuel, but do not fear for Lariah. She is none of your affair. I will protect her. We are leaving now.

Do not try to stop me," Ontius warned, his hand resting ominously on the hilt of his sword. Then to Lariah he said, "Come, daughter. We are going home."

"Ontius, please, we . . ." Samuel began.

Ontius stopped and faced Samuel again, glaring at him in dislike. "I know you consider yourself the leader here. If others would follow you, let them, but I will not!" he said, and with that he strode off, dragging his daughter along by one of her slender arms.

* * *

Jath overheard the conversation between Ontius and Samuel. For reasons he could not explain, he was saddened. Lariah had said nothing during the entire exchange. In fact, she had said nothing to Jath since their encounter in the darkness three days before. But several times he had felt as though he were being watched, and each time he had turned to find her clear green eyes gazing at him like a young animal. Always, when he looked at her, she would lower her eyes and turn her head. But he imagined that her perfect white skin glowed a mild shade of pink, and he wanted to reach out to her, but he did not.

As Ontius dragged her away, they passed within a few paces of where Jath stood leaning against a tall palm at the fringe of the trees. Lariah turned her eyes toward him, and to Jath's surprise, a brief smile crossed her pretty face. She even raised a slender arm, the one her father was not dragging her by, and waved shyly.

Then she was gone, and Jath felt like his heart had just been torn from his chest. He wanted to shout at her to break away from the terrible grip of her father and come back where she would be protected, but he did not.

An errant tear wet his eye, and he angrily brushed it away before someone should see it. Then he felt the arm of his father fall across his shoulders. "Pretty girl, isn't she?" Samuel said.

"Who?" Jath asked.

Samuel chuckled and said only, "I didn't realize Lariah's father was so foolish."

"Me either," Jath mumbled, and his father's arm held him tightly for a moment. Then Samuel walked quietly away, leaving Jath to stare dumbly at the spot where Lariah had disappeared into the trees.

CHAPTER 3

Antium refused further doctoring to his wound. Shecum reluctantly removed his latest bandage and viewed the angry red line that marked a path down Antium's face. "But it has barely begun to scar," he said. "Just a little longer—"

Antium pushed him away as he rose to his feet. "You act like an old woman, Shecum. You fuss over nothing. I scarcely feel any pain. Gather the men. It is time to strike."

It was true that Antium's wound hurt him very little. He was one who healed rapidly and had a high tolerance for pain. The fact that he was not overly sensitive to pain may have contributed to the impunity with which he inflicted injury to others. That, and his callous heart, of course.

Coiled neatly at the base of a large flowering tree was a long roll of supple but strong leather. Antium reached for his whip and shook it out to its full length. Three times the length of his body, Antium's braided whip tapered from a broad, woven handle to a tip not as wide as his little finger. With a sudden snap of his wrist, Antium cracked the whip and smiled.

With this very whip, Antium had struck terror in the hearts of Hagoth's people until they had driven him from their island. And with it he vowed to make Samuel and Gadoni pay for the death of his father. A second time he cracked the whip, and his men scurried from the trees and surrounded him. Several had felt the terrible sting of Antium's whip, and none wished to provoke him to anger now.

"Men," he began when they had all assembled, "it is time to begin our sweep of the colony on this island and identify and punish Samuel and Gadoni. We have left the people withering in their homes after I succeeded in killing Captain Baronihah. They know not when or where we will strike again." He paused and chuckled as he surveyed the faces of his band. They were eager, and evil danced from their eyes.

"Pagros, you will take half the men and go to the last home to the east," he ordered as he snapped his leather whip in the direction where Ontius lived and the one home beyond his. "I will lead the rest, and we will go beyond the last home to the west." Again his whip snapped as he indicated the direction.

"We will take the families one at a time from each end of their colony and bring them here. You are to kill no one, for I want Samuel and Gadoni alive, and some of the others may have to be forced to identify them for me," he said, stroking his whip as though it were a living thing.

"But, Antium, you said that only the women, the younger ones, would be kept alive," lanky Zermanah protested.

"That is right!" Antium snapped. "But that will come after punishment and torture. Once Gadoni and Samuel tell me what they did to my father and have been appropriately punished, then you men may do with the others as you desire."

That answer pleased the carnal nature of his men, for they smiled at his words, grunting in satisfaction. Antium went on. "We must move with stealth, for I do not want to provoke an attack by the people of this place."

Little did Antium know that Samuel had gathered his people, and that an attack was just what he planned to carry out as soon as he could locate the invaders.

Pagros led nine men east, including the wiry Shecum, who, no longer required to treat Antium's wound, was anxious for action. Antium trekked west with the other nine following behind him, including Migroni, the Lamanite, and Zermanah, the lanky one. Not once did it occur to Antium that his plan was not a perfect one or that there was even a remote chance of failure.

When, several hours later, he and his little band surrounded the farthest home to the west in the dusk of evening, he was surprised to find it abandoned. When one of his men suggested, "They must be smarter than you thought," Antium rewarded him with a painful welt across his back. Had it not been for the man's leather vest, the whip would have laid the flesh open like a knife.

"They are just visiting and cowering with someone else. They'll be back," Antium snarled. "We'll wait inside this house to greet them when they come. We'll still be there to meet Pagros and his men in the morning when they bring a family from the east to feel the sting of my whip on their tender flesh."

* * *

The fiery exchange did not go unobserved. Antium and his men stood outside Samuel's house, where, hidden in a large stand of ferns a few paces away, Samuel and Gadoni stood watching. This was no coincidence. Samuel had earlier decided to leave the rest of the men to provide protection to the women and children in the event of an attack while he and Gadoni searched the near parts of the island in an attempt to discover the hiding place of the invaders.

They had narrowly missed walking right into the path of the ten men they had then followed to the deserted home of Samuel and Ophera.

"There are others besides these ten men," Samuel whispered with a worried glance at his dark-skinned companion.

Gadoni nodded grimly. "Unless they have gone to the home of Baronihah, they will have found only a deserted house for their efforts, as these men have done," he said.

"Unless . . ." Samuel paused, thinking of the stubborn Ontius and his beautiful little daughter.

Gadoni finished his thought. "Yes, unless they find that fool, Ontius."

Samuel nodded, his stomach tight with worry. He said, "I wish I could see the face of that man holding the whip."

Gadoni met Samuel's gaze in the fading dusk. "His voice sounds familiar. Where could he . . . I mean, where could they have come from?"

Samuel shook his head as he silently parted the fern leaves to watch his house now filled with invaders. Gadoni did the same.

As they watched, the leader, carrying his long leather whip in his hand, came to the door. Samuel's heart lurched, and he heard a horrified gasp from his companion. Both men stared in dumbfounded silence until the big, hook-nosed man turned and disappeared inside.

Samuel let the fern leaves fall back into place before turning his head toward his companion. He had never seen his brown-skinned friend so pale. Gadoni's eyes were wide, and he was trembling visibly. "Did . . . did you see what I saw?" Samuel asked him in horror.

"Sam. You can't . . . kill . . . a ghost!" Gadoni stammered.

"That was no ghost!" Samuel countered, but he spoke with less than full conviction.

"He's dead, Sam!" Gadoni said, wiping his hands across his eyes as if that might somehow erase what he had just seen.

"Yes, old Antium is dead, my friend, but—" Samuel began.

"Sam," Gadoni interrupted. "That had to be him. It looked just like him. That was Antium."

With two good eyes? No, you and I buried him with our own hands," Samuel reminded him.

"Then it is his ghost." Gadoni tried unsuccessfully to smile.

"Maybe it is one of his relatives," Samuel suggested sensibly. Then, upon hearing footsteps leaving the house, he again parted the fern leaves as he said, "Shh," to Gadoni.

Two men had emerged, and again the likeness of the renegade with the whip to Samuel's enemy of long ago took his breath away. When the big man spoke to his companion, it was in the same raspy voice that had haunted him as a young man. The companion the renegade spoke to was a Lamanite, as dark as Gadoni and of similar build, stocky and not too tall.

"Migroni," said the dark, hook-nosed man. "We will find Pagros and the others while these men wait for the family that lives here. When they come, and it should not be long, Zermanah and the others will have no trouble with them, I am sure. I just hope it is Samuel or Gadoni!" he hissed with unveiled hatred.

Again, Gadoni gasped, and the horror in Samuel's breast grew.

"They will feel the sting of your whip, Antium!" Migroni asserted as the two moved toward the trees to Samuel's right.

With a sinking heart and trembling hands, Samuel let the fern leaves fall back into place. He again turned to Gadoni.

"Antium!" they whispered in horrified unison.

Through the soft leaves of the ferns, the only too familiar voice reached them. "Yes, Migroni, I will learn from them what they did to my father—how they murdered him and where. I will enjoy torturing them and their families until they tell me what I want to know. Then they will suffer my wrath and die."

"It is Antium's son," Samuel exclaimed softly. "And he somehow knows we are on this island. I never imagined Antium had a son."

Gadoni looked grim. "But he has, and he hates us as badly as his father did. Sam, we must destroy him! You and me and our families are in grave danger as long as he lives."

Samuel nodded in agreement, and then he asked, "Did you notice the wound on his face?"

"Yes. A nasty one. Nearly got his eye."

"Then he would have looked exactly like his father," Samuel agreed. "It must have been him that Dara struck with her knife. Come, we must warn the others, and maybe we can come back and defeat the others who are waiting here to ambush me and my family. We mustn't disappoint them," he said grimly, then added, "and we must begin tonight to eliminate this terrible threat to our lives and our peace."

"Samuel, maybe one of us should follow this new Antium," Gadoni suggested. "He will most likely lead us to his hideout."

"You go, Gadoni. I will bring some of the others back here and deal with those renegades in my house," Samuel said. The two friends solemnly embraced and parted.

Samuel found all well at Baronihah's when he got back there a short while later. No one there had seen or heard anything out of the ordinary. Samuel explained what and who he and Gadoni had seen, and then he selected several men to accompany him back to his house to do battle with the eight men waiting so smugly there to ambush his unsuspecting family.

Into a peaceful moonlit evening he led his brother, Oreb, an expert marksman with a bow, and his brother-in-law, Nemti, an experienced soldier. His son, Jath, and his half-brother, Uri, had insisted on coming, and with reluctance, Samuel had given in to them. Three others completed his hastily assembled and well-armed squad as they moved out to launch a fierce surprise attack against the unsuspecting men of Antium.

His last glimpse of his people as he left brought pain to his soul, for he saw in their faces a fear they had not known in over a decade. But what haunted him worst of all was the horror that tarnished the beautiful face of his devoted wife, Ophera. With her and the others in mind, he stopped his small band a little later and led them in a solemn and fervent prayer. He pled with God to preserve the lives of his people and restore them to their peace. Then they proceeded steadfastly to help God answer their prayer of faith.

Soon they arrived at the fringe of the forest in front of Samuel's house. Surrounding it silently, they prepared to do battle in the moonlight.

Samuel called out, imitating the familiar, raspy voice of Antium, "Come at once, men. Pagros is under attack and needs your help!"

Immediately, the renegades began to pour from the door. Oreb loosed the first arrow, and one man fell without a groan. A second and third fell to the sudden onslaught of arrows before the invaders realized they had been tricked. They scrambled in confusion, some trying to get back in the house while others ran for the trees. But two more invaders fell heavily to the ground before one wisely shouted, "We surrender!" and threw his hands in the air.

Samuel immediately shouted the order to quit firing arrows. Then they bound the two men who stood with raised arms. When it was learned that one of the five men who had fallen was still alive, Samuel ordered that his wounds be attended to.

When that was done, Uri approached Samuel and said, "There were eight, weren't there, Sam? We can only account for seven."

"Yes, there were eight. Check the trees and see if an injured man might have crawled off while we were attending to these others."

One of the prisoners laughed. "You will waste your time. Zermanah will find the other men, and you will regret your treachery tonight," he said.

Samuel turned on the securely bound invader in anger. "Treachery? It was you who were in my house waiting to destroy me and my family!" he shouted. "And you dare to accuse me of treachery?"

"Antium warned us of you. You are Samuel, aren't you?" the man asked calmly.

"I am. And my people and I have lived on this island in peace until you came. Who are you? Where do you come from?"

The captive smiled smugly and refused to say anymore. The other two prisoners followed his example when Samuel asked them the same questions. Seeing that he was wasting his time, he brusquely ordered his men, "Cast the dead into the sea! These three we will hold as our prisoners."

Samuel had no desire to waste manpower guarding these evil men while there were still others to fight in future battles, but he had no alternative except to hang them, and he was revolted by this idea. So he led his men and the captives back to the gathering of his people at the home of Captain Baronihah.

Samuel stood watch for the rest of the long night, hoping each hour to see Gadoni return with news of the location of the hiding place of

Antium and the rest of his band of renegade invaders. But daylight came and Gadoni did not.

* * *

Gadoni was in trouble. Not serious trouble—yet. His vast knowledge of the island could save him if his strength and endurance held out. Right now, he was involved in a frantic chase, and he was the chased.

After having successfully followed Antium and Migroni to the hideout in the tiny alcove, Gadoni was in a rush to return and see how the battle at Samuel's house had gone and to let Samuel know of the hideout. His hurry, coupled with over a decade of peace in which he had been far removed from danger, caused him to be careless. He ran right into the path of Pagros and his returning band.

They had found no one at home to the east and were in foul moods. The sudden sight of Gadoni emerging from the trees into the bright moonlight ignited their hatred and lust to kill. "After him!" Pagros had ordered.

That had been several hours ago, and Gadoni had eluded them. It was daylight now, and Pagros was proving that he was an able adversary and good tracker. Deeper and deeper into the uninhabited mountains toward the center of the island Gadoni fled. He had hunted and roamed every part of this rugged, densely wooded area and was in no danger of becoming lost, but he had to throw his pursuers off his trail if he were to safely return to his people anytime soon. Gadoni knew that both his family and Samuel would be worried about him, but he also figured that the longer he kept Pagros and his band away, the better chance Samuel and the other men had of defeating the rest of Antium's men. So, with that in mind, he made no attempt yet to circle back toward the inhabited shores of the island.

The vines, shrubs, and trees were so thick that Gadoni had to fight his way through. Suddenly a wild hog snorted and jumped from its resting place when Gadoni surprised it. Because of the denseness of the foliage, he could not see but could only hear the hog as it tore a frantic path down the hillside for several hundred paces.

"There he goes! I can hear him running," he heard one of the invaders shout.

Gadoni listened with relief as his pursuers crashed through the foliage after the hog. He took advantage of the distraction, knowing that Pagros would soon enough discover their error and begin looking for him again. He climbed as rapidly and silently as he could, stopping more frequently than he liked as his breathing became labored and his legs weak.

Gadoni was in good shape for a man in his early forties, but he was not as strong as he used to be, and this worried him. Eventually, long after he could no longer hear his pursuers, he allowed himself a prolonged rest—one he badly needed.

When he moved again, he headed toward the rim of a volcano that usually rumbled, blew a little smoke, and even belched some flame occasionally. He had spent many hours in the past few years on the high rim listening and watching as nature snored deep in the mysterious, smoky hole that was the center of the volcano.

Located several miles from the settlement, it had never posed a danger to Samuel's people. In fact, it had provided them with a source of fascinating entertainment from time to time. But this day it was quiet. Even the snoring sounds from deep down were still. It was almost as though it were holding its breath while peace was restored to the island it claimed as home. The stillness here was most unusual, Gadoni mused thoughtfully as he worked his way around the rim, staying mostly in the bushes that lined it.

He stopped occasionally and listened for his pursuers, but hearing nothing, he finally decided that he had lost them, and he chuckled again over the lucky advent of the wild hog. Perhaps, he decided, he should return and report to Samuel, so he turned and worked his way slowly back along the rim looking for an easy place to descend. Gadoni was hungry and very exhausted.

* * *

On the rim across from him, two persons peered at him through the shrubbery. They watched him until he disappeared, and then glanced momentarily at each other. Then they left and slipped silently into the thick forest that guarded the rim of the slumbering volcano. The smaller one, grasping a strange but deadly weapon in one hand, followed the larger one.

CHAPTER 4

Antium clenched his coiled whip in his hand. Migroni, the stocky Lamanite, eyed the whip, which would bring to an end the patience he usually exhibited with his leader.

"Not one captive yet!" Antium shouted. "Where could the men be? Pagros should have been back hours ago! He knows we should not be out in the daylight."

Antium's men exchanged nervous glances for they knew his anger could easily be showered upon them all.

"Maybe the people of Samuel have fled inland," Migroni suggested mildly.

Antium looked at him and narrowed his eyes in thought, then nodded. "Perhaps they have," he agreed. "Samuel is a shrewd one. But still—that does not explain why Pagros has not returned with his men. He would not have gone inland without the rest of us."

"Unless he was in pursuit of someone," Migroni said flatly.

Antium looked startled. He had not considered this. "Well, since we don't know where he is, we might as well seek out Zermanah," he said. "The crazy fool may still be waiting for someone to return to the abandoned house. He should realize that they might not be coming back." He glared at his men and snarled. "Looks like I have to do the thinking for everyone in this band. Come, Migroni, and we'll go see why he has not brought his men back."

Just at that moment, there was a rustling of leaves, and the men looked up warily. As the bushes parted, Zermanah stumbled through the foliage and fell upon the ground before Antium. The broken shaft of an arrow protruded from the back of his bloody leg.

Antium cursed. "Zermanah! What have you done now?"

Zermanah was very weak, and he spoke without lifting his head from the grass. "Ambush. The one called . . . Samuel . . . and others . . . attacked us."

"Attacked you?" Antium scoffed. "You were supposed to be hiding inside the house. What did you do, you fool, let yourselves be seen?"

"He called us in the voice of Antium." Zermanah paused, gulping in a great breath of air. "It sounded just like you, so we came out, and they began to slay us."

"Where are the others?" Antium demanded in alarm.

"Some dead. Some captured," Zermanah groaned.

"Fools!" Antium shouted. "How many are dead?"

"Four."

"And three captured?"

Zermanah grunted in agreement.

As Antium began to pace back and forth, cursing the stupidity of his men, Migroni kneeled beside the injured man.

"Help me," Zermanah begged. "Pull the arrow out."

"Do it!" Antium ordered. "We can't afford to lose him, too, even if he is so foolish as to allow himself to be injured. We have already lost too many." With that, Antium stormed into the trees.

Migroni shook his head remembering the wound Antium himself had received, and at the hands of a woman! However, he wisely kept his thoughts to himself as he began to care for the wounded man.

A few minutes later, the bushes parted again. One of the men of Pagros stepped into the clearing and sank to the ground in exhaustion. Migroni looked up. "Where are the others?" he asked. "Antium is furious that you are so slow."

Before he could answer, a second man entered the clearing and sank wearily beside the first. Almost as if he had known they were coming, Antium reappeared and began questioning the two men. Migroni continued his task, saying nothing as Antium scolded and cursed. *Although men follow him,* Migroni said to himself, *he is not a leader one can respect.* As always, he kept his thoughts to himself.

* * *

Back at the home of Captain Baronihah, Gadoni finally made his appearance. His pretty wife, Laishita, burst into tears at the sight of her scratched and dirty husband. She took him in her arms and brushed a gentle hand against his cheek. He managed a wan smile for her.

"I'm all right," he assured her.

"But you've been gone for so many hours," she said. "We were so worried about you."

Gadoni's story caused quite a stir. "At least they didn't get Ontius and Lariah," Samuel said with some relief when his friend had finished. "But unless that foolish man returns to the safety of the group, they may yet get to him."

Jath, leaning casually against a palm, listened carefully to every word. His thoughts of young Lariah were far from casual. When Samuel spoke her name, Jath determined to act immediately. He knew his father and mother would be upset, but nevertheless, he slipped away from the crowd. He carried his sword, bow, and quiver of arrows with him. He spotted Uri, who was on guard. As he crept into the forest, he was careful not to let Uri spot him, for he knew his young uncle would not be happy at what he was doing. So Jath waited until Uri's back was turned, and then he swiftly and silently ran past him.

As he ran, feelings of guilt began to assail him. *Someone has to help Lariah,* Jath justified himself. It had never occurred to him that Lariah's father could protect her. He thought only of how near her home Antium's men had been and the danger she was in. "Lariah and her father must be warned," Jath whispered to himself. "Antium's men will surely return."

As Jath came closer to his destination, he began to worry. Ontius would not be happy to see him. It did not occur to Jath that he might not find anyone at the house when he got there, but that is exactly what he did find. As his voice echoed through the deserted house, he was nearly overcome with fear as he considered that Lariah and her foolish father might have been taken captive . . . or even worse.

Frantically, Jath searched for tracks to see in which direction the invaders might have taken Lariah and her father. When he found none, he realized that the invaders had not been here at all, which could mean only one thing; Ontius had taken Lariah someplace else. *Maybe her father will take care of her,* Jath thought. *Maybe she is safe at this very moment. But where could they be?*

Just to reassure himself, Jath made a wide swing around the house, and then made a still larger one. He found no sign of the invaders although he did come across a seldom used trail with fresh tracks. Jath was certain they were no doubt the footprints of Ontius and Lariah. Impulsively, Jath followed the tracks, which led toward the center of the island. Even though he tried to convince himself that Ontius would take care of his daughter, he decided to follow the footprints a short distance. *Just to make certain they have not encountered Antium's men,* Jath told himself.

Why he kept going, he did not know. Drawn forward by some mysterious force, he continued up the trail. So intent was he on his task that he was surprised when darkness overtook him. He would have been even more surprised had he known that he had been seen and was now being followed.

Jath was not particularly hungry, for he had picked fruit along the way and eaten it, but he was tired. For the last two hours the darkness had grown thicker and more intense. Unaware of any danger, he decided to rest until the moon rose, and he curled up in the undergrowth beside the trail. He was soon asleep.

* * *

Pagros and Shecum were on a mission of their own. It had been sanctioned by Antium after much bickering and anger. Jath had not been part of their mission, but by following the trail of Ontius and his pretty daughter, he had placed himself in grave danger. Pagros and Shecum had also been following the trail and had spotted his tracks and, after a time, his light brown hair. With the fall of darkness, they had lost him.

Earlier they had also seen Gadoni, but when they had closed in on him, they had found only a wild hog. Disgusted, they had returned to Antium empty-handed. Now they were eager to close in on their prey, but the two men could hardly see each other in the darkness although they were but an arm's length from each other.

"Shecum," Pagros said, "let us rest until the moon rises. Then we will be able to see whoever is following the trail taken by the girl and her father."

"He who made these tracks is not the same man we saw earlier," Shecum said. "That man was a large man. This other is still a youth, no doubt one of Samuel's men."

Pagros snorted. "Of course it is, you young fool. And we shall soon catch him. Then we will tie him up and take him to Antium."

The two were silent for a moment. "The girl is very pretty," Shecum said at last.

"And the man is very foolish for not staying with the others," Pagros responded. "Antium will be most pleased when we return with the captives. Of course, if they resist, we may have to kill one of them. Samuel and Gadoni are the only men Antium insists we bring to him alive."

The two men had spotted the man and girl at the silent volcano earlier. Antium's two men had expected to easily overpower them, but like a wisp of smoke both had vanished. After searching for a short while, Pagros said, "We would do better to seek his permission to come back and complete the search."

They had returned to Antium, obtained the permission they sought, and had come again in pursuit of the man and his beautiful daughter.

* * *

Jath had no idea how long he had been asleep or what had caused him to awaken. The moon was shining brightly overhead, and he wisely allowed his ears to attune themselves to the sounds of the night before he made any movements. A light breeze rustled the leaves about him. Jath could hear water falling from the mountains beyond him. Something scraped the earth nearby, and a small rock rolled.

Jath felt a tremor of fear and apprehension, feelings that intensified when he heard the sound of someone clearing his throat.

"He can't be far," a gruff voice said. "His tracks have vanished. Let's check the bushes. He is probably asleep, but be careful, Shecum, in case he is not."

Jath held his breath and tried to still his pounding heart. It would not take them long to find him, for he was not far off the trail.

"I'll start down here, Pagros," a second voice said. Jath thought it was the voice of a much younger man than the first. The first man, the one called Pagros, began beating about in the undergrowth just down the hill from him. The second man began to poke in the foliage across the trail from Jath's hiding place.

As silently as he could, Jath gathered his weapons and crept to the edge of the trail. Fortunately for him, the invaders were making just enough noise to cover what little sound he made. The moon, however, was brighter. As it shined down through the trees, it cast eerie shadows around him. He paused to listen. One man was working his way up the hill and would be upon him in a few minutes if he remained much longer. The other man had vanished into the trees straight ahead.

It's now or never, Jath told himself as he eased his body onto the trail. His impulse was to go downhill, the direction he had come from, and he would have done just that had one man not called out to the other, "I know he's here. It's too dark to have gone far."

The other agreed. "Let's find him quickly so we can get after the man and his daughter."

Those words galvanized Jath. They were after Lariah! Jath's heart pounded in his ears like the surf, and Lariah's face appeared before him, as if to urge him onward. Jath ran up the trail.

"There he goes! After him!" the men shouted.

Jath gained a few minutes as Antium's men were forced to make their way through the foliage and onto the narrow trail. By then, Jath was running swiftly. He made good time, and was steadily increasing the space between him and his pursuers until his foot hit a loose stick that sent him sprawling. His sword flew from his hand, and the arrows spilled from his quiver.

Jath frantically began to search for the sword, tears of frustration stinging his eyes. Pounding feet closed on him quickly. He wanted to jump up and run again, but not without his weapons. The invader apparently in charge—undoubtedly the younger man—was almost to him. Jath's hand fell on the dry stick that had tripped him.

It was not too long, but very sturdy. He grasped it and stepped into the shadowy bushes and waited. When the invader came running, Jath swung.

Shecum fell with a groan. Jath pulled him off the trail and listened. Pagros was still coming, so he picked up the stick again and, a moment later, sent Pagros sprawling on the trail.

Jath pulled the sword from the sheath of Pagros and tried to shove it in his own sheath, but it was too large. So he unstrapped the belt from the waist of the fallen invader and removed the man's sheath and replaced his own with it. He then shoved the sword in place, grabbed the arrows from the quiver on Pagros' back, and darted up the trail.

Only after he had gone several hundred paces did it occur to Jath that he should have bound the two unconscious men, but he was not about to go back now. He hurriedly stumbled on, hoping that he was still following the route taken by Lariah and her father.

He forced himself at last to stop and search for their tracks in a spot where the moon flooded the ground with light. It was rocky here, however, and he could find no sign of tracks, human or animal. With fear gnawing like a rat at his stomach, Jath proceeded up the mountain.

* * *

Pagros had not taken as hard a blow as had Shecum and was the first to regain consciousness. When he did, he soon discovered that his face was bloody, a tooth was missing, his arrows were gone, and someone had taken his sword, sheath and all. Shecum woke up to the accompaniment of a stream of vile oaths as Pagros vented his anger on the still night.

Both men were upset, injured, and frustrated, but Shecum tried to stay calm and talk some sense into his enraged companion. "Maybe we should forget about him for now, Pagros," he said of the young man they had been following. "If we don't, we may not get the man and girl at all."

"He stole my sword and arrows and knocked out a tooth!" Pagros ranted, pointing at his damaged face. "I will not rest until he pays with his life!"

Shecum wanted revenge, too, but he was distracted by the pretty girl with the long black hair and milky skin. "He may lead us far from them, Pagros," he said. "They may get away from where we saw them before if we follow this man."

"Shut up, you young fool!" Pagros snarled as he buckled on the empty sheath that lay on the ground and began searching for the sword that would fit it. He eventually found Jath's sword and several arrows that lay loose on the trail. He sheathed the sword and cursed that it was smaller than his own. He dropped the arrows into his empty quiver and started up the trail, ordering Shecum to follow.

Without another word of protest, Shecum fingered his battered face and followed Pagros. They soon faced the same difficulty that Jath had faced as the trail became so rocky they could see no tracks. Neither invader had any idea where Jath might have gone. Even the trail itself faded and was no more.

"We will return to the place where we saw the man and his daughter," Pagros announced at last.

Shecum smiled to himself and agreed with the older man, but they disagreed about which way they should go. Pagros won again, and the two men continued uphill. "For," Pagros reasoned, "we must reach the lip of the dead volcano, and that is upward."

So upward they went until fatigue and pain finally forced them to stop and rest. They curled up in a dense thicket and were soon both sound asleep.

* * *

Jath knew his way better than the invaders. Even in the uncertain light of the moon, he managed to reach the rim of the slumbering volcano. He circled the entire area one time before he was so exhausted that he too had to stop for rest. He made his bed in the bushes just a few paces from the rim. There he slept soundly, and much longer than he had planned.

CHAPTER 5

When Samuel awoke at dawn to discover that Jath was missing, he was at first mystified. Then he grew angry, an emotion which was soon replaced by concern. Ophera was distraught.

"Something terrible must have happened to him," she sobbed. "Jath would not just run off. Antium or some of his men must have gotten past the guards and taken him!"

"No, dear, I don't believe so," Samuel said thoughtfully. He was developing suspicions, for he knew that the young girl, Lariah, had sparked strong feelings in his son. He feared that Jath might have gone after her, hoping to help her.

"We've got to find him," Ophera said.

Samuel agreed calmly. "I'll get Oreb and Josh, and we'll—"

Samuel did not finish his sentence, for he was interrupted by a warning cry from one of the men on guard in the trees surrounding Baronihah's house. "Attack!" the man screamed.

His meaning was clear, and the men scrambled to defensive positions as the women herded the children into Baronihah's house for safety. Samuel had ordered logs cut and stacked as barriers behind which the men could crouch and fire arrows in the event of an attack. It was from those positions that they now defended themselves. Antium and his band, with their numbers reduced, sent only a few arrows at them from positions of safety in the forest. One man made the mistake of exposing himself for a moment, and one of Oreb's arrows reduced the enemy's strength by one more man. Before too long the voice of Antium rang through the forest, calling for a retreat.

A short while later, they attacked again, then once more pulled back. After still a third attack, it became apparent to Samuel that Antium was going to harass them as long as he could. As badly as he wanted to slip away in search of his missing son, he could not do so now.

* * *

Several miles away, Jath lay on his belly in the dense foliage just below the lip of the ancient volcano. He was peering from the shrubbery as the two men who had been following him crept past.

"Shecum," said one. "We will continue to search until we find some sign of the man and his daughter. They are here somewhere. They cannot have simply vanished. If we do not deliver them to Antium as we promised, he will be very angry."

"I do not care to feel the bite of his whip, Pagros," wiry Shecum said. "Antium has never struck me, but I fear my luck may one day run out. But this young girl . . ." he said thoughtfully, then paused. "I can't wait to have my arms around this girl and carry her squirming and wiggling through the trees."

For a moment, Jath was tempted to string an arrow and send it into the small man's back, but only for a moment. He thrust the thought from his mind, because he felt it would be wrong. Even though these men were plotting terrible deeds, Jath could not shoot them in the back. That would be murder, he told himself. They passed from view, and he could no longer hear their voices.

Crawling silently from his place of concealment, Jath followed the two invaders. If they found Ontius and Lariah, he wanted to be there, for then he would be able to fight without his conscience bothering him. He would defend and protect Lariah at any cost, he brashly promised himself.

It proved to be very difficult for Jath to follow the two men and not be seen by them, for they kept looking back. Occasionally they drifted out of sight into the trees and shrubs below the rim. Once, Jath came into sight just as Shecum stepped out of some trees ahead. He dove headlong into the foliage to avoid being seen. After that, he lagged farther and farther behind, wincing a little over his bruised elbows and knees.

After some time had passed, Jath could no longer see the invaders, and his heart sank. They had lost him.

The rim of the volcano was not a perfect circle. In fact, it was jagged and broken so badly in places that it was difficult for a person to walk. It was rough and broken up all the way around its entire circumference. Several places were sloughed off to the inside, making it possible to climb down into the slumbering crater a short way and move around below the rim.

Jath had never ventured into these areas during the many trips he had made to the rim with his father. Always, smoke and flames stirred below, and Samuel said it would be too dangerous to descend even a few feet into the interior. This morning, however, all was still in the mysterious depths, and Jath crept across the rim, dodging from rock to rock and crevice to crevice where he could hide until he was ready to dart out and scurry to the next available place of concealment. In this way, he worked his way down into the massive crater as far as he could go. Beyond him, it fell away into dark and foreboding depths.

He crouched, feeling fairly well hidden, as he peered over the dangerous, sheer drop-off. The sun was nearly at its apex for the day, and it lit the giant cavity below. Far down, he could detect just a trace of smoke, but other than an occasional purr, like a big cat, it remained relatively silent. There were no flames that he could see, but there was also no bottom visible through the wispy smoke.

Never in the ten years that Jath and the others had been on the island had the volcano been so quiet. He felt the hair stir on the back of his neck, and his heart began to pound. Everything seemed so peaceful and still, but there was something sinister about this great volcano, and it frightened him. Maybe what life there was left in the ancient island-builder was finally dying out forever. In that case, there was certainly nothing to fear.

So absorbed had Jath become in the mysterious silence of the volcano that he had failed to notice the activity a few hundred paces away and on about the same level he was at below the rim.

Alerted by the clatter of a falling rock, he looked up. What he first saw brought him bounding to his feet. As he jerked the bow loose that he had slung snugly across his back, his eyes rapidly scanned the scene. He spotted a young woman standing with her back against a high, vertical wall that reached to the rim above. He knew, even at this distance, that it was Lariah. She was holding what appeared to be a long and slender stick. A few feet to her right, a man, undoubtedly her father, Ontius, was crouched, holding a strange instrument in his hands. Again, due to the distance that separated him from them, Jath could not tell what Ontius held.

His eyes returned to the spot a few hundred paces farther to the right where he had first spotted his enemies. Pagros and Shecum were also below the rim and sheltered by a huge outcrop of volcanic rock. They must have been responsible for the falling rocks, for they were on the go, moving ever closer to the girl and her father. Ontius and Lariah appeared to be trapped, for the uneven shelf they were on ran out where a crevice cut all the way to the sheer wall that ascended to the rim. This crevice divided the shelf they were on with the one Jath had climbed down to. Both shelves, at the crevice, dropped straight into the center of the volcano.

Jath could see that, given time, the invaders could reach Lariah and her father. Jath, on the other hand, could get to within a short distance, but could not reach them without climbing onto the rim, passing beyond them, and dropping down near where the invaders were.

Jath feared that Ontius and Lariah were doomed. He strung an arrow, knowing how hopeless it would be for him to shoot at Pagros and Shecum from this distance. But he felt he had to do something, for Ontius and Lariah were in danger and helpless.

So it seemed, at least. Then, to Jath's surprise, Ontius raised the strange contraption he held in his hands, and a moment later, Pagros yelped with pain, his voice echoing across the cavern.

Jath turned his eyes from Ontius and Lariah toward Pagros, who was tugging at a shaft in his arm. When Jath turned his attention back toward Ontius and his daughter, they were gone! In that brief instant in which his eyes had been averted, they had vanished. Apparently Shecum was equally surprised, for he shouted his dismay.

Pagros, however, was distracted by his injury and called for Shecum to come to his aid. Jath relaxed the tension on his bow. Pagros and Shecum were too far away to shoot at with any accuracy anyway. For that matter, Jath suddenly realized, Ontius was too far from Pagros to have shot an arrow with any hope of hitting his mark. The strange instrument must have been a weapon, and it must have launched the arrow, but how? Jath wondered. It certainly was not a standard bow.

Jath stood wondering for too long, and Shecum spotted him. The young invader shot an arrow just as Jath dropped out of sight. The arrow fell short, and Jath listened to it strike the rock below him.

Only a few moments passed before Jath peeked around the boulder in front of him. Shecum was busy assisting Pagros. With the two invaders temporarily preoccupied, Jath stole quietly from his hiding spot and moved as silently as he could toward the area where Ontius and Lariah had so mysteriously disappeared. He realized that he could not get there, but he hoped to reach a point where he could see where they might be concealed.

He covered more than two-thirds of the distance to the crevice before Shecum and Pagros, his injury bound up, started to inch their way over rocks and along the shelf that eventually brought them to within accurate arrow range of the spot where Ontius and Lariah had stood.

Jath moved a little farther and then stopped, for he was no fool. He was not a match for Pagros or Shecum with a bow, and he was well within their range now. But the thought of pretty Lariah and where she might be after having so suddenly vanished kept him from retreating to a safer distance. Ontius and Lariah had to be trapped in some unseen crevice within a very short distance of where they had stood, Jath concluded. He took some comfort in the knowledge that the reclusive father of Lariah was quite capable of defending himself and his daughter.

The amazing speed and deadly accuracy with which Ontius had launched his arrow still made Jath shake his head in wonder. What sort of weapon did the man possess that enabled him to shoot so far with such accuracy? There was little doubt that the only thing that had prevented Pagros from receiving a fatal wound had been the distance. If Ontius were to suddenly reappear as magically as he and Lariah had vanished, distance would not save Pagros again. Pagros and Shecum were quite close to the spot where Ontius had stood earlier.

Jath hunched low, fearing that the invaders would spot him. They would almost certainly hit him now if he let them see him long enough to shoot an arrow at him. He continued to hunch down where he listened, rather than watched, as the invaders closed in on the spot below the wall where Ontius and Lariah had vanished. Each step his enemies took brought them closer to him. Soon they were so close that he had no trouble hearing every word they said as they conversed in hushed tones. He was glad that the narrow, deep chasm separated him from them, even though it also separated him from Lariah and Ontius.

"They've got to be there, Pagros, just beyond that rock ahead. It is too steep for them to have climbed out over the rim, and I'd have seen them, anyway," Shecum said.

"Then move ahead and we'll find them. There is no other place they could be, unless . . ." Pagros said, and his voice trailed off.

In the silence that followed, Jath could hear only an occasional whispering of the slight breeze as it swirled from the rim above him and the gentle murmur that rose from the depths below. If Pagros and Shecum were still advancing, they were doing so without a sound.

Some very slight noise above him caused Jath to look up. His heart leaped. There, at the top of the sheer wall beneath which he was crouched, stood Lariah, her black hair swirling around her face and shoulders in the breeze. She was looking right at him, a triumphant smile on her face. Her right hand clutched a long, perfectly straight section of bamboo—the stick she had held earlier. She lifted her left hand to her face and pressed one finger over her lips in a gesture of silence. Her skirt twirled playfully in a sudden gust, then hung straight to her sandal-clad feet in the calm that followed.

Her eyes left his and searched the rugged, rocky volcanic terrain below her and in front of Jath. He knew the exact moment when she spotted their common enemies, for the smile left her lips, and her face became alert. As soundlessly as the beating of a butterfly's wings, Lariah brought the bamboo tube to her lips, and she blew into it forcefully.

The voice of Pagros erupted in a fierce yelp of pain, and he began to curse. Lariah silently hunched down until Jath could see only her head, and he knew that she must now be concealed from the view of the invaders. Again, she smiled at Jath, a shy friendly smile, and his heart surged.

He wished that he could scramble up the solid rock face that rose to where she was crouched and join her, but it was impossible. Once more, a finger touched her lips, and he smiled at her. The milky skin of her face was suddenly tinged with pink, and her smile grew broader.

So enraptured had Jath become at the appearance of Lariah, that it had not occurred to him to question how she had come to be above him. Only when the angry voice of Pagros again broke the stillness and smothered the murmuring of the volcano, did Jath wonder.

"Something struck me in the shoulder, Shecum," Pagros whined.

Lariah waved at Jath, smiled again, and was gone. His eyes lingered on the spot where she had been, but his ears listened carefully to the invaders' voices from across the narrow chasm.

Pagros cursed again. "It feels like a fire burns in my shoulder, and I can't move."

"Maybe it is from the arrow," Shecum suggested.

"The other shoulder, you fool!" thundered Pagros, and Jath knew the two were still separated, and that Shecum had not gone to the older man's aid.

Jath's thoughts turned back to Lariah. He puzzled over how she could have ever gotten, unseen, from across the chasm to the rim of the volcano. He wondered at her triumphant smile. He also could not figure why she was alone—why her father had not appeared there with her. For several minutes, he thought about it, but no answers suggested themselves to him. By all rights, she could not have been there above him. But she had been!

A desperate shout caused Jath to turn back to Pagros. "Shecum!" he cried. "Help me! I can't move."

"Just a moment, Pagros," Shecum answered. "I may have discovered where the man and girl went."

"Forget them!" Pagros pleaded.

"Ah! There is a large opening here. It goes into the rock," Shecum said excitedly. "It is a tunnel. They must be in there."

"Shecum!" Pagros begged, his voice shallow and weak.

"I'm coming. I'm coming," Shecum announced. "But we must hurry and find them. The hole in the rock cannot be very deep."

Only then did Jath finally rise from his hiding place far enough to peer across the narrow chasm. Shecum was scrambling toward Pagros, who was lying dangerously close to the edge. Shecum arrived and pulled him back far enough that he was no longer in danger of falling into the yawning jaws of the sleeping volcano.

"Pagros! What's the matter with you?" Shecum demanded in sudden alarm.

Pagros was beyond speech, and his body made no movement. Jath again crouched out of their view as he grappled with the mystery of the illness of Pagros. *The tiny dart!* he thought. *It must have been dipped in some kind of poison.*

Jath looked up at where she had stood when she had blown the tiny dart with such deadly accuracy, hoping that understanding would come to him.

It did not.

But better by far, Lariah again appeared. As before, she gestured for Jath to be still. Once more, she brought the long bamboo tube to her lips and blew. It was Shecum who yelped this time, and Jath rose and stared at him.

Shecum spotted Jath and screamed in rage, "You! I'll get you for this!" But when he attempted to raise his bow to carry out his threat, his arms did not respond, and he sat down heavily beside Pagros, a strange mixture of fear and rage on his face.

Jath watched him for just a moment longer, then dropped to his knees and glanced up. Lariah had vanished again. His eyes lingered on the rough black rock where she had stood, as if willing her to return.

She did. The bamboo reed in her hand had been replaced with a length of vine that she dropped down to Jath. "Come," she urged in a whisper.

That single word was like a call to heaven, and Jath quickly grasped the vine. He tugged and it held firm.

He climbed the vine, hand over hand, until he reached the edge. Reaching a hand to him, Lariah helped him scramble up beside her. He sat for a moment as he caught his breath, a dozen questions for Lariah churning around in his head. But when he turned to speak, she once again touched a finger to her lips and beckoned for him to follow her.

Jath hesitated, glancing down at Pagros and Shecum. Both men lay as still as death on the hard lava rock. He turned and followed Lariah, who was almost across the rim to the shrubs that bordered it on the far side. She waited while he crossed to her, then they entered the shrubs together, his dozen questions now organized and ready to erupt.

Lariah once more gestured him to silence as she sat and pulled him gently down beside her. She spoke in a whisper that thrilled him. "Jath, why did you come all the way up here? Was it . . ." she paused delicately, "was it to help me?" Her clear green eyes were wide with wonder as they searched his face.

"Yes," he whispered, puzzled over why they were whispering. He was not about to do anything to upset the girl who had so completely captured his heart. He smiled and softly added, "Not that you needed any help."

"Jath," she said urgently, leaning toward him until her mouth was only a hand-span from his ear. "My father will be very angry if he finds that you are here."

"Where is he?"

"Near. But he mustn't know you are with me or that you came to help me," she said.

Jath nodded, then began to ask the first of his burning questions, "Lariah, why did you kill—"

She touched a finger to his lips, silencing him. "They are not dead—only sleeping. Father prepared a poison, but it is mild. When they awaken they will be very angry."

Lariah placed a hand on Jath's arm and, for an exhilarating moment, leaned against him as they continued to softly converse. "I must go to Father," she whispered.

"Where is he?"

"In the tunnel Shecum found. He slipped and hurt his head and I had to stop the invaders before they found him. But now I must hurry and get Father away, for the one called Shecum has discovered our hidden tunnel."

"Why are we whispering?" Jath asked as she began to rise.

"The tunnel is close. It comes out down there," she said, pointing down the hill into an especially tangled thicket of shrubs and scrubby trees. "Father is not far inside and his ears are like those of a wild animal. He can hear anything. He would be so very angry if he knew you were on our mountain."

"Your mountain?" Jath asked, raising an eyebrow while getting to his feet.

Lariah blushed. "Father calls it ours, and he is angry when others come here. This is a sacred place to him."

"I have never seen him here before."

"He has seen you and the others, and it upsets him. For you to be here with me would throw him into a terrible rage. He must not know you are here or even that you were here," she whispered urgently.

"But . . . but surely he saw me when he saw those other men, and—"

She interrupted him impatiently. "Yes, he saw you, and had you been closer, he would have shot you. He thought you were just another one of the invaders."

"Oh, I see. And did you also think that?" he asked, still whispering very softly, for he certainly did not want to invoke the wrath of Ontius.

"No, Jath. I knew it was you," she replied as she bent and retrieved her bamboo rod.

"How?" he asked, but even as he did so, he remembered seeing her and knowing it was her, even though he could not make out her features.

"I don't know. I just knew," she answered, and he understood. "I must go now. Don't follow me, Jath. And please be careful as you leave, and don't let Pagros and Shecum get you," she urged.

With that dismissal, she stooped, kissed him lightly on the cheek, and left him standing stunned and thrilled as she vanished into the thicket below. Only after she had gone did he realize he had let her get away with most of his questions both unasked and unanswered.

CHAPTER 6

Antium persisted in his plan of short, harassing attacks upon Samuel and his people. So far, none of the islanders had been injured, but the men were growing weary and irritable. Samuel was unable to fully concentrate upon the fighting as he continued to worry about Jath. He desperately wanted to go in search of him, but he could not. However, he felt it was unlikely that any of Antium's men were somewhere else when they were needed here for the fighting. He hoped and prayed that he was right, but still he worried.

Inside Baronihah's crowded house, the tension hung like a dense fog, choking and smothering the women and children. Ophera, despite her worries, struggled to maintain order.

"Please," she urged. "We must pull together and have faith." The women agreed, but the children, not understanding fully how desperate their situation was, continued to bicker and whine at an alarming tempo. "Please, children!" Ophera cried. "Captain Baronihah lies very ill in the next room. I know there is scarcely space to move in here, but you must be still so he can get better."

A hush fell over the crowded room, and for a moment, Ophera thought the children were responding to her urgent plea. Then she realized that all eyes were directed beyond her, and she turned to see what they were watching.

Captain Baronihah stood in the doorway, clutching Dara's arm. His flowing white beard and thick crown of equally white hair seemed to glow as he smiled and spoke. "God bless you all. These are trying times to which we are not accustomed. Ophera is right, my young friends. Only God can preserve us from the hands of our enemies. Come, let us all kneel."

Ophera watched as Baronihah, though pale and weak, gently moved through the room as everyone dropped to their knees. He smiled at the little ones and touched each head in turn. Finally, still holding firmly to his wife's arm and with his own son and daughter beside him, he knelt and bowed his head.

At that moment, Samuel entered the house. His eyes swept the room, stopped on Baronihah's kneeling form, and then returned to Ophera, registering surprise. She beckoned him to join her and a moment later, with Maribel between Samuel and Ophera, they bowed their heads, and Baronihah prayed.

He prayed fervently and with great faith for their deliverance from the men who had invaded their peaceful island. A reverent hush remained when he had finished. Without rising from his knees, he spoke. "The Lord will bless us, but we must wade through trials and afflictions first. The men must fight, and you women and children must support them with your faith until they conquer," he said.

Ophera attempted a smile at Samuel, but the weight of the trials she was undergoing was too much. Only tears came and through a mist, she saw Baronihah, his wife, and their two children as they slowly made their way to the doorway that led to the small room where Baronihah had been recovering.

At the light bamboo door, the captain paused and turned to face the women and children. "Perhaps we have had it too easy here," he said. "We will be a better people and a stronger people when we, with God's help, conquer our invading enemies."

He then left the room, his broad shoulders drooping and his head bowed. Not a sound from anyone in the house was heard for several minutes after his departure.

* * *

Jath stayed where Lariah left him for over an hour. The desire to find her and help move her father to a safer place was very strong within him, despite her warnings of her father's anger. Lariah had intended for Jath to return to the other islanders, but he did not know how badly Ontius was injured. This raised a serious question in his mind concerning Lariah's safety.

Jath finally decided on a compromise. He would do something to detain Pagros and Shecum. That would give Lariah time to move her father to safety somewhere. But where, he wondered, did she have in mind? He wished she had told him. And yet, she had hinted, had she not? For she had said her father claimed the mountain. So surely it would be somewhere on the mountain and most likely, not far from here.

Finally, having made up his mind what he would do, Jath scrambled from the bushes and back onto the rim. He looked around cautiously although he didn't really expect to see anyone. After binding Pagros and Shecum securely, Jath planned on returning to Samuel and the others. They could decide what to do next with the two invaders and free Jath of that concern.

He stepped to the very spot where Lariah had stood and launched her little darts. As he looked over the edge, a nasty surprise met him.

Pagros and Shecum had vanished!

Jath had waited too long, and the effects of the poison had apparently worn off. The other possibility was that Pagros and Shecum may have been rescued by other invaders!

Jath rapidly scanned the twisted and broken lava rock below him and looked around the rim. Seeing no one, he hurried back to the other side and scurried into the protection of the bushes. There he tried to think. The more he thought, the more worried he became. Finally, Jath made another decision.

The opening to the tunnel that Lariah and her father had used to escape from Pagros and Shecum was somewhere in the dense thicket of shrubbery and trees just a short distance down the hill from where he sat. Risking the unreasonable anger of Ontius, Jath went in search of the tunnel.

As Lariah had said, it was a dense thicket, and he struggled to make his way through it. If Pagros and Shecum had come out of the effects of the poison, they could well be in the tunnel or in the thicket at this very moment, for Shecum had discovered the opening at the far end. For Lariah and her father, if they had not yet gotten away, it would be disastrous.

The opening was well concealed, and Jath only succeeded in locating it by looking for and finding bent branches and broken leaves. It did not appear that Lariah or her father had used this opening often. When he finally found it, he had to part a large flowering shrub. Several of its broad leaves were bent and broken where someone had gone through before him.

Despite its small opening, the tunnel, once Jath entered it, was much larger than he had expected. He was able to stand without hitting his head, but the floor was rough, twisted, and broken. It was very easy to see how Ontius may have fallen, for little light shone from the openings, and the lava was ragged and sharp. Someone who was hurrying through here could easily trip and fall, and injury would almost certainly result.

He did not hear a sound in the tunnel other than his own labored breathing. It appeared to be empty, but he pulled his sword and crossed to the far end, searching as he went. The opening at that end was very small, and he had to crawl through. The bright sunlight outside made him squint, and it took a moment for his eyes to adjust so he could look around. There was no sign of Shecum or Pagros, or anyone else, for that matter. It was a mystery where the two men had gone. Jath knew it would be hopeless to try to track them, for no one left tracks on the rough, porous surface of the lava rock.

Jath reentered the tunnel and looked more closely for signs that might indicate where Ontius and Lariah might have rested for a few hours. There was no trace of anything to betray their having been here at all. With a sinking heart, he exited the tunnel and sat for a long while in the dense thicket, thinking.

He hoped that Lariah and her father had made it to another hiding place in safety. He was still convinced that Lariah had had a spot in mind when she left him, and he was also sure it was close by. The nagging fear that Lariah had failed to safely move her father tortured Jath.

Had the two invaders entered the tunnel and taken Lariah and Ontius captive? If so, they must have taken them out the other end of the tunnel, for there was little to show where they might have come out this way. If they had, it would have been impossible to do so silently, and Jath would have heard them. But, of course, they could have taken them the other way.

The sun was slowly sinking, and Jath finally started down the mountain. He had finally determined that he should return to his father and ask for help and advice. He had not gone more than a few hundred paces when he stopped and gazed back up the mountain toward the rim of the silent volcano. Why had the flames and smoke ceased? he asked himself once more. But worry over the beautiful girl he had come here to protect crowded the mystery from his mind.

To leave now, with her fate unknown, would be to desert her in what could be the hour of her greatest need. Oh, if only he had not waited to tie up Shecum and Pagros, he lamented. But what he had done, he had done, and in waiting, he had failed Lariah. By leaving now, as he was doing, would he be failing her again? Fiercely, he slapped his forehead and clenched his fists. He could not, would not, fail her again!

So, trying not to think of the worry his absence must be causing his parents, Jath retraced his steps, vowing that he would not leave the vicinity of the volcano until he had either found Lariah again or found evidence to convince him that both she and her father were gone. If they were gone, he was sure, it would not be of their own accord, for he was more convinced than ever that Lariah and Ontius had more secret spots on this mountain, and that they felt safe here.

So, if Lariah and her father were still free, they would be nearby. If they were still free and still on the mountain, then it only stood to reason that Pagros and Shecum would be searching for them.

* * *

Jath was quite mistaken.

Pagros and Shecum were not searching for Lariah and Ontius. They were searching for Jath! No one could be more angry and murderous than those two were as they prowled about the mountain. After awakening from the effects of the poison arrows, they had searched the tunnel. Finding it abandoned, Pagros had decided that the man and his pretty daughter could wait. Their young tormentor, Pagros informed Shecum, must be found and put to death. It was just too dangerous having the young man running about with his poison darts.

* * *

Antium the Younger was not a patient man. The advantage had been his. The harassing attacks against the islanders had not resulted in any injuries or deaths, except to one of his own men, and his people were becoming frustrated and weary. Antium wanted to end the affair here and now, so he gathered his band together.

"As the sun is setting, we will make another attack, only this time we will not retreat. We will push on and wipe out the men of Samuel and Gadoni," he said fiercely.

"But I thought you wanted to capture those two," one of his men said.

"If possible, yes. But if not, then they can die with the others."

"Antium, we are outnumbered," the man complained. "Would it not be wise to wait until Pagros and Shecum have returned to bolster our forces?"

Antium glowered at the man in anger. Then, without warning, his wicked whip snaked out. The unfortunate invader attempted to duck, but Antium's whip was like lightning, and it cut the man savagely across the face, parting the flesh as neatly as a sword might have done. Blood gushed out, and the man grabbed his wound with a whimper.

Turning from him, Antium spoke again. "Does anyone else care to question my judgment?" he demanded.

If any did, they wisely chose not to admit it. If any were angered by Antium's vicious attack on one of them, they did not voice that opinion, either.

Antium's eyes fell upon his victim again as the man attempted to stop the flow of blood. He spoke once more. "Good. I'm glad you all agree with me. This is what we will do." He went on to give his orders. When he turned his back on his men after finishing, they cast doubtful glances at one another, but none dared cross Antium unless they all did. None of them trusted the others enough to suggest such treason for fear another might carry the tale to Antium, so they all sat sullenly and awaited the moment of their final attack.

* * *

Samuel encouraged his men. Some were not much more than boys, and all were accustomed to peace. This siege, at first something of an adventure to the younger ones, had lost any appeal it might have had. The result was unrest, anger, fear, and frustration. Samuel was determined to channel their anger and frustration into productive fighting at the next attack. In doing so, he hoped to reduce the numbers of the enemy and also reduce the unrest and fear of his people.

From barricade to barricade he slipped, giving instructions and expressing his hope and faith. The last barricade was manned by Gadoni and Kim.

"We must draw Antium's men from the trees," he said as he had told the others. "We have got to make them think that their arrows are hitting some of us. A few screams of anguish and someone jumping up and then falling to the ground as if wounded might encourage them to close in and expose themselves to our arrows. When they do, we will fight back with determination. It is time we end this thing."

Gadoni nodded grimly. He did not need a pep talk. No one felt more keenly the desire to protect the women and children than this sturdy man of Lamanite descent. He was angry. "Antium must be stopped, even as we stopped his father," he said with a frown on his broad brown face. "Kim and I will do our part. Of that you can be sure."

Kim's youthful face was serious. "I will fight to the death if I must," he vowed.

Samuel fondly placed a hand on the young man's shoulder. Kim and his brother Kib were experts in the use of slings. As young boys in Zarahemla, they had practiced faithfully. When escaping the torment of the Gadianton robbers, they had used their skill to great advantage. Samuel had no doubt that they would do so now, if and when Antium or any of his men presented themselves as an unsuspecting target.

Suddenly, from the far side of Baronihah's house came the now familiar cry. "Attack!"

Samuel dropped to the ground beside Gadoni and Kim. All three men watched the thick forest ahead. An arrow came as if from nowhere, narrowly missing the log barricade behind which they were sheltered. Kim wasted no time in following Samuel's advice. He cried out, jumped to his feet and, writhing in mock agony, fell to the ground. He crawled quickly back beside Samuel, grinning broadly.

"Well done," Samuel said.

A moment later, another scream of agony came from a point not too far away. But not one of the enemy ventured into sight yet. A third scream, followed by a shout of genuine alarm, came from beyond Baronihah's house.

"Fire! Fire on the roof!" someone cried.

Samuel turned his head just as a flaming arrow sped from the forest and passed overhead. It struck the grass-thatched roof of Baronihah's house, instantly igniting the sun-dried grass on the near side of the roof. Flame from an earlier arrow was already spreading quickly on the far side.

Samuel's blood ran cold, for he knew in that instant what Antium was planning. No sooner had the thought struck him than several men bolted from their places of security to go to the aid of the women and children in the burning house. Even Gadoni whirled as if to go, shouting, "Sam, our families!"

"We can't go, for they will attack now," Samuel warned. And attack they did.

A cry of pain, this time a genuine one, came from somewhere near the house, and Samuel knew that the islanders had just suffered their first casualty.

One of the attacking invaders came straight toward the barrier behind which Samuel lay. With a cry of anger, Kim surged to his feet, whirled his sling in a powerful arc, and released a stone, cutting the man down. Screams and crying from the house alarmed Samuel. The grass and wood were burning rapidly, and for the first time, Samuel wondered if Antium's invasion and takeover of the island paradise might succeed.

Just as quickly as the doubt arose, he thrust it from his mind. "Stay here, Gadoni and Kim," he ordered. "I'll go help at the house and return the other men to the battle."

Twisting and turning to make a difficult target of himself, Samuel scrambled toward the house. An arrow grazed his leg and another tore by his head, but he ran on, ignoring the danger.

At the burning house, arrows were flying everywhere, although to Samuel's relief, most of the people were already out. "Everyone lie down!" he shouted. "Men, turn and fight before it is too late!"

At the sound of Samuel's voice, the confusion cleared. The men turned to face the oncoming invaders just in time, swiftly driving the men of Antium back. Several of the invaders fell to the ground under the fierceness of the attack.

Leaving the fighting to the others, Samuel dashed into the burning house in search of anyone who had not gotten out. He found Dara helping Baronihah slowly across the floor. "Samuel, help us!" Dara cried out.

Samuel was big and strong, as was Baronihah. But the captain's injury and brief illness had caused his huge frame to shrink. With a groan, Samuel gathered the captain in his arms and staggered for the door, following Dara.

Burning grass and sticks from the roof fell all about them as they went. A hot ember lit and smoldered in Baronihah's beard. Another burned Samuel's bowed neck, but he crashed through the door like an enraged bull, carrying Baronihah to safety.

"We were the last," Dara assured him as he placed Baronihah gently on the grass.

It was good they were, for a moment later the house collapsed, and flames shot far into the darkening sky. Dara cried and brushed the smoldering ember from her husband's beard.

Samuel ran to join the fighting, but it was over. Antium and his surviving men had vanished into the forest.

During the dark hour that followed, several men stood guard while the others helped the women care for the wounded. Samuel assessed the damage they had suffered. One of the islanders, a close friend of Captain Baronihah, had died in the attack, leaving a widowed wife, a teenage son, and an infant daughter. Uri was injured, but not too seriously. Laishita had suffered a burn to her arms, and two children were also burned. Another child had been grazed with an arrow. One of the young girls had broken an arm when she fell in the rush to escape the burning house.

Ophera's brother, Josh, had engaged one of the invaders in a fight with swords. He had been victorious, but had suffered several nasty flesh wounds in the process. Others had minor cuts and bruises, but nothing needing attention. The house of Captain Baronihah, along with much of the supply of food the islanders had carried here when they gathered, had been destroyed in the fire.

Oreb reported to Samuel that the captive invaders had been cut loose, but one of them later turned up dead along with three more of Antium's men. One man was left behind in the invaders' retreat. He was severely wounded, and had been unable to drag himself away. He died before the night was over.

Samuel's people had been dealt a blow, but they consoled themselves in the fact that Antium and his men had been dealt a bigger one. As the wounded were cared for and a few shelters hastily constructed for the women and children, Samuel prowled the perimeter of their encampment. He was seething in righteous anger. Antium must be stopped!

* * *

Antium was also seething. His men had failed him. In failing, their numbers had dwindled. A quick count revealed that only nine men had returned from the battle. Of those nine, three, including Zermanah, who had scarcely had the strength to join in the attack, were badly injured.

Antium cursed when he realized that he only had eleven men left. And that included Pagros and Shecum who had not yet returned from their pursuit of the two islanders who had fled inland. He could only hope they were still alive and would soon return to aid in the fighting.

Daylight came, and it found Antium pacing and cursing his men, especially Pagros and Shecum, who still had not returned. The men lay in a tight bunch, tired and sore from the battle the night before. They listened to Antium's tirades without response.

Suddenly, his whip snaked out and snapped like a sharp clap of thunder. The men came to attention—all but the three who were seriously wounded, that is. "Men, we will attack again as soon as Pagros and Shecum return with their captives. If you will do as I order this time, we will succeed."

Not once did Antium consider the fact that his planning was flawed. Failures were always the fault of his men. Those men were feeling defeated now, and they were not anxious to engage Samuel and his men again, but none of them said so to their leader.

Had it not been for Antium's fierce hatred for Samuel and Gadoni, his unreasonable desire for revenge, and his men's fear of him, the big double canoe that lay concealed just a few paces away would be floating on the sea in a permanent retreat. But Antium was firmly in charge, and to give up now, even in the face of his humiliating losses, would go against his cold and calculated hatred as well as everything his evil father had taught him.

* * *

While Antium and his men nursed their wounds and cursed their bad luck, Samuel was moving his people. Not knowing how much longer Antium would continue to pursue his sinister purposes, the people decided they should go to one of the other houses. Samuel's was not too far distant, so that was where they were now headed. For safety's sake, they traveled in one body. Men acting as guards moved ahead and behind, watching for any sign of the invaders. They arrived safely, and by noon they had settled fairly comfortably in and around Samuel's house.

Food was gathered and new barriers erected to protect the men in the event of further attacks. Samuel worried as he worked, for Jath had not yet returned, and when he did—if he did—he would find the encampment at Baronihah's place abandoned and have no idea where to go. He might even think they were all dead or taken captive by Antium.

Ophera prayed for her son. In the heart of this loving mother lurked a premonition of impending disaster. She knew that something terrible was about to happen.

CHAPTER 7

Jath could not be blamed for allowing himself to get distracted, for strange things were happening in the huge volcano. It had simply been a bad time to venture to the edge and look in. He was trying to determine why the soft purr had turned to a hair-raising growl deep in the bowels of the ancient crater.

Actually, it sounded much like a giant pot of boiling stew. Jath could not see much because of the foul-smelling smoke and steam that arose in ever increasing volume. Something frightening was going on in that crater, and Jath didn't like it.

He had failed in his efforts to locate Lariah and her father. He hoped, if they were near, that they too could hear the changes that were occurring. Having had no experience with volcanoes, he didn't know what this all meant, but he was afraid.

Jath had also not seen anything of Pagros and Shecum or any of the other invaders. He wondered if they had decided to rejoin Antium and his band. When Jath straightened up and turned away from the dangerous precipice over which he had been leaning, he wondered no more.

Pagros and Shecum were only a few paces away!

As they approached Jath with drawn swords, he quickly drew his own, but Pagros only laughed. "You don't know how to use that," he scoffed. "Anyway, it is not yours. It is mine. I want it back before I send you into the molten lava bubbling below."

Jath's hand gripped the sword tighter, and he took a step toward his advancing tormentors—away from the edge of the crater. "Get out of my way!" he shouted, hoping to startle them. He hoped they didn't hear the tremor in his voice.

"Throw that sword down!" Pagros ordered gruffly, advancing to within about three paces of Jath before stopping.

Shecum stood only a step behind Pagros, and on his face was a gleeful smile. "Let me throw him in the crater, and then the girl will be mine," he said.

Jath's throat constricted in terror, and he could scarcely breathe. The taste of fear was bitter in his mouth. He imagined his body tumbling into the scalding mass of molten rock below. He tried to think a prayer, but it was short.

"Drop the sword or I'll slice your hand off!" Pagros warned, his poised sword glistening in the sunlight, ready to carry out the threat. A drop of sweat rolled across Jath's eyebrow and into his eye, blurring his vision. With his free hand, he rubbed it, clearing his sight. Pagros took advantage of Jath's distraction and lunged forward, jabbing with his sword.

A sudden surge of energy flowed through Jath's veins and into his arms, and with a powerful swing of his sword, he deflected the sword of Pagros. He followed with a quick jab, drawing blood across the big invader's knuckles.

A cry of rage accompanied a powerful stroke of the sword of Pagros, and he knocked the sword from Jath's hand. It clanked on the rock, bounced, and came to rest, poised at the brink of the precipice.

"Now you will fall to your death and burn!" Pagros shouted. "And I will have my own sword again."

Jath stepped back, stumbled, and fell. He landed so close to the edge of the crater that his head leaned back over the edge. Steam and smoke swirled about him. A hand grasped his foot and shoved. Jath kicked and pulled himself free. But then a hand grasped his other foot. He kicked again but felt himself slipping over the edge. His head hung farther, and his neck strained painfully as he attempted to lift his head high enough to see his tormentors. Death waited but a few heartbeats away for Jath.

He did not want to die! Desperately, his fingers dug into the sharp edges of the hardened lava as the two invaders attempted to shove him to his death. With strength born of desperation and the desire to survive, Jath gripped the lava tighter and held on despite the pain of the rock tearing his fingers and palms.

Pagros placed one of Jath's feet against his belly and leaned over so far that Jath could see the cruel light that burned in his eyes. Shecum was pushing the other foot up, but Jath clung to life with his hands, refusing to give up. He struggled and tried to kick. Pagros was a big man, and his twisted, hateful face bent closer toward Jath, shooting intense pain through his leg. Shecum was lighter, and Jath, with a tremendous surge of power in the leg Shecum held, sent the small man sprawling on his back, freeing the leg.

Then, for no reason that Jath could understand, Pagros let go of the other leg, and the great bulk of his body came forward, crushing Jath's chest and driving the breath from his lungs. Jath heaved himself upward, and Pagros rolled off Jath's body. Then, with a terrible scream of terror, he tumbled head first past Jath's eyes into the steaming, churning crater. His scream was swallowed up in the bubbling and boiling lava below Jath's own head and shoulders.

The sound of Shecum's voice rose above the din. "Pagros! Where are you?" he shouted. "I'll kill you for this," he told Jath angrily.

But he did not. Instead he ran, and Jath could faintly hear the sound of his fleeing footsteps above the racket coming from below. Jath strained and managed to pull his head up far enough to catch a glimpse of Shecum as he disappeared across the rim.

Alone and baffled at his sudden deliverance, Jath began to use what strength he had left to wiggle and scoot his battered and torn body away from the edge. He was making steady but very slow progress when a voice said, "Give me your hand, and I'll help you."

Jath recognized the voice. "Lariah?" he choked.

"Yes, Jath," she responded urgently. "Give me your hand."

Slowly and painfully, Jath released his grip on the lava with one hand and reached up. A soft, warm hand gripped his hand and pulled. Jath tensed the muscles of his stomach and gave Lariah all the help he could. As his head and shoulders rose, he saw her.

Never had anyone looked more lovely. Moisture glistened from her face, which was strained with the effort of pulling on Jath's hand. Her long black hair hung to one side in a straight, shining mass. Jath did not take his eyes off her until he was in a full sitting position. Then, all his strength faded in a surge of relief at his miraculous release from the jaws of death, and he slumped forward.

Lariah was instantly beside him, one arm across his back and the other beneath his chest. There she steadied him, held him, and comforted him while the terror of his close escape drained away and new strength pumped into his limbs.

After a while, he responded to her gentle urging and let her help him to his feet. He stumbled forward, away from the ugly death that licked at his back, and let her guide him to safety and concealment in the trees and bushes below the rim.

While his strength slowly returned, Lariah slipped away, promising to return in a moment. When she came back, she was carrying Jath's sword in one hand, the one he had taken from Pagros. In her other hand was the strange weapon with which Ontius had injured Pagros the day before.

As he stared in fascination at the weapon, a realization of what had caused Pagros to fall came to him. He looked away from the bow, for it was a bow of sorts, and into the glowing green eyes of Lariah. "Did you use this just now?" he asked.

"Yes." Her eyes glistened with tears as she looked at Jath. "I had to shoot Pagros. He would have pushed you into the crater, Jath."

Jath touched her cheek. "Thank you, Lariah, for saving my life."

"I didn't want to lose you," she murmured, her eyes lowered. "You are my only friend, Jath."

Jath smiled at her, then suddenly frowned. "What about Shecum? One minute he was threatening to kill me, and the next he was running away."

"He must have seen me holding Father's bow," Lariah speculated, "and thought he would be next."

"Would you have shot him?" Jath asked in amazement.

"It would have been too late to save you," she said and looked away.

"Why? Your aim was good enough the first time," Jath protested.

"It's not my aim," Lariah smiled. "Father has taught me well. It is just that this bow is very powerful, and it takes me a long time to string an arrow. But, fortunately, Shecum wouldn't have known that."

"How does this thing work?" Jath asked, gingerly taking the bow from her with his scraped and bleeding hands.

At the sight of his hands, Lariah cried out, "Your hands! We must wash and bandage them."

Jath shrugged. "They'll be fine. Please, tell me about this bow. Did your father build it?"

"Yes," she answered, "he designed and built it. The wood is very strong."

Jath examined the bow as Lariah explained how it worked. The bow part itself was much like any bow, only the wood was a little thicker. Fastened to the center of the bow was another piece of wood, a cross-piece. It was about the length of a man's arm. "It is designed to fit snugly against your shoulder when you want to shoot." She took the bow from him and demonstrated.

"What are the notches for?" he asked, referring to a series of small notches in the cross-piece near where it was designed to fit against the shoulder.

"They are to hold the string back when it is ready to shoot," she explained. And then she demonstrated by placing an arrow in two rigid loops of carved bamboo that were fastened to the cross-piece. Then she placed the notch at the end of the arrow over the string. "Help me," she said. "I can hardly pull the string back. That is why it takes me so long to get ready to shoot."

Jath stepped behind her and reached around. He felt her tremble lightly as they stood close together, and he helped her pull the string tight, pretending that his fingers didn't hurt. When it was pulled back, she slipped the string into one of the notches where it held the bow in its bent position.

The arrow stayed in place, and she showed Jath how she could aim the bow without having to strain as she would if she were holding the string back with her hand. The cross-piece did that for her. "It increases your accuracy," she said as he stepped from behind her and took the bow that she held out toward him. Pressing the cross-piece to his shoulder, he sighted down the arrow.

"When you're ready to shoot, you just flip the string with your finger," she explained.

Jath was impressed. "This is a very fine weapon. Your father is a smart man, Lariah."

"Yes," she agreed. "But he's . . . well . . . not very friendly."

"I guess I can't blame him too much. He's just protective of you," Jath said as he helped Lariah free the string on the powerful bow, releasing the tension. As they worked, fresh blood oozed from his torn fingertips.

"Jath, we really must clean and bandage your hands." She took his arm firmly, adding, "Then we must help Father."

"We?" Jath asked. "Do you mean he will let me help him?"

"He must. He fell in the tunnel and hurt his head. He hit hard and cut himself deeply. When he stands up, he is very dizzy and falls unless I support him. He said he can't see anything very clearly. His head aches terribly, too."

"Where is he?" Jath asked. "We better hurry, I don't like the way this old volcano is acting."

Lariah dismissed Jath's fears with a shrug. "Father says not to worry about it. He says he's not afraid."

"Well, I am," Jath admitted.

Lariah smiled. "I must admit that I am afraid, too. We must get Father away from here. Come, he is not far."

Ontius was sleeping when Lariah led Jath to a well-concealed cave several hundred paces down the mountain. The cave was small and damp, but it was well stocked with food and water-filled gourds. Lariah grabbed one of the gourds and led Jath out of the cave and into the dense jungle that surrounded it.

"Hold out your hands," she said.

Jath did as she instructed, and Lariah bathed his hands. They were badly torn, but none of his injuries were very deep. He refused to let her bandage them. "We haven't time for that," he protested. "Anyway, they'll be fine in a day or two."

When they re-entered the little cave, Ontius was awake and sitting with his back against the wall. He eyed Jath suspiciously. "Who's this?" he demanded of his daughter. Jath was surprised that Ontius didn't remember him until he recalled that his vision had been impaired by his fall.

"Jath," Lariah answered simply. "He is here to—"

"I told you to stay away from my daughter!" he roared.

Jath stepped back, but Lariah grabbed his arm and tugged, pulling him beside her again. "He came to help us, Father. Pagros is dead. He fell in the crater. But Shecum is still—"

Ontius interrupted angrily again. "Then send Jath to his father where he'll be safe, and we'll stay right here. Off with you, boy. You're not welcome here."

As Ontius spoke, the earth began to tremble lightly, but it was not his angry voice that shook the ground. A rumble seemed to ooze from the very walls of the cave as the trembling increased. Jath glanced at Lariah in alarm. Her eyes were wide with fear.

"The volcano! We must hurry and get away from here!" she cried.

"It is nothing, Lariah," her father grumbled. "Send the boy away and help me get something to eat. My stomach is complaining."

Jath ventured to speak. "I came to help Lariah move you to a safe place. I don't know much about volcanoes, but this one is acting—"

"Don't be a fool, boy," Ontius cut in. "It's just stretching its muscles. There is nothing to fear."

Jath turned to Lariah. "Help me get your father to his feet."

"You keep your hands off me!" Ontius growled.

"Father!" Lariah cried. "Get up. We've got to get away from here. It isn't safe."

"We are not leaving," Ontius said stubbornly.

"I am going with Jath, Father, whether you come or not," she said with a firmness that surprised even Jath.

"I command you to stay!" Ontius thundered in response.

"No, Father," she said. "I will not stay. It is dangerous here. We are leaving now. Are you coming?"

The face of Ontius was black with anger, but he could see that he was powerless to stop her. So he reached for her hand, and she helped him to his feet. He stood shakily, swaying like a palm tree in the wind. Jath reached out to support him, but Ontius shook him off.

"I'll get the weapons and a few supplies," Jath said.

Lariah nodded at him and led her father outside. Jath joined them a moment later. "I think it is going to erupt," he said.

"Yes, it is," she agreed. Her father swayed dangerously, and she struggled to support him. "I just hope we're not too late," she added.

Ontius stumbled, and had Jath not dropped his armful of supplies and caught him, he would have fallen. "I'll help him now," Jath said firmly, and Ontius made no further protest.

Lariah gathered up the supplies Jath had dropped, and together they made their way down the mountainside and into the dense jungle below. Jath was not thinking about what direction they were traveling. His only concern now was to get as far away from the volcano in as little time as possible. Safety lay in distance, as much as they could get before it erupted.

They traveled through jungle so dense that the sun scarcely penetrated, which created a dark and gloomy atmosphere. The earth beneath their feet continued to tremble, and the rumbling behind them became more intense. Even Ontius quickened his pace.

* * *

Had Jath been able to see what his family now watched from in front of their house, he would have been terror-stricken, but the jungle hid the volcano's plume of smoke and flames that shot into the sky.

Samuel and the others watched in awe as the plume grew higher, then died away momentarily before shooting up again even farther into the sky. "Are we going to die, Father?" Maribel asked fearfully.

"No, we're safe here," Samuel replied. "The volcano is a long way off."

Ophera expressed his worst fear, though, when she said, "I just hope Jath is not near that horrible mountain!"

"Oh, that stubborn fool Ontius," Samuel muttered in helpless frustration, placing the blame for Jath's disappearance where he felt it justly belonged.

"But Jath should not have gone," Ophera reminded him.

"I would have done the same thing for you," Samuel countered softly.

To that, Ophera could not argue, for she knew it was true.

"Take Maribel inside, Ophera. I must see to the men. It would be just like Antium to attack when we are all watching that old volcano show off," Samuel said, squeezing her fondly and patting his daughter on the head.

* * *

Samuel need not have worried right then, for Antium and his men were not yet ready to attack again. Pagros and Shecum had not returned, and Antium was purple with rage.

Hidden as deeply as they were in the heavy jungle beside the cove, Antium's men were unaware of the flames and smoke that were shooting from the high mountain behind them. After Antium's latest tirade had run its course, Migroni, the young invader of Lamanite descent, stalked from camp. He muttered and cursed to himself over Antium's harsh treatment.

In time he became aware of a rumbling in the distance. He ignored it at first, but it seemed to grow louder as he walked through the dense forest. At last Migroni's curiosity got the best of him, and he stepped out of the jungle into a large area of shrubs and grass.

His eyes bulged when he saw a mighty burst of flame shoot into the air from a tall mountain peak. Smoke filled the sky as the flame died out. Then it shot up again with even more force than before. Having never before seen a volcano, Migroni knew nothing of them. To him, what he saw was more terrifying than anything he had ever experienced—including the whip of Antium.

Like a frightened animal, he returned to the trees and fled back to camp in terror. "The mountains are breathing fire!" he announced at the top of his voice as he raced into the encampment. "The island is going to burn. The gods are destroying the island!"

Antium's men gathered around Migroni and tried to calm him down. But Migroni became more frightened as he talked, and soon he was just babbling and pointing. His fear passed like a fever through the men. Antium snapped his whip and shouted at them to not listen to Migroni's foolish babbling, all to no avail.

One of the men shook Migroni roughly and said, "Show us what you saw!"

Migroni pointed in the direction of the fire-breathing mountain. The men shoved him roughly, and he finally led the way to where the erupting mountain could be seen. All but the wounded men followed him.

Even Antium went along, grumbling, "It is probably only a trick of Samuel's. He is trying to frighten us."

When the fiery mountain came into sight, even Antium realized that Samuel could not possibly be responsible. The sky was dark with smoke, and each time flames shot skyward from the top of the mountain peak, they went higher, and more smoke filled the sky. The invaders watched in mute horror until Migroni turned and fled. Then they followed.

Antium was not alarmed. He alone, of all his surviving band, knew what a volcano was, and he had no fear. But when his men started pulling the boat from its place of concealment amidst cries of "We must get away from here!" he cracked his whip furiously. Several men felt the biting sting of his whip before they finally submitted and pushed the boat back.

"We will wait here for Pagros and Shecum, just as we planned. Then we will attack. The mountain is only an old volcano that is erupting. It is too far distant to be of danger to us," he explained angrily.

"But the gods—" Migroni began breathlessly.

"There are no gods!" Antium thundered, letting Migroni feel the bite of his whip.

The young Lamanite gazed steadily at Antium, then walked away. If he lived through this terrible thing, Antium would regret what he just did, Migroni vowed to himself.

* * *

Shecum was battered and bruised from his terrified flight down the mountain. When he had realized that Pagros had been shot by the pretty girl and had fallen into the bubbling crater, he had fled. His first concern had been that the girl would shoot him as well. His second was that the death of Pagros had left him alone and vulnerable.

He had only intended to flee a short distance where he could hide and wait for a better chance to capture the girl, but when flames began spurting into the air from the wide crater and the earth began to tremble, he fled for his life.

The terrain was rough, and he stumbled many times, bruising his knees, his arms, and his hands. Branches tore at his clothing, and his body was covered with scratches and cuts. He could think of nothing but getting back to Antium and the other men and sailing far away from this dangerous island.

After several miles, Shecum had been forced to stop and rest. His legs hurt, his lungs burned, and his head pounded. After he had caught his breath, he looked back toward the volcano. To his surprise, the shooting tower of flames had disappeared. Only a drifting blanket of smoke that dimmed the sun gave evidence of the fire that had erupted from the mountain.

Then the earth began to tremble and a strange rumbling swept across the island. It reminded Shecum of distant thunder. He needed to go on, but he could not draw his eyes from the mountain he had so recently walked upon. A huge tower of liquid fire then climbed hundreds of paces into the air. The noise was deafening, and a wave of heat smothered the island. Shecum stood in dumb shock as he watched the molten rock reach an astounding apex far in the smoky sky before it came crashing back to earth, burying the old crater in an orange sea of flames.

CHAPTER 8

Nature's mighty show of force was a spectacular but frightening thing for the islanders as they stood outside Samuel's house. Even Baronihah, weak and thin though he was, insisted that he make his way to the door where he could watch. "I always wanted to see one of those go off," he said with a twinkle in his eye that demonstrated to the others his lack of fear and bolstered their own courage. "Shows just how puny we little people are. If we could imagine all the things God can do, even this erupting volcano would seem puny."

When they were over their initial shock, the children were fascinated. Not that they weren't frightened, for they were, despite the courage of Captain Baronihah. The ground rumbled and shook beneath their feet. Oppressive heat hung in the air, and the cry of fleeing animals reached them from the forests. Despite it all, they stood in awe as a great column of lava continued to shoot far into the sky.

Samuel and Ophera clung to one another, silently praying for the deliverance of their son, the girl he had so rashly gone to save, and her stubborn father.

* * *

That stubborn father was not being stubborn at the moment. He had seriously delayed his flight through the jungle, and he and his daughter and Jath were still dangerously close to the unleashed fury of the volcano.

Supported by Jath's arm, Ontius stumbled down the mountain to safety. Lariah found it necessary to abandon some of the supplies she had been carrying. But it didn't matter. They were fleeing for their very lives.

The first initial blast had deposited burning lava close behind them. Trees and bushes burst into flaming torches from the searing heat waves that surged before the lava as it flowed down the mountain. The heat that surrounded Jath's little group was intense and suffocating. Had they waited just a few more minutes before leaving the little cave, they would have been consumed by the rolling lava or roasted by the heat itself.

Even after the eruption halted, the molten rock continued to seek lower ground. It filled the valleys, sent huge clouds of steam into the air from the streams, and drove the surviving wildlife from their chosen territories near the fatal mountain.

When even the force of terror could not overcome fatigue and burning lungs, Jath, Lariah, and Ontius sank to the ground on a lightly forested ridge. The older man stretched out on his back on the ground, eyes closed, while Jath and Lariah watched with relief as the volcano's eruption slowly diminished.

"I wonder if Shecum got away, too," Lariah said.

Jath had had the same question. "We did, so I suppose he could have," he said.

Lariah gazed at the fiery mountain. "You saved our lives," she said quietly.

"You saved mine first," Jath said with a grin. "Otherwise I wouldn't have been here to help you." He glanced at Ontius and asked, "Is your father asleep?"

"Probably," Lariah said, giving her father a tender look. "No doubt he's exhausted. And starved as well. I am, and I know you must be."

If Ontius was awake, he made no effort to prove it. Lariah was right about hunger. As darkness was not far off, Jath decided to do something about it. On this island, food was not a problem. Fruits, coconuts, roots, edible herbs, and wild game were plentiful. Although Jath wondered sadly how many beautiful animals and birds had died that day from the volcanic eruption. His father had taught him to love and respect the animals and birds of the island and to kill only what was needed for food and clothing.

As Jath lifted his bow to go in search of game, Lariah rose and stood beside him. "Jath, did your family know you would be gone so long? They must be worried about you."

He felt his face redden. Her eyes opened wide, and she looked at him accusingly. "Do you mean . . . you didn't . . . they didn't know you were leaving?" she asked.

"I was afraid they wouldn't let me go if I told them, so I didn't," he admitted sheepishly.

"They must be sick with worry!" Lariah scolded him. "Jath, you must hurry back to them and let them know you are all right."

"You mean, we must," he responded. "I can't leave you and your father out here by yourselves. He's still not well, and—" he began.

"We'll manage, Jath," she said sternly. A wistful look spread across her face, and her eyes searched his face. "It's almost dark. You could get hurt if you try to go tonight. Anyway, you are too tired after helping us escape. You better not try to go until morning."

"We'll all stay here tonight," he agreed. "And when we go in the morning, it will be together."

Slowly, Lariah shook her head. "Father will not go, and I cannot leave him," she said, her eyes brimming with tears. "You must go back without us."

"Back in the cave, you told your father that you'd leave without him if he didn't come," Jath reminded her.

"That was because our lives were in danger," Lariah explained. "I thought it would make him come, and it did."

"What would you have done if he had still refused?" he asked.

"I would have stayed with him," Lariah answered calmly.

"But you'd have been killed!" Jath exploded.

"Jath, he's my father. He may be stubborn and unfriendly to strangers, but he is still my father, and I love him," she said firmly. "I know that we are no longer in danger, but I still can't leave him."

"No longer in danger?" Jath asked incredulously. "Do you really believe that Shecum will give up? He's determined to capture you, Lariah. Can't you see that? And there are a lot more invaders just like him, too. You may not be in danger now of the volcano hurting you, but you are still very much in danger, Lariah. And so is your father!"

"That is not your affair, young man!" Ontius said with a roar from the ground, startling both of the young people. They spun toward him. He was propped up on one elbow, scowling fiercely. Jath wondered how much of their conversation he had heard.

"I am not ungrateful for your aid," Ontius continued, "but your presence now is offensive to me. You are to leave. Now!"

"But I was just going to get some meat—" Jath began.

"My daughter and I have managed just fine all these years without your help—without anyone's help," Ontius growled. "We can certainly manage now."

"Father! How can you treat him so harshly?" Lariah said reproachfully. "He saved our lives from the eruption."

Ontius laughed. "You both thought I was asleep, but I was not. I heard every word that you said. Lariah, hand me my quiver."

She quickly obeyed as he struggled to sit up. He counted his arrows. "Aha!" he thundered when he had finished. "There is one missing. Lariah, did you shoot Pagros with it?"

"Yes, Father," Lariah admitted, "but he was—"

"About to kill the son of Samuel, I'm sure," Ontius said with a sneer. "I understand fully. You see, young man, we can manage quite well without you. You are the one who needs protection, and we cannot continue to give it. So leave!"

Jath could see that Ontius would not be satisfied until he left. After a quick look at Lariah, he bowed his head in submission. "Yes, sir," he said.

"It would be better if he waited until morning, Father," Lariah argued tearfully.

"That's enough, Lariah!" Ontius said sternly.

For a moment her green eyes glared mutinously at her father, then, like Jath, she too bowed her head. "Yes, Father," she said finally.

Without a word, Jath gathered his weapons and started off the ridge. Lariah stood motionless, staring after him. "Good-bye, Jath," she called out, her voice choked with emotion.

Turning back, Jath gazed at her for several long moments. Although she was stained with dirt and her long black hair was tangled, he had never seen anyone so beautiful.

"Good-bye, Lariah," he said before he turned and strode briskly out of her view. His heart had never ached like this before. Had he stayed a moment longer, she might have seen him cry and he could never have let that happen!

Behind him, the voice of Ontius thundered through the trees, arresting Jath with its ferocity. "Don't you ever come back looking for my daughter again, you son of Samuel! Do you hear me, boy? Never again!"

Jath heard, but he made no reply. Instead, he muttered angrily, "We should have left you in your cave." Tears stung his eyes and he regretted his words, grateful that Lariah didn't hear him, for he did not really mean it.

Then he muttered something he did mean, and he meant it with all the youthful power of his soul. "I will be back, Lariah. Neither your father nor anyone else will ever be able to stop me!"

"You hear me, boy?" the angry voice called again, as if in reply. "I mean what I say!"

"And so do I!" Jath murmured, having no idea where his rash promise might lead him in coming days. "And so do I!" he called out fiercely.

* * *

The sun settled over the western sea, shrouded in a great cloud of smoke and ash that painted the sun a dull red. As it sank into the distant waves, the island emitted a glow of its own that was reflected by the dark waters of the sea.

Shecum stared for several minutes at the ocean. Then he cast his eyes upon the mountain that had swallowed his friend and had nearly taken his own life. Bright lava still rolled slowly from the glowing summit. The slopes emitted a dull orange light that seemed to give life to the mountain—an evil, destructive life.

As Shecum watched, he wondered if the pretty girl, the one he wanted for his own, had been consumed by the hungry flow of lava. Or had it spared her life? If so, he would yet claim her, he vowed. He would find her and she would be his.

As Shecum turned and directed his path into the trees and down the slope, he wondered if Antium and the others would be in the secluded cove to greet him. Or would he find himself alone?

In a short time he decided that he would rather have found himself alone! For it did not take Shecum long after being confronted by an enraged Antium to realize this. Not only was Antium furious because Shecum had been gone for so long, but Antium even blamed Shecum for the death of Pagros! But Shecum could consider himself lucky, for all he received was a terrible tongue-lashing. Antium merely shook the whip that was coiled tightly in his fist.

This was evidence that Antium did, in fact, favor Shecum somewhat over his other men. But so furious was he at the verbal assault Antium flung at him that he turned his back on his leader and stalked away.

At any moment, he expected to feel the sting of Antium's whip, and he berated himself for being a fool. *Antium has killed men for less,* Shecum thought as he held his breath, waiting for the crack of the whip.

But it did not come, and Shecum breathed a sigh of relief and tightened his hands into fists to stop their trembling.

He soon found himself at the water's edge in the cove. Due to the darkness that had settled in, he was unaware that he was not alone until he was startled by the voice of Migroni behind him.

"So you finally returned," Migroni said.

"I'm lucky to be alive," Shecum responded dramatically, turning to face the shadowy figure behind him.

"Is Antium still angry at you and Pagros?" Migroni asked. "He was certainly in a rage at your failure to return earlier."

"He is angry. If I'd known he was so unreasonable, I might not have come back at all," Shecum said darkly.

"We all know of his anger and his whip," Migroni muttered.

This was no surprise to Shecum, who knew that Antium favored him. However, he also knew that the day would come when he might, unexplainably and irrevocably, fall from his precarious position. "He has never whipped me," Shecum grunted, "except with his tongue, and that's bad enough."

"He will whip you one day, Shecum," Migroni predicted. "You will not always be his favorite."

Shecum shuddered, for deep down he knew that Migroni was right. No one, no matter how favored, was guaranteed to always be safe when Antium was angry.

Migroni said half-resentfully, "But I have no doubt that Pagros received his share and more."

"Pagros is dead," Shecum said dryly.

Migroni's face showed his surprise. "Dead? How did he die?"

"He was swallowed by the mountain, the one that shoots fire in the sky," Shecum answered briefly. He did not plan on telling anyone what really happened on the mountain that day. How could he ever explain about the girl and her weapons? The others would simply laugh at him.

Migroni only nodded. "The mountain is evil," he said. "It is a bad sign. Nothing but bad luck follows us."

Shecum felt a chill creep down his spine. "Why do you say that?" he asked nervously.

"There was more fighting while you were gone. Men died. Some are badly wounded. With Pagros gone, there are only eleven of us left alive. Three are unable to fight. They need time to heal. While we have lost so many, our enemies have lost but few. Ours is a losing cause, I fear," Migroni finished soberly and looked in the direction of the volcano, which was hidden from their view by the trees in the cove. "The mountain is angry at us for coming to this place where peace has prevailed."

Shecum looked at the deeply shadowed face of the young Lamanite. He wondered if Migroni was right. But he felt compelled to defend Antium; although Shecum feared him, he also respected him. "Antium is smart," he said briskly. "We will win, Migroni, and the island will be ours."

Migroni said nothing as he turned away.

The night had grown still except for the gentle, rhythmic lapping of the waves on the shore and what could only be described as a steady moan from the direction of the deadly volcano.

The two young men faced the sea and stared out at the distant orange reflection of the molten mountain that it threw back at them. Neither fully trusted the other, and each wondered if he had already said too much. Shecum finally seated his battered and weary body on the sand and gazed again at the sea. Sitting beside him, Migroni said after a while, "I suppose we will fight again soon."

"Yes. Then I can go after the girl again," Shecum said with a sigh. "If she escaped the fury of the mountain, that is."

"It is not after them. Only us, the invaders," Migroni warned.

Shecum shrugged. "Maybe. But I will find her, and I will kill the boy if he still lives."

"What boy?" Migroni asked.

Shecum did not respond. He had already said too much.

* * *

The boy he referred to had grown too weary to go on. Jath had fallen asleep in a soft bed of rotting palm fronds. There he slept much of the night away.

When he awoke, it was to the pungent odor of stale smoke and ash and cooling lava. The air was still, and the smoke lay like a blanket over the island. Jath looked up from his cool bed, but all he could see beyond the dark leaves and branches overhead was more darkness with only a pale sheen of the moon trying in vain to shed a cheery light over the island. The smoke had grown so thick that it even hid the stars.

A gnawing hunger tormented Jath's stomach, and he felt the aching of his bruised and stretched muscles from his encounter with Pagros and Shecum. Even worse than his physical pain was the ache in his heart at having to leave Lariah. Ontius would be no match for Antium's men, should they find Lariah and her father.

Jath sat up and felt for his bow and quiver with his torn fingers. They lay where he had placed them. His sword, the one he had taken from Pagros, was still strapped to his side. He had his weapons but no food or water. Jath had not eaten since before his encounter with the two invaders, nor had any water to drink since his wild flight from the fury of the erupting volcano.

The dim glow of the moon through the veil of smoke did not give enough light for Jath to find roots or fruit, but he did find a small stream that flowed nearby. The water was not sweet and cool as he had hoped but was tainted by the lava and ash of the eruption. Jath drank anyway, and then he collapsed beside the stream and again fell asleep.

When he awoke, the sun was burning through the thick layer of smoke to the east. In searching for a ridge where he could inspect the volcano, Jath was surprised at how high the cone had grown during the night. The flow of lava had nearly stopped, and Jath stared in fascination at the stately, newly created mountain crest. When he finally turned his back on it, it was with a mixture of wonder and relief.

Jath's first concern now was in satisfying the hunger that tormented his stomach. He craved meat but settled for fruit. When he had driven the edge from his hunger, he undertook a serious study of the terrain. The hurried retreat from the advancing lava had led Jath, Lariah, and Ontius far from the settled area of the island. He was not lost, but he was anxious to determine the most direct way home, for the sooner he got back, the sooner he could attempt to persuade his father to allow him to go in search of Lariah again. He finally settled on a route and started out.

Thoughts of Lariah troubled him as each step took him farther from where he had last seen her. Anger flooded through Jath again as he thought of Ontius and his foolishness. It was not so much Ontius' foolishness that angered him, but the simple fact that the man was so intent on keeping Lariah and Jath apart. The thought startled Jath. Yes, that was it, he nodded as he muttered under his breath.

His anger gave him strength that quickened his step and reaffirmed his resolve to somehow, sometime, find Lariah again. He consoled himself a little with the hope that Ontius was feeling better and would protect his daughter from the invaders. For surely, Jath thought, Ontius would lead Lariah still farther away from the settlement and the invaders.

* * *

Jath was badly mistaken.

Ontius and Lariah were at that very moment following a route that was similar, almost parallel, to Jath's. There were things that Ontius wanted from his home, and being an impatient man, he wanted them now.

They moved slowly, with Lariah still required to support her father from time to time. Although he was feeling stronger and better, waves of dizziness attacked him without warning. Lariah was convinced that he was wearing himself out and told him so.

"You worry too much, Lariah," he responded testily. "We haven't time to spare, so we must hurry."

"Why, Father?" Lariah said reasonably. "What are you after that we must hurry so?"

Ontius was evasive. "Just some things I want before we establish our new home on the far side of the island."

"New home?" Lariah was stunned. "Father, the invaders will be gone soon, I am sure. Samuel and the others will succeed in driving them off. Then we can return to our house and live in peace again."

Ontius stumbled, and Lariah caught his arm, steadying him before he fell. He said nothing for a few more steps. Lariah pressed him for an explanation, hoping the sinking feeling in her heart was misdirected.

It was not.

"The invaders don't worry me, Lariah," Ontius said, shaking his head. "I believe they will be defeated. No, it is not them I worry about."

Lariah looked at her father in bewilderment. "Then why do you speak of a new home far from the other people?" she asked. "We would never see anyone else if we lived clear across the island."

Her father's face wore a look of satisfaction. "Exactly! We don't need anyone else. That is why we are going to build a new home. I don't want anyone disturbing us again."

"But Father," she began, then paused. She wondered how to say what she wanted to say, but her father continued speaking.

"And especially not that Jath! He certainly is a nosy young man. He is too much like his father, and I don't like either one of them."

Lariah looked at her father sadly. "You don't like anyone, do you, Father?" she asked.

"You are wrong, my daughter," Ontius said softly.

"I am? Then name someone," she challenged.

His voice was tender. "You, my daughter."

"I . . ." she stammered, then cast a glance at her father and could say no more. She was the only one he had in the world. *Maybe I have been too hard on him,* she thought. *Truly he has suffered much.* Lariah was deep in thought when her father spoke again.

"We will not stay at our house longer than it takes to pack what we need and leave," he said.

She nodded, wondering which of the things she treasured he would allow her to take and what she would be forced to leave behind. The thought of leaving her home saddened her. There were birds she had tamed and wild animals that came near whenever she sat quietly watching. There were memories, sweet and clear, of her mother and sister. It would be so hard, so very hard. But she must not cause her father more grief. She must think of him.

Ontius again broke into her thoughts. "No one must see us," he said. "No one can know that we have been home. That which we do not take we will leave undisturbed. It must appear as though we never returned. Maybe then Samuel and the others will think we are dead and not search for us. The sooner they forget about us, the more likely will be our lasting peace and seclusion."

Lariah studied her father's face with misgivings. She saw that he was growing weary. His steps were faltering, but his face remained grim and determined. He glanced at her and then spoke again. "We must rest. I don't want to tire you unnecessarily, Lariah. You must have enough strength left when we get back to our house to help me pack a few things and leave again quickly. And when we leave, we must travel far."

Gratefully, Lariah sat down and leaned back against the trunk of a great mango tree and closed her eyes. She fought back the tears that lurked there, but her thoughts flowed on. Ever present in them was Jath. Quietly, she prayed for him—both that he would be safe and that he would understand her father. But her prayer lacked faith, for she herself did not fully understand him. Nevertheless, despite her lack of under-standing, she would obey.

* * *

The men of Antium also obeyed. They obeyed Antium, but for several, their obedience was increasingly more from fear and mistrust than a belief in the mission that Antium had appointed for them. They started to mistrust not only their vicious leader, but each other as well.

Preparations were made for another series of harassing attacks. "This time we will succeed," Antium said confidently as he led seven of his men from the hidden cove. Three were left behind. They were too badly wounded to be of any help this day.

"We will strike and withdraw, strike and withdraw," Antium said. "And if you men will show a little courage, we will wear the people of Samuel down until we are able to finish off every man and boy of them in one final assault."

He bore a triumphant look on his scarred face, and his beady black eyes shone with unholy glee, for Antium was not a man who gave up easily. Nor was he the kind of man who recognized shortcomings in himself. He would *make* his men give him the victory he sought and help him to avenge the death of his father.

Disappointment awaited Antium at the burned-out dwelling of Baronihah, the last place Antium had seen Samuel and his people. They were gone! Angrily, he ordered his men to follow him until they discov-ered where the islanders were now preparing to defend themselves. Disappointment did not lesson Antium's anger. "We will search out every dwelling," he commanded. "And when we find them, we will attack as planned. They will know the wrath of Antium!"

* * *

What Antium did not know was that the islanders, seeing no sign of the invaders during the early hours of the eruption, had left for a distant part of the island. There, they would prepare a strong defense and then send several men in search of Antium and his evil band of invaders. They would not rest until they found them and destroyed them from the face of the earth.

After that, a search would be conducted for Jath, Ontius, and Lariah, for whom they all prayed with great faith.

CHAPTER 9

A black mound of ashes greeted Jath's eyes as he peered from the trees at the place where the home of Captain Baronihah had stood. The thought of what it likely represented brought Jath to his knees with grief. His first thought was that his people had suffered total annihilation at the hands of Antium and his band.

Several tense minutes passed before Jath was able to force himself to approach the area of destruction and examine it closer. He found no charred bones as he sifted through the ashes. By the time he had abandoned that effort, he was black from head to toe. Soot and ashes filled his nose with a nauseating stench. His eyes were smudged from rubbing them with blackened hands, and his mouth was full of grit.

Several mounds of fresh dirt indicated unmarked graves, hastily dug and covered over. As he stood gazing at the moist brown mounds, he wondered with awful dread whose bodies lay there. He grieved for whoever had died even as he recognized with a slight lessening of his sorrow that for anyone to have been buried meant that there had been survivors to bury them; he was certain that was something Antium would not do.

As Jath backed away from the graves, his eyes still drawn to them with somber anxiety, it did not occur to him that they might contain the remains of some of the invaders. He could think only the worst; after his close encounter with Pagros and Shecum, he truly feared Antium and his men.

Forcing himself to turn his eyes away from the mounds beyond the ashes, Jath faded into the trees, shivering with the sudden realization that he had carelessly left himself exposed to the peering eyes of any enemies who might have been near. He knew he must be more cautious.

From the destroyed home of Baronihah, Jath directed his feet toward his own home. When he arrived, he cautiously circled the entire yard, looking for anything suspicious. He did observe the log barriers that had been constructed and immediately recognized that as the work of his father. So they had been here and prepared a defense, but Jath could see no evidence of a battle having been fought here, and the place appeared to be deserted. Dread again filled his weary soul.

After checking once more to see that he was alone, Jath dashed to the house and entered. The sight that greeted him was heartrending. Everything of value in the house was destroyed! The furniture Jath and Uri had helped Samuel construct lay in scattered pieces. Broken shards of pottery covered the floor, and the walls had been hacked to shreds. Clothing lay torn and scattered everywhere, and everything that could be damaged was. Even Maribel's carved dolls had been broken and hacked to pieces. At the sight, Jath felt sickened to the core.

He wondered how long it had been since the invaders had vented their wrath on this place that his mother had worked so hard to make a joyful home. And where had they gone after they left here? He would not solve that mystery by standing dejected in the pathetic remains of his family's belongings. So leaving the house, Jath entered the green forest again.

Loneliness pressed on him like a giant hand, and he longed for his family. Were they still alive? Were they now fleeing from the bloodthirsty invaders, or were they making a stand somewhere else in the settlement? It had been a long, hot day, and despite Jath's desire to find his family and the answers to his questions, he knew it would take many hours to check all the homes. Even then, he might not find them if they had fled to another part of the island. It would soon be dark, and that would make such an endeavor impossible until morning.

I'll wait until morning, he decided. *Then I'll try to find them.* They could not travel fast, that he knew, for there were many women and children, including some babies. And Baronihah, unless he filled one of the unmarked graves, would certainly slow them down. Yes, Jath could catch up with them quickly, wherever they had gone. Of that he was quite certain.

* * *

Samuel and the islanders were indeed making slow progress. They moved at the pace of a tortoise. For Baronihah, the travel was pure torture, but he did not complain. The children thought it was an adventure. The women quickly grew weary. The men watched continually for the invaders and covered their tracks the best they could in the hope that they would not be followed. Samuel sought a route where they would leave the least possible sign of their passing. They built no fires during their frequent rest stops. They ate only raw fruits and roots and a little dried fish that Samuel had brought from his home.

A stiff wind arose from the west as night set in, driving the smoke and ash out to the open sea, clearing the island of its oppressive cloud. With the rain-scented wind came clouds of a different nature, and as they opened up and generously scattered their burden of rain over the island, the people gave thanks. The rain would help to erase the sign of their passage, and though it was uncomfortable, it brought a measure of security to them in their laborious travels.

* * *

Antium and his men had not been successful that day in locating the islanders. It had not occurred to him to look for tracks, and none of his men chose to suggest this, for fear of Antium's anger. They just did as they were told and pretended not to think.

"They must be at one of the most distant homes to the east. We will find them and attack before noon tomorrow," Antium said confidently as he led his ragged band back to their camp in the cove. There they found that their numbers had dwindled again. One of the wounded men had died during the heat of the day. But the other two appeared stronger.

Migroni again sought seclusion near the water's edge where he grumbled to himself as rain washed over his sweaty, aching body. Of the twenty men who had come to this island to take it by force for themselves, only half now remained alive. He wondered how many, if any, of the other invaders had acquired doubts about their mission, as he had.

To plunder and fight did not bother Migroni a great deal, for his conscience had been dulled by his association with Antium and his kind. The senseless destruction at the home of Samuel had not made sense to him, and he had not participated. To take what someone else owned and make use of it was a way of life with Migroni, but he had never destroyed useful things just for the sake of destroying. As he thought of those members of the band who had died, Migroni knew it was not part of his plan to allow himself to be killed because of Antium's desire for revenge. Several times that day, he had been tempted to slip away and desert Antium, but he had not, for to do that meant being alone on the island with people who viewed him as an enemy or to travel alone by sea. Either could be disastrous.

Migroni smiled to himself as he thought of something he had observed that day that Antium had not. There was no sign of the islanders having come east through the scattered settlement from Samuel's home. Unless he was mistaken, there would be no fighting tomorrow, for the islanders had left the settlement. Migroni had nothing to fear by staying with Antium for now—nothing but the whip, that is, and he had no intention of feeling its sting again, not if he could avoid it.

* * *

The volcano still issued a small amount of lava from its towering cone. Lariah was amazed at its staggering height. Stark and black, it rose far above its old level. The fresh lava flowed from the top and cooled rapidly, adding still more bulk and height. The sun glistened from the newly formed rock, and a few lingering clouds passed below the summit, sending dark shadows racing across the lower slopes of hardened lava.

Birds sang in the trees, and wild animals played in the bushes. A small stream of clear water gurgled nearby, and the grass and leaves still dripped with moisture from the night's abundant rainfall. Lariah's world had the appearance of beauty and peace, but it was a cruel facade. Evil forces were at work on her island paradise. As much as she hated to admit it, her father was more on the side of evil these past few days than good. Otherwise, he would be helping the other islanders, not deserting them in the darkest hour of the island's history.

"Lariah!" Ontius called from nearby.

"I'm coming, Father," she responded obediently, wondering if obedience was the best course. Had she not resisted his wishes when the eruption was nearing? She had and would be dead now, her body burned and buried somewhere in that huge ebony cone, if she had not. It was true that their lives were at stake then, but much was still at stake; if not their lives, then certainly her future happiness!

"Come, daughter!" Ontius ordered gruffly. "We have a hard day ahead of us, and we'd better get started now."

As far as she could tell, the effects of his fall were gone. Her father seemed strong and steady this morning. As if reading her thoughts, he said, "I feel good today, Lariah. My headache is almost gone, and there is no dizziness at all."

"I'm glad, Father," she responded dutifully.

"I'll lead the way, Lariah," he said, and he proceeded to set a blistering pace. He seemed determined to make up for the time they had lost the day before when he was still weak.

By shortly after noon, the sun had dried the soaked grass and leaves, and oppressive, humid heat sapped Lariah's strength. Her father, who was so weak the day before and had called for frequent rests, allowed very few today. Her feet were blistered, her lungs burned, and her muscles ached, but they pressed on relentlessly.

Lariah hung back when they approached their home about noon. She had not forgotten the evil etched in Shecum's features and feared meeting him or any of the other invaders. Ontius might have forgotten all about the invasion the way he plunged recklessly from the trees to the door of his house. Lariah had not, and she approached the house with caution.

It was still and quiet inside, and a thick layer of volcanic ash and dust covered everything. Lariah recalled her father's warning about leaving no sign of their having been here, and she stood quietly just inside the door. Ontius, however, seemed to have forgotten, for he left glaring marks in the dust as he touched and then discarded item after item.

Lariah finally moved softly through the house and entered the door of her room where she stood and surveyed the contents. Several intricately carved wooden dolls sat where they had sat for years on a shelf over her bed. Beside them were several colorful seashells that she had found and with which she had played for many contented hours. On one wall hung a dozen necklaces made of colorful seeds, beads, tiny shells, and white sharks' teeth. Lined up on the floor against the west wall was an array of gaily painted gourds of various sizes and shapes.

Hanging in her closet were several colorful skirts and dresses of finely woven cloth that had been her mother's. They fit Lariah loosely now. Beside them were several grass skirts, creations of her own nimble fingers. Beneath them were a dozen pair of leather sandals, most of them having been made for her by her father.

There were other things as well. As she gazed at them and remembered with simple pleasure the joy each item had given her, tears misted her vision. There was nothing that she wanted to part with. The thought of leaving the things that had given her joy in her loneliness tore at her already aching heart.

She had not moved when her father said from behind her, "Are you about ready, Lariah? Take only what you can carry."

How could she ever choose? "I'll be a moment, Father," she replied sadly.

"Put what you are taking in this," Ontius said, dropping a large sack made of woven grass on the floor beside her. "I'm almost ready, so hurry," he added as he left her still standing and staring at a lifetime of carefully collected, simple, but wonderful things she must choose from.

Finally, she gritted her teeth and began. Two wooden dolls, intricate in feature, one male, the other female, were the first items to go in the sack, wrapped quickly in one of her dresses to protect them. One large seashell of light blue and pink and a half-dozen small ones were also wrapped in one of the colorful skirts and gently placed into the sack. Into a gourd her mother had painted the year of her death, Lariah put the most colorful of her necklaces and added them to the sack. She also included a gourd the size of a baby's head that contained her mother's jewelry: precious stones and priceless items of gold and of silver. These had come from far-off Zarahemla. Also included in the large gourd before it went into the sack were some pure white combs carved from bone for her hair.

Three of the most comfortable pairs of her sandals were selected, followed by two grass skirts. Finally, she deposited in the top of the sack several items of clothing along with an assortment of pieces of beautiful cloth she had been saving. That done, Lariah quickly changed into a colorful red and yellow wrap-around skirt with a matching top. She put on her newest sandals and stood again, gazing around the room.

To Lariah's dismay, the spots from which the selected items had been removed were clearly visible in the thick layer of dust and ash. A cursory glance would tell anyone that she had been here. A careful study would reveal to the discerning eye the identity of much of what was now deposited in the bulging grass sack on the floor.

"I see you're finished at last, Lariah. So am I. We will go now," Ontius said from her doorway.

"Father," she began, "I was careful, but the ash made it impossible not to—"

"Never mind, daughter. It can't be helped. We must go now."

Lariah lifted the sack and groaned. It was heavier than she had imagined. But there was nothing to do but take it, for she could not bear to part with even one thing that she had selected. After only a few steps from the house, she remembered something she had forgotten, and dropped her sack to run back inside. From beneath her mattress, she retrieved a small steel knife that had also been her mother's. It had come across the great sea with her from the land of Zarahemla. It was enclosed in a sheath of soft goat leather. A supple belt of matching leather was attached. Swiftly, she opened her skirt and secured the belt around her bare waist. After folding the skirt back in place, her knife was well-hidden.

As Lariah turned to leave the room, she was startled to hear her name in a low-pitched voice. "Oh, it's just you, Amoz!" she exclaimed, whirling about to smile at the beautiful bird perched on the windowsill watching her. It was a parrot with a bright blue back, a breast of fiery red with long tail feathers to match, and wings of blue and yellow. Its head was red and its beak was white except for the tip, which was as black as Lariah's hair. It stared at her with intense black eyes.

"Lariah," it said again in its throaty, sing-song fashion.

"You're back!" she cried. "Where were you when Father and I left for the mountain? I searched for you and called you for an hour. Father said you must be dead. Oh, Amoz, I am so glad you are alive. I can't leave you again. Come, Amoz." She tapped her shoulder in invitation and the parrot flew from the window and lit as lightly as a puff of air on her shoulder.

"Food. You must have food when we travel," she said as she dropped to her knees beside her row of gourds. She had gathered and filled one of them with seeds of many varieties, using the seeds to tame Amoz. She lifted the gourd, rose to her feet, and ran from the house with Amoz swaying gracefully on her shoulder.

Her father was just coming from the forest, an angry scowl on his face. "Where have you been?" he demanded.

"I forgot something," she said meekly as she forced the gourd full of seeds into her already overfilled sack.

"That bird? I thought he was dead!" he thundered.

"He is fine, and he wants to come, Father," Lariah responded hopefully, choosing to say nothing of the little knife she carried concealed against her thigh.

Ontius' face softened. "Oh, all right. Bring Amoz if you like. But hurry now. I want to be away from here."

"Thank you, Father," she sang with relief. For the first time since Jath had left them on the ridge, she felt a little gladness in her soul. Lariah loved this resplendent parrot, who, with very limited vocabulary, would be a welcome friend in her hours of loneliness that lay ahead.

She hoisted her sack. It felt lighter, somehow, with Amoz clinging to the cloth on her shoulder. Then, without a backward glance, she skipped after Ontius.

For several minutes they trekked quietly along. Ontius was bent beneath his heavy load. He toted a sack much larger that Lariah's. In addition, he carried his bow and arrows and her bamboo blow-tube, as they called it. When they paused to rest for a few moments, Lariah said, "I'll carry the blow-tube, Father."

Without a word, he handed her the stout bamboo reed and small leather pouch of darts. As he turned back to the trail, she swiftly secured the pouch beneath her skirt to the belt that carried her knife. With the poison darts secure next to the knife, she scurried to catch up with Ontius.

A short time later, he suddenly changed his course, heading directly for the seashore. "Father, I thought we were going to cross the island to live," she said.

"We are, my daughter, but we'll go by canoe. I don't want to have to build another one, and anyway, it will be much faster," he explained. "The shore is only an hour's walk from here."

"Of course," she said, wondering why she hadn't thought of that earlier. Ontius always kept his canoe hidden in a rocky cave just a few feet above the shoreline. He kept it stocked with a few supplies, including such food as coconuts, dried reef fish, arrowroot flour, dried skipjack tuna, sugarcane, dried bananas, and a variety of dried herbs as well as several large gourds of drinking water.

When he planned a long trip, one out to sea, he always added some green bananas, green breadfruit, pandanus fruit, yams, taros, and pastes made of several of these fruits and roots. For a trip around the island, they wouldn't need a lot, for the shore was always close and fruits and roots could be found about anywhere, so she doubted that he would take time to add any of those things.

As badly as she hated the thought of seclusion in the rocky, high ledged areas of the far side of the island, Lariah certainly favored a canoe trip over three or four days of arduous hiking. She followed Ontius without voicing any complaints, despite the disturbing thoughts of Jath—gentle, sturdy, handsome Jath.

* * *

"There is nobody here, either," Antium complained as he peered from the forest at a neat, tightly built house in the foothills.

"There is only one dwelling left, if we have discovered where they all are," one of the men said. "It is farther east and nearer to the sea than this one."

"Then that is where they are," Antium declared confidently, and he rubbed his hands together in relish of the revenge he was sure would soon be his. Migroni smiled to himself, for he knew they would not be there. He was continually amazed at Antium's arrogance and ignorance.

Migroni watched as Shecum approached Antium and whispered something in his ear. Antium scowled but nodded before moving back into the trees, shouting for his men to follow. Migroni's eyes followed Shecum as he walked quickly toward the deserted house. On a rash impulse, Migroni darted after him and nearly ran into Shecum, who stood inside the house surveying the main room.

"Are you looking for something?" Migroni asked casually. Shecum spun around as if he had been stung, an angry scowl on his face. But upon seeing that it was Migroni, a smile replaced the scowl. "I'm just looking. I know this place," he said.

"You have been here before?" Migroni inquired dubiously.

Shecum gave a sly grin. "It is the house of the man with the beautiful daughter with hair as black as yours and skin as clear and white as a puffy cloud," he said.

"And what do you expect to find? Surely she is not here," Migroni scoffed.

"Perhaps not. But perhaps she has been recently." Shecum smiled and started through the house, looking everything over carefully as he went.

Migroni followed Shecum through a bamboo door that led into a small room at the rear. There Shecum's face broke into a broad smile, and he nodded his head several times.

"She was here, Migroni, and so was her father," Shecum said.

"Of course," Migroni answered gruffly. "You said it was their home."

"So I did," Shecum agreed with a smirk. "But I mean they have been here—since the mountain spewed fire and smoke. See for yourself," he said as he pointed at the row of gourds along one wall.

Understanding dawned on Migroni, and he, along with Shecum, examined the room closely. He could see where items were missing by the clean, ash-free spots which revealed where the items had lain.

Shecum fingered the few remaining items of clothing. He touched them softly, gently, as if the warm, vibrant body of the girl were in them. Then he turned to Migroni and said in a husky voice, "She is mine. I will have her!"

"But she is gone."

"Yes, and so is her father, but they can't be far. We must find them."

"How?" Migroni asked.

Shecum gave an evil smile. "The way we could find the people of Samuel, or could have before last night's storm."

Migroni nodded. So Shecum also knew what Antium had failed to see. And the sturdy Lamanite's estimation of Shecum grew. Yes, that young Nephite, though favored by Antium, had also observed that the islanders' tracks had not come this way, but he had chosen to remain silent on the subject.

Why?

Migroni thought he already knew the answer. It was because of the girl. Yes, he was determined to find her and did not seem to feel that following the islanders would lead him to her.

Shecum spoke. "Migroni, you are a better tracker than I am. Will you help me?"

Migroni shook his head. "Antium will be angry."

"Antium!" Shecum scoffed. "He's a crazy old fool!"

Migroni smiled now. "That is a dangerous thing to say. What if I were to tell Antium what you—" he began.

Shecum's face momentarily revealed a fear Migroni had never seen before, but Shecum cut him off with a wave of the arm. "You hate him, too, Migroni. I've been watching you. And you know that he would probably whip you. Come, let's find them."

"Antium expects us to catch up with him soon," Migroni ventured.

"Us?" Shecum asked with a laugh. "No, he expects me to catch up. I told him I was coming in here, although he did not know why. You, my dark-skinned friend, are the one in trouble with our fearless leader." His eyes gleamed with satisfaction.

"But did he expect you to go after the girl?" Migroni asked.

For a moment Shecum looked uneasy. "Of course not. He doesn't even know whose house this is."

"Then you shall also be in trouble with Antium," Migroni pointed out. "Perhaps he will not spare you the whip this time, my friend with the flaming hair."

Shecum's eyes blazed momentarily with anger—and with fear as well, thought Migroni.

Shecum turned on his heel and stomped toward the door. "Oh, quit fussing, Migroni," he muttered. "We understand each other, you and I. Let us find the girl and her father and take them captive. To appease the anger of Antium, we will tell him that Samuel went inland."

"And what if Antium claims the girl for his own?" Migroni asked.

Shecum looked back at Migroni, his expression dark with anger. "She will be mine," he said in a tone that brooked no opposition.

"Very well, Shecum," Migroni said softly. "We will follow them."

Thus was born a fragile trust and shaky friendship, and once again Lariah was in grave danger.

Leaving the house together, the two men gave no thought to the tell-tale sandal prints they left behind in the ash and dust on the floor.

CHAPTER 10

The house of Ontius and Lariah was a popular one that day. Another visitor entered and read the signs left in the dust and ash. He looked around and exited the house hurriedly, his heart in his throat and his temples throbbing.

She had been back! That stubborn old fool Ontius had brought Lariah back to this house after having had her safely removed a long way from the invaders. The strange prints indicated that two of the invaders had been into the house and knew that the occupants of the house had been there recently. The invaders would have to have been blind or stupid not to see that the smaller prints were those of a woman. Clearly imprinted on the floor, the prints from the invaders' sandals now followed the very route taken by Ontius and his innocent daughter. In horror, Jath realized that either pair of footprints could easily belong to Shecum, the man who had vowed to obtain Lariah for his own!

Jath was furious—both at Ontius for his foolishness and at Shecum for his evil designs on Lariah. His anger made him bolder. It also made him more careless. Most significant, it made him more dependent on himself and less on God. Now his anger spurred him on as he hurriedly followed the tracks leading away from Lariah's home.

What surprised Jath was the direction taken by Ontius and Lariah.

To the sea!

Jath was certain of it. And since he did not really know Ontius well, he could only assume that he had a seaworthy vessel of some sort hidden somewhere along the seashore. Jath had no doubt that the men who followed Ontius and Lariah realized this as well and intended to overtake them before they could get a boat into the water. Once again Ontius had foolishly put his innocent daughter in jeopardy, Jath fumed to himself as he raced to the seashore.

Earlier that day, Jath had gone from home to home, hoping to locate his father and the other islanders. Since the home of Ontius and Lariah was out of the way, much farther removed from the sea than any of the other houses on the island, Jath had almost bypassed it. He could not imagine his father using it as a place to make a stand against the invaders; Ontius had made it plain that he did not welcome their company!

But a nagging thought kept coming to his mind, urging him to go there. Now that he had discovered the danger Lariah was in, he was sure he knew the source of the thought that had steered him there.

It was from God.

Jath felt reasonably sure that he had received a prompting. As he hastened now to intervene in Shecum's evil plan, Jath prayed that God would help him know what to do when he overtook the two invaders. He was confident that He would, for why else had he been quietly directed by the Spirit to go to Ontius' house and discover the man's blundering foolishness?

Jath had much to learn. One important thing that he had been taught, but had either forgotten or simply did not understand, was how God worked to help men help themselves. When He inspired someone to take a certain action, it was likely that He would further inspire him to another when the first was acted upon. But many times men erred by following the first prompting but then failing to listen for the next. That is exactly what Jath had done.

* * *

Ontius was stubborn. At times he was downright foolish. As is the case with all men, he had many faults and shortcomings. For a man who had been taught the principles of the gospel at his mother's knee, some of those faults were rather glaring ones.

Regardless of his faults, however, he loved his daughter greatly. However misguided others might consider him to be, he loved Lariah and thought his actions were in her best interest.

He was also skilled with the powerful bow he had designed and built, and he was prepared to use that skill in Lariah's defense. To his credit, Ontius admitted to himself that his stubborn reluctance to leave his cave on the mountain had nearly cost Lariah her life. He was determined not to let that happen again.

Ontius was close to the area where his canoe was hidden. Although aware of his daughter's fatigue, Ontius had pressed her to hurry. The sooner they reached the sea, the sooner he could get her to the safety and seclusion awaiting them in the rugged terrain on the far side of the island.

He had not forgotten the invaders and was alert to every sound about him. Not until he was almost to the cliffs overlooking the lagoon where he kept his canoe did he find cause for alarm.

The lagoon was surrounded by high ledges which in turn were backed up by a steep and rugged hill covered with thick forest. To enter the sheltered area required a short but difficult descent through a naturally disguised, narrow, and rugged break in the ledges.

It was down this jagged and twisting trail that he led an exhausted Lariah. He dared not slow their pace, for he was sure that he had heard falling rocks from the steep hill above and behind them. Now convinced that they were being followed, he urged his daughter to quicken her steps and Lariah did her best to comply.

Below them the lagoon rested in perfect tranquility. The clear blue water lapped gently at the narrow strip of black volcanic sand that rimmed the water in a circle which almost closed where the lagoon joined the sea. The opening to the sea was straight north of where Ontius and Lariah now descended. Narrow and guarded by huge rocks above the water and dangerous reefs of coral below, the lagoon required the greatest skill to navigate to the open sea beyond.

Ontius had the skill. But he first had to reach the canoe that was hidden in a shallow cave at the base of the ledges. Then he would need to pull it across the sandy beach to the water, load Lariah and all their supplies, and paddle several hundred paces across the shimmering lagoon to reach the narrow opening. If someone was behind him, it could be a very dangerous undertaking, for he and his daughter would be exposed to the arrows of an expert marksman for several minutes.

"Why do you keep looking behind us, Father?" Lariah asked as Ontius paused near the bottom of the pass and searched the ledges and tree-covered slopes above them. "Is there someone there?"

"Oh, it is nothing, daughter," he replied casually, angry with himself for being so obvious.

She was not about to settle for that answer, but as her lips began to form another question, Ontius cut her off.

"I like this spot, Lariah. I will miss it. Your mother and I used to like to come here often. You remember, you and your sister came with us several times. No one else ever found the way down here, although I think some of the other people may have viewed the lagoon from above," he said, pointing upward and using that moment to rapidly scan the rocky, tree-covered mountain. "I was lucky to discover the way down. I doubt if anyone else ever will."

Ontius almost never spoke to Lariah of her mother or sister, for the loss still ran deep and bitter in his soul. He mentioned them now only as a desperate ploy to block any further questions.

It worked.

Tears formed in Lariah's eyes. "I wish Mother and my sister were still here with us," she said softly.

Ontius seldom allowed his own grief to show in his eyes or his voice, but he couldn't help it now. "So do I, Lariah," he said. "So do I."

Another swift glance behind him went unnoticed by Lariah who was brushing away her tears. Seeing no one, he led the way to their canoe. After walking about a hundred paces along the beach, he stopped and dropped his sack; however, he retained his bow and quiver of arrows. Lariah dropped her sack beside his and laid her blow-tube on the sand. Amoz left her shoulder and flew out over the shining water as Ontius and Lariah trekked up to the cliff.

A distant movement far above and to the east brought Ontius to a standstill. A figure appeared at the top of the cliff, well away from the last of the trees. A second figure joined the first. They both carried bows. The first man pointed at them, and Ontius heard his daughter gasp.

He pulled back the string of his bow with a mighty heave and slipped it into a notch on the cross-piece. "Father, it is the invaders. We are trapped!" she cried.

"We are not trapped. We have the canoe, daughter," he said as he fitted an arrow on the string and raised the bow to his shoulder. "And I have this."

"You knew they were behind us," she accused her father as he took careful aim. It was to be a very long shot. He must make it count.

The two figures darted from sight before he was ready to shoot. "Run to the canoe," he ordered softly as he lowered his massive bow.

She seemed not to hear him, and her eyes continued to scan the cliffs above and the trees and craggy hills beyond. "Run to the canoe!" he said again, more forcefully.

Distance was in their favor. So was the near impossibility of the men finding their way down. It was rocky and rugged along the top of the cliff, but if the men worked their way back into the trees and then west, they could come out on the cliff directly above where the boat was concealed. There they would be in range to easily shoot him and his daughter. He hoped they would continue to search for the pass down, for if they did, he and Lariah would have time to get the canoe in the water and row a safe distance away.

* * *

Jath was both confused and worried. The forested hill was rocky, and tracking anyone had become impossible. He knew the sea was fairly near although far below, for he could smell the salty air and hear the crash of waves against the shore. Jath had never approached the sea in this area, and he knew nothing about it. He did know that the two invaders were around here somewhere.

His confidence had waned, but not his determination. Leaving the comforting cover of the trees, Jath strode quickly toward the lip of a mighty cliff, carrying an arrow in one hand and his bow in the other. He looked behind himself frequently until he reached the edge, where he peered down in amazement. Far below was a lagoon of perfect blue, peaceful and serene, bordered by glistening black sand. He glanced about him and back toward the trees. Seeing that he was still alone, he looked down again at the breathtaking beauty below.

Where were Ontius and Lariah? *They must have gone down there somehow,* he reasoned.

Then he saw them as they came into view almost directly below him. Ontius was pulling and Lariah was pushing a fairly good-sized canoe. Ontius glanced up and Jath realized he had been seen. Lariah turned as well, just as a brightly colored bird lit on her shoulder. Jath raised a hand, the one holding an arrow, and waved at her, his heart beating rapidly at the very sight of her long black hair and slender body clad in red and yellow.

He was so wrapped up in watching the girl he adored as she raised a hand shyly to him in greeting, that he failed to realize what Ontius was doing. It was only when Lariah lowered her hand and turned toward her father that Jath realized he was staring death in the face. The powerful bow of Ontius was directed at him!

He heard Lariah's cry above the wind that swept across the cliffs. "No, Father!" she screamed and lunged toward Ontius just as the string came free of the notch and the arrow sped toward him.

* * *

Lariah hit the black, sandy ground and rolled over, Amoz squawking a strong protest from the air where he had taken flight as she lunged. She looked up at the cliff where Jath had stood a moment before.

He had vanished.

"Father, you hit him!" she cried in anguish.

"I hope so. He was much closer than the other two. He could easily have killed either one of us, Lariah!" he raged. "If I missed, it is your fault! Why did you—"

"Father," Lariah interrupted with a cry. "That was Jath up there! Didn't you recognize him?"

Ontius was preparing his bow for another shot, and at first Lariah thought he had not heard her. "That was Jath!" she said angrily.

Although Ontius had heard her clearly, he said, "You are badly mistaken, Lariah. It was one of the invaders. Now push and let's get this thing to the water before another one appears."

Blinded by her tears, she pushed as Ontius pulled. Amoz again took up his rocking perch on her shoulder. They were not quite to the water when Ontius suddenly stopped again and grabbed his loaded bow from the canoe in one easy movement and took aim.

"Father, please," she begged. However, she did not look up, presuming that once again her father was aiming for Jath, who had somehow miraculously lived through her father's first attack.

When her father ignored her, she lunged at him fiercely, sending her parrot once more protesting into startled flight. Her outstretched hand touched the bow just as Ontius released the arrow.

* * *

Migroni yelled, "Look out!" Shecum felt a burst of air rustle his beard as Ontius' arrow sped by.

Both young invaders dropped to their stomachs and crawled out of sight, back from the cliff's edge. "That was close," Shecum exclaimed. "He almost got me with that arrow."

From down below, the sound of the man's shouting voice carried clearly to Shecum's ears. "Lariah! What is the matter with you? They are our enemies and intend to kill us."

Her voice, as well, ascended clearly though not as loudly. Shecum could not make out what her reply to her father was, but he loved the sound of her voice.

"She saved my life," Shecum whispered to Migroni, then added, "Lariah. What a pretty name. At least I know the beautiful creature's name now." He grinned at his Lamanite companion.

The voices continued to drift over the rim of the cliff. "Get that worthless son of Samuel out of your head, Lariah!" the man's voice continued loudly. "All you can think about is Jath. If he is wise, he will never come near you again as long as I live."

"Who is Jath?" Migroni turned to Shecum, whose eyes narrowed.

"You heard that man down there, Migroni," Shecum spat angrily. "He is the son of Samuel, the one I was telling you about. He is the one who throws poisonous darts."

"It seems that the girl's father doesn't like him any better than you do," Migroni commented. "Perhaps he doesn't like the darts, either."

Shecum chuckled. "It is just as well, for Lariah will be mine, and there soon will be no Jath, son of Samuel, to cast his darts."

Migroni gave Shecum a puzzled look and asked, "How does this boy Jath throw the poison darts? You say you felt them and then, after a little while, blackness smothered you. Did you see him throw them?"

"No, but I know it was him. I don't know how he makes them fly so straight and so fast, but he does. Right after I was struck, I looked up and saw Jath standing above me."

"I see," Migroni responded, but it was clear he did not. However, he said only, "Let's see where Lariah and her father are going."

Cautiously, the pair crawled to the edge of the cliff and peered down. Lariah and her father were just pushing the canoe into the water. The man helped Lariah into the canoe and steadied the canoe with one hand while he swung first one sack and then the other into the canoe. He glanced repeatedly at the cliff behind him as he worked. At last he passed his bow to Lariah, then took from the sand what appeared to be a long, narrow rod and handed it to Lariah as well.

"What is that thing?" Migroni asked as the man pushed the canoe into deeper water and leaped in behind his daughter.

"I have no idea. A stick, I guess," was Shecum's response.

* * *

Even though he could not see it, Jath knew what it was, and he wished he had it in his hands right now. Lariah had already used it once to defend him. If only she were here beside him now with her slender weapon. She would not miss.

Jath clenched his hands in frustration at his helplessness in the face of danger. Beside him lay his broken bow. He had fallen on it, snapping it in two, when the arrow fired by Ontius had sped toward him. For the second time, Lariah had saved his life. Had she not lunged and spoiled her father's aim, the arrow would not have missed him. Of that he was certain. He guessed that she had saved Shecum in the same way, thinking she was again trying to save him.

Jath had narrowly escaped being seen by Shecum and this Lamanite he called Migroni. Had they not been talking as they approached in the trees, they would have come upon him lying in the very spot where they now lay as they watched the lagoon. He had gathered up his broken bow and bounded into the shrubs in the nick of time.

Now he could do nothing but watch the two men as they discussed how they might still capture Lariah and her father and save themselves from the anger of their leader. Several minutes passed before Shecum said, "They are out of the lagoon and into the open sea."

"And they are heading west," Migroni added.

"Come, we can overtake them in Antium's boat," Shecum suggested. "We will have the advantage of our sails, for he has none."

Jath understood that advantage, for Captain Baronihah had taught the islanders to build sails by weaving leaves together and securing them on poles held fast with coconut-fiber ropes. A moderate breeze in those sails would send a light canoe literally skimming across the surface of the sea. Jath remembered that Ontius had not been there when the good captain had explained and demonstrated. Perhaps he did not understand the advantage.

With a surge of guilt, Jath remembered thinking that he should run to the sea, locate one of his father's canoes, and sail to this part of the island.

That thought had come earlier as he started after Shecum and Migroni in his anger. But he had been so sure of himself that he had thrust the thought from his mind and pursued them on foot. How he now wished that he had listened to that prompting, for if he had, he would be far ahead of Shecum and Migroni and could sail to the aid of Ontius and Lariah.

And he would still have his bow!

Shecum and Migroni retreated from the cliff at a trot. Still determined to do something, Jath waited until they had vanished from his view, then he set out to get one of Samuel's canoes. He had failed Lariah once. He must do all within his power not to fail her again.

Darkness had set in by the time Jath succeeded in getting a small canoe in the water and loaded with a few coconuts, several bananas, a large bunch of pandanus fruit, a few lengths of sugar cane, and one large gourd full of fresh water. He set the sail, pushed the canoe into deeper water, and scrambled in.

A few clouds drifted overhead, and a breeze filled his sail as it roughened the briny water with little caps of white foam. He steered with a paddle, keeping the black mass of the island in sight to his left. Cool ocean spray soaked his light clothing and bare legs and arms, chilling him to the bone. With grim determination, he gritted his teeth and prepared for a long and sleepless night.

* * *

The hidden cove was saturated with a black fog of profanity. Antium was out of control with rage. His men had fled into the trees to avoid the sting of his whip. Even the wounded men found the strength to crawl away from his unholy wrath.

Having failed to find the islanders in the settlement, Antium was already in a dangerous mood when he led his men back to their hideout. He had returned, expecting to find his two truant men there. Upon discovering that they were not, he began his vicious tirade.

After he had finally settled down and ordered his small company to assemble about him, he suggested that they take to the sea and sail around the island looking for smoke or any other sign that might give them a clue as to where the islanders had gone.

That brought a fearful confession from young and injured Zermanah that the double canoe was gone.

"How can it be gone?" Antium had demanded.

"Migroni and Shecum sailed in it just before you returned."

"Why?" Antium demanded.

"They went in pursuit of two of the islanders," Zermanah responded. "A man and his daughter."

A scream that would have put the fiercest wild animal into a flight for its life came from Antium's throat. His whip cracked and flew. That was when his men fled from their outraged leader. No man alive would be safe in the face of Antium's wrath that night.

CHAPTER 11

Lariah was cold despite several layers of clothing she had pulled from her sack and put on. She watched in alarm as her father's head nodded, and the paddle slipped from his tired hands. She tried to retrieve it, nearly falling from the canoe in her haste and sending her parrot, Amoz, into frenzied flight.

Ontius jerked awake and looked back at the paddle as it drifted away. He muttered angrily, for that was the second paddle he had lost, and it was his last. He pulled off a layer of clothing, removed his sandals, and dove into the thrashing water of the sea.

The sun was slowly rising from the east, concealed for the moment by the cone of the volcano. The ocean current had pulled the canoe several miles west of the island, and from there the red capped cone was the most prominent feature in view.

Under pleasant circumstances, the sight would have been exhilarating, but Lariah was too cold and frightened to notice it. Her eyes were on her father. He was thrashing weakly in the water, gaining no distance on the bobbing paddle.

A large swell lifted the paddle high, balancing it for a moment on its crest, while Ontius struggled to keep his head above water. Then Ontius was lifted up by the wave and the paddle vanished from Lariah's view.

"Father, come back!" she screamed, fearing that he would disappear in the next trough as the paddle had done, leaving her alone, drifting at the ruthless whim of the broad sea to a slow but certain death.

Ontius, weak and exhausted, did turn and begin to swim slowly back toward her. She caught one more glimpse of the paddle as it poised for a moment atop another, more distant wave. Perched on it was Amoz, who seemed not to notice their plight. Then he rose into the air, and the paddle disappeared completely.

Several minutes passed as Ontius struggled to get back to the canoe. At times he seemed to drift even farther away from her. With her hands in the water, Lariah attempted to paddle as best she could and managed to move the canoe a little closer. They were able to close the gap to a short distance, but then Ontius began to flounder in the water. Thinking quickly, Lariah grabbed his bow from the bottom of the canoe and extended it to him. His head sank beneath the water, his hands thrashing desperately.

Lariah prayed for him with all the fervor of her frightened soul. His head reappeared. "The bow, Father. Grab the bow!" she shouted.

"The bow," Amoz repeated from near her head in the air.

One hand extended toward her, and she reached as far over the side of the canoe as she could and swung the end of the bow into his outstretched palm. He clamped his fist tightly on it, and she pulled with all her strength. Slowly, very, very slowly, she inched him closer to the safety of the canoe. When at last she got him there, she took hold of the hand that clenched the bow.

"You can let go of the bow now, Father," she instructed.

His hand remained tightly clamped, as if he were holding on to life itself. Holding his wrist with one hand, Lariah reached for his other one, nearly tipping the canoe over in the process. Leaning back to balance the light craft, she placed her father's hand on the canoe's edge. Then, with one hand on the bow and one on the canoe, Ontius rested for several minutes to allow new strength to fill his exhausted limbs.

At last he let go of the bow, allowing Lariah to set it aside while she helped him into the canoe. Heaving great breaths and trembling from the chill and exhaustion of his recent effort, Ontius collapsed on the floor of the canoe.

As he rested, the little vessel continued to drift with the ocean current, moving ever farther from the island. Amoz again perched himself on the shoulder of his pretty mistress. He had no fear.

* * *

The sea was giving Shecum and Migroni a difficult time. Antium's boat, built of two large canoes with a wooden platform secured between them, was designed to be manned by several men. Shecum and Migroni struggled to steer with a paddle while keeping its sail set to keep them moving around the island. They were carried far off course several times and struggled to keep the shoreline within a reasonable distance.

They had seen nothing of Lariah and her father since the sun had risen. Migroni wondered if they might have passed them in the darkness. For that matter, he knew they could easily have missed them in the hour since the sun had risen. Ontius' little canoe had no sail, and even at a few hundred paces, it would be invisible if Lariah's father were able to keep themselves hidden behind swells for a prolonged period.

Migroni was beginning to regret his alliance with Shecum, even as he regretted his alliance with Antium. He could imagine Antium's wrath even if they returned with two captive islanders, and that was looking less likely all the time. To return empty-handed would be to invite certain death.

Migroni's body was numb with cold from the constant spray of briny water, and his arms and back ached. He was also very sleepy. A quick glanced revealed that Shecum was standing near the front of the boat on the platform of hewn planks that were bound between and to the top of the two canoes, making them as one almost unsinkable vessel. Shecum held onto one of the stout coconut fiber ropes that ran from the top of the right side of the sail to the platform. His head, with its thick mane of reddish hair, was bent with fatigue and discouragement. Shecum had yet to confess it vocally, but he was concerned about the outcome of this little venture, too.

The boat rose to the top of a huge swell, and Shecum let out a whoop of delight. "There they are!" he cried, pointing to the southwest excitedly.

Migroni looked, but already their craft was sliding into a trough and all he could see was water. Shecum worked his way back and squatted in front of the sturdy Lamanite. "They are out there, Migroni. It has to be them."

"How far?" Migroni asked.

"Quite far," Shecum admitted. "I only saw the canoe for a moment, and it was just a dark speck on the sea, but it had to be them."

"Maybe," Migroni muttered, not at all convinced that it was not simply a piece of driftwood. "If it is them, as you suggest, what are they doing way out there? It makes no sense. They can't be prepared to sail to some other island, not in that tiny vessel. But if they are going to the other side of the island, they are certainly making a long trip of it."

Shecum nodded. "I wonder, too. But no matter. We must steer our craft that way and take them captive."

"If we can," Migroni said. "We need more men. We haven't done so well steering this thing, you know."

"We'll make it," Shecum said optimistically. "I'll help steer. We cannot fail."

"Have you forgotten the strange and powerful bow of Ontius?" Migroni asked with a scowl, for he had not forgotten its awesome power. "Lariah may not try to save you a second time. This time she will know you are not her friend Jath, the son of Samuel."

Shecum tugged at his straggly beard thoughtfully. "That is a problem. But we can solve it later. For now, we'll work on getting closer to them, then we'll worry about the bow."

Their vessel was sailing at a fairly good rate, despite the rough sea. Both men crouched in the rear, one in each canoe. There, except when they had to bail some water out, they bent their backs to their task, keeping their broad paddles in the water, attempting to steer a course that would lead them to Lariah and her father. Twice, over the next hour, they caught a glimpse of the canoe they sought. Each time it was closer, a bigger spot on a broad expanse of rolling blue water. As they sailed laboriously on, the island grew more distant to the east.

* * *

Migroni and Shecum were so intent on closing the distance on their suspected quarry that they failed to notice a small craft approaching them rapidly from the rear. However, the waves were tall and rough, which would have prevented them from seeing the small boat, even if they had taken the time to look back.

* * *

Jath, on the other hand, was well aware of the big vessel he was chasing. Its sail was much larger and taller than his own, and he was able to see the top of it much of the time as it rose above the swells. His canoe, one designed by Captain Baronihah but built by Samuel, was easy to steer, light upon the water, and very fast in comparison to the larger vessel.

The fatigue fell away from him like rain from the clouds as the chase went on. Whether they had seen him or not, he did not know. Why they were taking a course so far out to sea was also a mystery. He could only suppose that they could see something he could not and were in pursuit of it, presumably the canoe of Ontius and Lariah. It was his intent to pass by the larger vessel and attempt to catch up with Lariah and Ontius and see if he could aid them in some way.

If nothing else, there was room for both of them in his canoe, and perhaps he could persuade them to abandon theirs and make a run for the shore with him. That Ontius could ever hope to paddle his canoe faster than Shecum and Migroni could sail their boat was not even a question. They could overtake the hapless man and his daughter almost at their leisure.

As Jath sailed nearer, he steered his little vessel wide to the west. He would be foolhardy indeed if he allowed himself to come within the range of the bows and obsidian-tipped arrows of the two invaders, for he had none with which to defend himself.

He was directly west of them, sailing lightly upon the waves, when they spotted him. Shecum gestured wildly and shouted something Jath could not hear over the noise of the sea and the roar of the wind in his sail.

It was several minutes later before he actually saw the canoe the invaders were pursuing. It was a long way off and was clearly moving farther and farther from the island. As he drew closer over the next hour, he could see the exhausted figures of Ontius and Lariah as they bailed water from the canoe, a chore he himself was required to fulfill because of the rough water. As he sailed close enough to see them more clearly each time they rose on a giant swell, it was apparent that no one was rowing. It was not difficult for Jath to guess why that might be.

Without paddles, and with Shecum and Migroni not far behind, they needed his help more than ever, and Jath's heart took courage. *Surely Ontius will welcome me this time,* he thought as he peeled a banana and took a sip of water from his gourd.

The sun shone hot overhead, and as the wind subsided the ocean surface began to smooth out.

When Lariah spotted Jath, she waved in excitement and relief, calling out his name with joy. Ontius, who had been slumped over for several minutes, sat upright at the sound of her voice. Then he reached down and came up with . . . his bow!

"Father!" Lariah cried in alarm, slapping furiously at the weapon, causing the bright parrot to leave her shoulder and fly in alarm over the sea.

"Ontius," Jath called. "The invaders are coming back there. I've come to give you assistance."

"I told you not to come around my daughter ever again, you son of Samuel!" Ontius raged in return as he struggled in his weakened condition to draw the great bow tight.

"Please!" Jath pleaded in alarm. "Get in with me. We can outrun the invaders." He was fearful, for Ontius seemed murderous in his intentions. No doubt the struggle of the long night after an exhausting day had taken its toll on both the body and mind of Ontius, Jath thought.

Having drawn his craft to within a short distance of the drifting canoe, Jath lowered his sail so he would not overshoot them. As Ontius continued to struggle with his bow, Lariah continued to shout at him to stop. Amoz, meanwhile, continued to lodge his protest from the air.

Somehow, despite his weakened condition, Ontius succeeded in pulling back the string and slipping it into a notch on the cross-piece. He pulled an arrow from his quiver in the bottom of the canoe and lifted it, dripping with water, and fitted it into his bow despite Lariah's struggles.

For a desperate moment, Jath had hope. But Ontius suddenly bellowed with rage. Swinging his arm in a great arc, he struck his daughter on the side of her head, and she fell back, releasing her grip on the bow and managing just barely to keep from falling out of the canoe. Ontius glanced at her, then brought the bow into position to fire his arrow at Jath.

Seeing that he was in imminent danger, Jath dropped flat in the bottom of his canoe and held his breath. He both heard and felt the impact of the arrow as it struck the side of his canoe just above the level of the water. To his amazement, the sharp obsidian point bore a hole clear through the wood and the arrow was stuck over a hand's width into the inside.

Assuming that Ontius would require some time to again pull the bow tight, Jath lifted his head over the edge of the canoe. But the demented man seemed to have gained strength in his madness, and already he was slipping the string into the farthest notch on the crosspiece. Another shot with the bow bent so far could send the arrow clear through the side of Jath's canoe and injure him seriously or even kill him.

Jath did the only other thing he could do as his canoe drifted closer to theirs. Slipping over the far side of his vessel and into the sea and taking a great gulp of moist air, Jath began to swim deep beneath the surface. Only when his lungs burned in their hunger for air did he allow himself to surface. As his head cleared the water, he drew a swift breath and dove again.

The second time he came up, he was nearly to the canoe of Ontius. He allowed himself a quick look up, hoping that Ontius would be confused and not see him at once. To his surprise, the bow was empty. Ontius had fired the weapon but had not pulled it tight again. Rather he was screaming at his daughter, and her parrot was screaming at him in return. Lariah crouched in the opposite end of the canoe from Ontius, who suddenly lunged at her! Her slender white arm flashed upward and whatever it was that she held, she flung into the sea.

It took Jath a moment before he realized that Lariah had thrown Ontius' quiver of arrows overboard. Ontius was crying with rage and Jath feared for Lariah's life. He took several powerful strokes and grabbed the edge of their canoe.

Ontius was hunched over, sobbing and muttering, "Why, my beloved daughter? Why did you disobey your father?"

She answered in a grief-choked voice, "Father, you would have murdered! You are not a murderer."

"But he . . . the son of Samuel . . . he came for you!" Ontius sobbed. "I can't let him take you from me."

"Father, he came to save us . . . both of us. We are adrift in the sea and have no paddles. Now he can take us in his canoe and help us flee from the invaders who . . ." Lariah was saying when she suddenly screamed. "Jath, your canoe!"

Jath had not been thinking of his canoe, and he turned his head, casting his eyes about. Then he gasped, for his canoe was drifting away. It was already too far! He would have a difficult time reaching it. Letting go of the canoe, he began to swim back toward his canoe.

He had not gone far before he knew he was in trouble—they were in trouble. His progress toward his vessel was painfully slow, and he was growing very tired, which necessitated occasional stops in the water while he floated and caught his breath.

For Jath, the whole world had become salty water, burning lungs, glaring sun, and exhaustion. But he persisted, and was over half of the way to his canoe when he became aware of Lariah's screaming and the agitated squawking of her parrot. Turning in the water, he looked toward her.

What Jath saw brought almost overwhelming despair to his soul. The great double canoe was almost upon Lariah and Ontius! And they were helpless. Ontius' arrows had been swallowed by the sea along with his paddles. But even more helpless was Jath himself. There was nothing he could do but watch as the two invaders bumped alongside the drifting canoe and took Ontius and Lariah captive.

Jath watched in despair as Migroni bound Ontius tightly and deposited him roughly in the left canoe, tying him to one of the cross-poles that held the platform to the canoe. Shecum tied Lariah's ankles together and sat her on the platform behind the sail. Then he bound her hands in front of her and stood up. He gazed down at her possessively as Amoz settled on her shoulder and began to scold her captor.

At last Shecum took his eyes off of his beautiful captive. Together he and Migroni turned toward Jath, who had been so involved in watching the capture that he had given no thought to his own plight. It struck him like a thunderbolt. He began to swim frantically toward his drifting canoe, but it was hopeless. In minutes, the large vessel of the invaders bore down on him.

"Jath, look out!" Lariah screamed in warning.

"Jath!" the parrot echoed.

Jath looked over his shoulder as he swam and caught a glimpse of Shecum. The wiry young invader was standing on the platform with his feet spread, fitting an arrow to his bow.

There was no place for Jath to go. Oh, he could dive, but when he came up, Shecum's arrow could easily get him. Jath stopped and faced his tormentors.

He uttered a frantic prayer.

Then a most amazing thing occurred. Migroni, who had been steering the big craft with his paddle from behind Ontius, leapt to his feet, lunged onto the platform, and wrenched the bow from Shecum.

"What are you doing?" Shecum cried in anger.

"The question is, what are you doing?" Migroni shot back.

"Jath shot me with a poison arrow. I'm going to kill him," Shecum returned.

"He did not!" Lariah cried. "I did."

Shecum swung and looked at her with shock on his bearded face. Then he smiled. "So, it was you, huh? One day I will let you teach me how you did it."

Then he turned back to Migroni. "He dies anyway, for he hit me with a stick, and he wants the girl," he said coldly.

Migroni spoke impatiently. "Don't be such a fool, Shecum. If we deliver the son of Samuel to Antium, then perhaps he will not be so angry at us and will spare our lives. We need Jath alive!"

Shecum seemed to think about that for a moment. Then he suddenly pulled his sword and thrust it at Migroni, holding the point poised near the young Lamanite's bare chest, directly over his heart. "Okay, Migroni, I won't kill him," Shecum said, causing Jath to sigh with relief. But his relief was short-lived, for Shecum added, "You will kill him, Migroni. Pick up my bow."

Migroni glared at Shecum, then picked up the bow, fitted an arrow, and turned to face Jath. The big vessel continued to drift.

"Go on, shoot him before it is too late. Antium will be pleased to receive the body of the son of the man he hates," Shecum said with a sneer.

"Don't! Please don't kill him," Lariah cried, the red and yellow of her skirt flapping in the breeze.

"Kill him!" Shecum countered.

Slowly, his muscles glistening in the bright sun, Migroni pulled back the string and pointed the arrow at Jath. Jath did not even flinch. Again he was staring death in the face, and he was paralyzed with fear, expecting at any moment to feel the painful impact of the arrow.

It did not come!

Migroni released the tension on the string.

"Shoot him!" Shecum hissed.

"Please don't," Lariah cried.

"Jath," Amoz added.

Migroni turned to face the outstretched sword of his fellow invader. "No," he said quietly. "Kill me if you think you can, but I will not take the life of Jath."

"You would sacrifice your own life for the son of Samuel?" Shecum asked in astonishment.

"Samuel has never done anything to me," Migroni responded. "He is Antium's enemy, not mine or yours. I have never taken the life of anyone, Shecum. I will not begin now, not by killing in cold blood."

"You are a coward, Migroni," Shecum growled. "Why did you come to this place with us, anyway?"

"The promise of an island of our own," Migroni said simply.

"That is all?"

Migroni laughed dryly. "And fear of Antium if I did not come with him when he asked me to."

"You fear Antium?" Shecum scoffed.

"Not anymore. I hate him. But you fear him, Shecum. If you kill me and this one called Jath, then you can be sure that Antium will kill you."

"He will never know how or why it happened," Shecum said boastfully.

"They will tell him," Migroni said, nodding toward Ontius and then Lariah.

"Then I will kill Ontius," Shecum responded.

"But you will not kill Lariah," Migroni said confidently.

Shecum slowly lowered his sword. "Get Jath aboard," he muttered in defeat. "We will do it your way and deliver three prisoners to Antium. He will execute Jath and Ontius in his own special way," he said.

Migroni nodded. "A wise decision, Shecum," he said softly. "A very wise decision. Now maybe we both will live."

CHAPTER 12

After Jath was safely on board and securely bound, Migroni spoke. "Before we return to the island, let's recover those two canoes," he suggested, nodding at Jath's, which had drifted some distance away, and pointing at Ontius' canoe, which was much farther away.

"Yes, and the strange bow and bamboo reed Lariah carries," Shecum gloated.

Recovering the two canoes was no small task for the two weary invaders. The wind had died down to nothing but a slight breeze, and the surface of the sea became transformed into a giant mirror. The big sail hung limp and useless beneath a blistering sun. The ocean current continued to ease all three crafts farther from the island.

Shecum insisted that they pursue Ontius' canoe first, for he wanted the bow and bamboo tube. With only the two of them to row the big craft, it took a painfully long time to reach the drifting canoe. By the time they had it secured behind their vessel, the sun was sinking low on the horizon. The island had almost disappeared to the east.

"We must hurry if we are to recover Jath's canoe before it is dark," Migroni said to Shecum who was standing on the platform examining Ontius' bow.

Shecum waved a hand at Migroni in irritation and asked, "Where are your arrows, old man?"

Ontius did not answer, for fatigue, thirst, heat, and delirium had overcome him. His chin rested on his chest. He was asleep.

Shecum started toward him, but Migroni, who was seated in the rear of the right canoe, said, "Forget that for now, Shecum. I need help rowing."

Shecum ignored him and kicked Ontius savagely on the shoulder. "Old man, I'm talking to you," he said roughly.

Ontius shook his head and lifted his eyes toward his tormentor and mumbled incoherently.

Shecum drew back his foot to kick again, but Lariah cried, "Don't hurt him anymore! His arrows are gone. I threw them into the sea."

"Why did you do that?" Shecum asked in amazement.

Lariah slowly shook her head. She was too tired and hot and thirsty to explain. She had turned Shecum's anger from her father, and that was all she really cared about.

Jath had watched it all with growing anger. He too was exhausted, and the sun, though now low in the west, still burned, parching his already dry throat. From where they had tied him in the canoe in front of Migroni and across the deck from Ontius, he could see Lariah's face. Her fair skin was burned, her lips were cracked and bleeding, and her green eyes had lost their luster.

Food and water were in short supply. No one had anticipated a long voyage, and Shecum was not about to share what there was with his captives. Migroni also ate and drank, but he did so more sparingly. Jath knew the young Lamanite had saved his life, and he was grateful. He called upon him now. "Migroni, it will soon be dark. There is food and water in my canoe, but unless you get to it while it is still light, we will never see it again."

"He is right, Shecum," Migroni said.

"I know that," Shecum responded haughtily. "But we have time. There is no hurry."

But the breeze had died away, and a perfect calm had settled over the sea. Only the invisible drift of the ocean current and the slow swish of Migroni's paddle kept the vessel moving, and that movement was almost imperceptible.

"We are thirsty, Shecum," Jath said. "We must have water. Without water we will die."

Jath had not expected sympathy from Shecum, but he hoped that he might get him to realize that when the little supply of food and water ran out, he too would thirst and starve.

"Please, Shecum," Lariah added in a plaintive whisper.

"You are all weaklings," he said contemptuously. "I feel fine."

No one made the effort to remind Shecum that he had not been deprived of food and water during the long, hot hours of the afternoon as Lariah and Jath had.

When Shecum again took up his rowing position, the boat picked up a little speed, but it was almost dark when they finally caught up with Jath's canoe. It was dark by the time they had it secured behind the bigger boat.

Paying no attention to the others, Shecum gorged himself on the food he found in Jath's canoe. In contrast, Migroni ate a little. When he offered food and water to the three captives, however, Shecum grabbed Jath's gourd and drank deeply, finishing off the water. Then he threw Jath's gourd into the sea.

"That was the last of the water," Migroni said in disbelief at his companion's foolish behavior.

"Yes, it was," Shecum said carelessly. "We'll be back on the island in no time. But first," he yawned widely, "I need a little rest."

Migroni's look of disbelief deepened. "Shecum, I'm just as tired as you are," he said. "In fact, I'm probably more tired, because I've done most of the rowing."

"I'll take over after I get some sleep," Shecum said as he stretched out on the planks of the deck. "You row until then. Just head straight for the island."

Migroni muttered something under his breath.

"What did you say?" Shecum demanded sharply.

"Which direction do we go to get to the island?" Migroni asked.

Shecum hesitated briefly before throwing his arm out and pointing in a northwesterly direction. His form was but a shadow in the dark night, lit only by the glittering stars of the heavens.

Migroni was doubtful. "Are you sure?"

"Of course I'm sure," Shecum scoffed.

Jath had heard enough. His plight, and that of Lariah and her father, was dim indeed. Unless they returned to the island, they had no chance of survival. He knew from the stars which direction the island lay. He spoke up. "Migroni, if you go that way, we'll all die.

"You are pointing northwest, but the island lies east of us."

"Don't listen to him," Shecum said sharply.

For the first time since their capture, Ontius spoke up. "You may not care if the rest of us die, young man, but you must care about your own life."

Jath looked across the deck to where Ontius was tied. He could make out his features just enough to discern that he was gazing into the star-speckled sky. Ontius had been delirious since before the capture, but his actions now indicated that his senses had returned.

Shecum had seen Ontius look up, and so had Migroni. But Shecum stubbornly resisted their advice. "The island is that way, like I said," he insisted, unaware that the vessel had turned slightly, and that he was now pointing almost directly west.

"Very well, then," Migroni agreed mildly.

Jath's heart sank as Migroni slowly turned the big craft until it faced away from the island and began to row.

Shecum was soon asleep. Jath too was terribly fatigued and was fighting to stay awake. Across the deck, Jath could see from Ontius' dark profile that his head was ducked and his hunched body motionless. Lariah was also slumped over, her head on her knees.

In the dark Jath heard a whisper. "Jath, are you awake?" It was Migroni.

Startled, Jath replied, "Yes, I am."

"Which way do we need to go?"

Relief flooded over Jath as he took a minute to study the stars and peer into the dark waters at the side of the boat before answering. He was surprised to find that the craft was nearly on course. Migroni had turned it in a big circle.

"You are close already," he answered. "Look at the stars and I'll try to tell you which one to follow for now."

Without the use of his hands, Jath had difficulty giving directions, but he eventually succeeded, and Migroni got the vessel headed on the right course.

"Cut me loose and I will help you row," Jath offered.

Migroni chuckled. "Just because I stopped Shecum from killing you doesn't mean I am a complete fool, Jath. I need you alive when we get back to the island, but I do not trust you. I'll row alone."

"Have it your way," Jath replied.

"Have it your way," a raspy voice echoed. Jath started, then laughed. He had forgotten about Lariah's parrot, Amoz.

Silence again descended, and sleep tugged at Jath's eyes. The only sound was the slow, rhythmic swish of Migroni's paddle. Before long, even that sound ceased. As Jath lost his fight to stay awake, his last thought was that Migroni had fallen asleep.

* * *

Lariah awoke to a deep, profound silence. There was no motion beneath her. If the vessel moved at all, it was only the ocean current that moved it. Her eyes strained in the darkness, and it was soon apparent to her that everyone was asleep. Even Amoz, perched lightly on her shoulder, was sleeping.

Her body ached, and her throat burned with thirst. She felt hopeless and helpless. She stared for a long time into the darkness as tears wet her tender, sunburned face. A thought seemed to nibble at the edge of her mind, but she could not quite pull it in. *Think,* she told herself. *What is it?* She fought the urge to sink back into slumber and struggled to bring the lingering thought into focus.

"I'm too dull," she mumbled. "If my mind were sharp . . ."

Sharp!

That word seemed very important, but why? She repeated it over and over in her mind, but nothing developed. Perhaps she was wrong, and it was not important at all. No doubt her mind was playing games with her. *Is this what it's like to die a lingering death?* she wondered calmly.

Sharp!

There it was again. What did it mean?

My mind is not sharp, she sighed to herself. *Knives are sharp. But what does it mean?*

Knife!

Lariah's groggy mind cleared. Of course. Now she recognized the thought that had been lingering at the fringes of her consciousness. She had forgotten the knife concealed beneath her skirt!

As she tore at her skirt with her bound hands, the motion woke Amoz. "Lariah," he said in his loud, raucous voice.

"Shh!" she said in alarm.

"Shh," he retorted.

Her groping hands finally found the hilt of her knife, and she slowly drew it out. Holding it tightly in one fist, she carefully straightened her skirt before twisting the knife and hacking at the cords that bound her wrists. It was slow and awkward, but she kept at it. When the sharp blade nicked her tender skin, she cried out and dropped the knife.

"Ow!" she winced.

"Ow!" Amoz echoed.

"What was that?" Shecum demanded in a sleep-slurred voice as he sat up on the deck in front of Lariah.

Alarmed and afraid, Lariah searched for a believable reason for her outburst.

"Who was that?" Shecum asked as he twisted his head around, scanning the darkness.

"It was just me. Lariah," she answered, trying to hide the fear in her voice. "I . . . I . . . I hurt myself trying to get comfortable. These planks are rough and hard. I'm all right now, though."

"Try to be still after this," Shecum directed her. "I was sleeping very well until you woke me up."

"Sorry," she murmured as he stretched out on the deck again.

Shecum made no response to her apology, but Lariah did not attempt to recover her knife until his even breathing indicated to her that he was again sleeping. After she had the knife back in her hands, she immediately began to cut at the coconut fiber cords. She nicked her tender skin again, but managed not to cry out or drop the precious knife.

She let out a sigh of relief and offered a silent prayer when the cords finally separated, freeing her hands. She swiftly cut her feet loose, then arose. For a moment, she was dizzy from fatigue and thirst and hunger, and her muscles were cramped and uncooperative. She steadied herself with the mast and flexed her muscles gently until she felt better.

Finally, she moved silently around Shecum's shadowy, sleeping form and stepped over to Jath. He was also sleeping soundly, so soundly that he did not even awaken as she cut him free. She arose and took a step across the deck toward her father but stopped as she remembered his angry attempts to slay Jath.

She turned back and kneeled beside Jath again. She shook his shoulder gently. "Jath," she whispered.

"Jath," Amoz rasped, incapable of a whisper.

"Shh," she scolded, her heart beating rapidly as she looked around to see if the parrot had awakened anyone else.

"What is it?" Jath asked in a groggy voice and one that was a little too loud in the stillness of the night.

Lariah placed a hand on his cheek and whispered, "Be very quiet, Jath. It is just me."

"Lariah?" he whispered in surprise.

"Yes. I cut my cords and yours."

"We're loose? I need my sword then."

"Come with me," she said, touching his lips with a slender finger and taking him by the arm.

"How did you—" he began.

"With this," she interrupted, pressing the handle of her little knife into his palm.

He accepted it without another question, and they crept together to the front of the boat where Shecum had deposited Jath's knife and sword and those of Ontius. After he was armed, he gave Lariah back her little knife. "Where did you get it?" he whispered.

"It was hidden beneath my skirt," she responded. Turning away from him, she opened her skirt and returned the knife to its soft leather sheath. With that done, she turned back to him, picked up her father's sword, and said, "I'll follow you."

They crept past the sail and knelt beside the dark, slumbering form of Shecum. Silently they stripped him of his weapons, but as Jath attempted to bind his wrists with a cord, he awoke.

"Migroni! Is that you?" he called out loudly as he attempted to sit up.

"It is Jath," Jath responded as he touched the young invader's neck with the tip of his sword. "You are now my captive."

"Migroni!" Shecum screamed.

"What is it?" the young Lamanite responded. "Is something the matter with you?"

"It's Jath. Kill him!"

Migroni's mind was still clouded with sleep. "Jath? Why should I do that?"

"He is loose, you idiot," Shecum fumed. "You were supposed to be awake."

"Be quiet, Shecum!" Jath ordered. "And don't move or I'll stain the sword of Pagros with your blood."

Lariah had quietly set her father's sword at her feet and now held in her hand her bamboo tube. Reaching within her skirt, she opened the bag that held her poison-tipped darts. Careful not to prick her finger, she removed one and inserted the dart into her tube.

"What do you intend to do now?" Shecum asked Jath in a scornful voice. "We're still quite a distance from the island."

Jath's voice was steady and calm. "Wait until it is light," he said. "Then we'll tie you both up and return to the island."

"You'll regret this," Shecum threatened. "Do something, Migroni, if you're not afraid."

Migroni scrambled from the canoe onto the deck. Even in the darkness, his figure stood out sharply. Lariah raised her blow-tube.

"Let Shecum go. He can row now," Migroni said in a stern voice.

Jath answered softly, but firmly. "No. And you sit down right where you are."

Migroni sat down with a surprised groan. Only Lariah, who had shot her tiny dart at him, understood why. As he slowly slumped over, Lariah had an idea. Once more she unfolded her skirt, grateful for the darkness that protected her modesty. After she had retrieved another dart, she slipped silently to one side and raised her bamboo tube again.

Shecum was not moving, for Jath still held his sword against the invader's throat. He was cursing Migroni, though, and ordering him to do something about Jath. He became especially angry when his partner failed to answer. Then he asked sharply, "What was that?"

"Be still, Shecum," Lariah ordered with a hint of mirth in her voice.

"Be still, Shecum," her raspy-voiced bird repeated.

Shecum soon became still. Lariah's second dart had done its job.

Jath turned to Lariah in surprise. "What happened?" he asked.

She stepped close to him and held up her blow-tube.

"Oh," he said. "Where did you find your darts?"

"Beneath my skirt with my knife," she answered. "Shall we tie them up? They may awaken before it is light."

"Then let's do it now," he agreed.

"Now," Amoz said, not attempting such a long phrase.

After they had securely tied both Shecum and Migroni, they pulled them to the front of the boat and tied them to a cross beam. Then they shared a banana, and each ate a pandanus fruit.

"I'm so thirsty," Lariah said.

"So am I, but thanks to Shecum's greed, we have no water until we reach the island, and that could be awhile if a breeze doesn't soon begin to blow. I guess I better get to rowing."

"I'll help you," she responded. "But first I must get Father to eat a little fruit."

While Jath worked to get the sluggish craft on course again, she knelt beside her father. He was awake but seemed to be out of his mind again, for all he would do was curse Jath and his father, Samuel, blaming them both for his troubles.

Lariah succeeded in getting him to eat some fruit. She tried to make him more comfortable but did not untie him. She feared he would start trouble with Jath.

Ontius cursed. "Cut me loose, Lariah. I will free you from the clutches of Jath."

Lariah's heart ached terribly that her father misunderstood Jath so badly, and a few tears of unhappiness slipped down her cheek. After a few moments, she wiped her eyes with her skirt and crossed the deck to Jath.

"I've left Father tied," she said.

Jath nodded in understanding.

"Where is the island?" she asked.

"I am headed for it now, Lariah. I'm sure we could not see it even if it were light. We have drifted so far," he explained.

"How can you be so sure?" she asked, afraid that he might somehow be mistaken.

"I have two guides. I only told Migroni of one, but both are present now, as they have been all night long. It seems that Shecum and Migroni are ignorant of them."

"What are they?" Lariah pressed.

"Well, the stars, of course, are one of my guides."

"Of course, but I don't understand them."

Jath smiled. "Someday, Lariah, I'll teach you, but not now."

"Is that a promise?" she asked, leaning near him.

"I promise, Lariah," he said, and let go of his paddle long enough to lightly touch her sunburned cheek.

She laid a hand over his, and her heart throbbed. *Could it be . . . love?* she wondered in awe. Maybe, she decided, but whatever it was, it felt good and it felt right. She smiled in the darkness as she asked, "What is your other guide, Jath?"

He gently freed his hand from hers and put it to the paddle again before answering. "Te Lapa," he said.

"What?" she asked, puzzled.

"Your father never told you of Te Lapa?"

"No, he didn't."

"Look over the side," he instructed. "Not on top, but deep down."

She peered into the black water. At first there was nothing, only blackness. She was about to say something when she saw it. Deep below the dark surface were streaks and flashes of light.

"Jath, what is it?" she cried in amazement.

"Jath," Amoz called from her shoulder, startled again by her loud cry.

"Te Lapa," he said again, smiling. "They are streaks of light that dart out from the islands. At night, even when it is cloudy, those lights show up deep in the ocean."

Lariah was astounded. "How far do they go?" she asked.

"Not too far. Maybe twice the distance from which one can see land from the sea. All I have to do now is follow those streaks of light and we'll come to the island," he said.

Lariah straightened up. "Thank you, Jath. I'll row now."

She crossed the deck and stepped into the rear of the far canoe where she began to row, quietly humming an old tune her mother had taught her. Then she stopped abruptly, pulled her oar from the water, and jumped onto the deck.

"What are you doing?" Jath called out.

"My darts. I didn't pull them out of Migroni and Shecum. I don't want to lose them. Father says they can be used over again. I must get them before they wake up."

After she had retrieved the darts, she again began to row.

* * *

At length morning arrived. Having recovered from the effects of the poison, Shecum and Migroni regained consciousness. While Shecum raged over the cords that bound him, Migroni sat silently in the yellow light of dawn, appearing to be in deep thought.

Lariah looked ahead and felt a rising panic in her breast. The stars were gone, as were the streaks of light in the water, and she could see nothing of the island. Only a vast and glassy blanket of clear, frightening sea surrounded them.

CHAPTER 13

"Today we will reach our destination," Samuel announced as he roused his people from their beds. "There we will fortify ourselves. Then we will take the fight to Antium and free ourselves of his aggression."

The side of the island to which they were traveling was rugged. Huge mountains had been thrust up from the sea in ages past, with steep, rocky slopes covered with thick vegetation: trees, shrubs, flowers, and vines. There were few flat places large enough for growing crops or grazing their few domestic animals. Streams of water cascaded down steep ravines and plunged over spectacular cliffs, creating huge ribbons of glistening silver as they fell toward the waiting sea.

Wild game roamed the deep canyons and scaled the rugged mountainsides. Most common were the wild boars which could be heard grunting and rooting but were seldom seen except by the most skillful hunters. Samuel had led hunting parties into those mountains, but no one had ever tried to live there.

His destination was certain. A place high up, it overlooked the sea but was inaccessible except by a narrow path from below. Set back on a small plateau and sheltered by huge cliffs that towered above, it was one place that could easily be defended by three or four well-armed men. There were trees bearing fruit, water, a few edible roots, and natural shelter from the sun and bad weather.

Samuel did not really expect an attack. Antium and his men would never find them there. In fact, Samuel hoped to forestall even the remotest possibility of attack by searching out their enemies and destroying them in the next few days. He could afford to use most of his men to fight if he could get his people into the high, natural stronghold to which he was directing them. Samuel was determined to succeed, for their lives and existence on this island paradise depended on the complete destruction of the enemy.

"It will be a difficult day," he warned the people as they prepared to start up the mountain later that day. "The climb will be steep and rugged, but safety awaits us up there." He pointed toward the summit of the mountain. "The smaller children will require help. They'll need to be carried much of the time. There are places that are narrow and dangerous, and we wish to avoid any accidents."

There was no grumbling, and Samuel's love for his people swelled in his breast. They were good people and God-fearing. With the glaring exception of Ontius, they were more than willing to share one another's burdens. Samuel was particularly proud of the rising generation, for they were all obedient and loving young souls.

One of them approached him now as the people began to shoulder their burdens and start toward the slopes ahead. "Hello, Limre," he said as the smiling, good-natured daughter of Gadoni and Laishita stopped in front of him and gazed up at his face.

"Hello, Samuel," she said. "Still no sign of Jath?"

Samuel shook his head sadly. "I'm afraid not, Limre."

"He'll find us," she announced cheerfully.

"I'm sure he will. His mother and I have prayed long and hard for him," Samuel said quietly.

"I know he will." Her matter-of-fact manner left little room for doubt.

Though Limre, now eighteen, was nearly a year older than Jath, they had always been very close friends. If it weren't for the difference in the color of their skin, they could almost be mistaken as brother and sister. But her skin was a deep brown while his was light. Her face was round and pretty with dark brown eyes that were always full of mirth. Long black hair cascaded over her shoulders.

Limre was the oldest child of Samuel's Lamanite friend, Gadoni, and his part-Lamanite wife, Laishita. Like her mother, Limre was petite, bubbly, and good-natured, but there was no visible sign of the Nephite blood in her veins. Her Lamanite features mirrored those of her father. Despite her youth, she was full of faith. People found it well to listen when she spoke, for her wisdom exceeded her years.

Samuel listened to her now.

"I have prayed long for Jath, too," she confessed. "And last night I felt the sweet reassurance I sought from God. He still lives and will return to us." Then, without waiting for Samuel's reaction to her words of faith, she asked, "Who needs help in climbing the mountain? Father said to ask you."

"Dara and Baronihah," he responded without hesitation. "If you would take their two children and escort them safely up the mountain, it would relieve Dara of a great burden. She will want to be beside her husband as we carry him."

"I will take good care of them," she promised, and stretching on her toes, she gave Samuel an affectionate peck on the cheek before going in search of Dara's children.

"Isn't she a dear?" Ophera said as she approached her husband's side and watched the pretty Lamanite maiden as she skipped away.

"She is that, Ophera. She'll make one of the young men a good wife," he said.

"Will she, Samuel?" Ophera asked.

Samuel turned to Ophera in mild surprise. "Of course she will, dear," he said a bit sternly. "Why did you say that?"

Samuel had learned to listen to Ophera, and as she matured into her middle years, she grew in her wisdom. Even though he questioned her at times and appeared to argue, it was really his way of getting her to say more.

So it was now. She had a reason for asking the question she had, and he wanted to know what it was. She answered him with another question, as she so often did. "Haven't you noticed her when she is around the young men, Samuel?" she asked.

As usual, he felt a bit stupid, for he knew that she was about to reveal something he should have already known and had somehow missed. She always seemed to observe things that should have been obvious to him but were not. "Well, yes," he answered thoughtfully. He was thinking back over the past couple of years, hoping for once to pin-point what his wife was about to reveal before she could do so.

Samuel had always taken pleasure in watching the young people at play, both when they were small and when they were older. He could not think of a time when Limre had been present that she was not in the very center of whatever they were doing. Everyone, including the young men, seemed to enjoy her company.

"Yes," he repeated. "I have noticed her, and there's not a young man on this island that doesn't like Limre. Why, even our Jath—"

"Exactly!" Ophera agreed triumphantly. "You have often said that they were like brother and sister. Well, is that not true of her and all the other young men?"

Then Samuel's eyes were opened. "Yes, I see now," he admitted. "There is no one who sees her as a woman, but only as a good friend."

"That's right, Samuel. If anyone—Uri, Kim, Kib, or any of the others—had any romantic interest in her, don't you think it would have manifested itself by now?"

She was right, as he had just admitted, but Samuel could be stubborn at times. He chose to be so now. "Ophera, there are not so many young people from which to choose a companion on this island. One of them will fall for her one of these days. You'll see."

She shook her head. "No, not one of our young men. She's a Lamanite, and they like her, but none of them will ever marry her. Now, her little sister, that will be different. She looks more like Laishita's father's people. But not Limre." Ophera spoke with such conviction that Samuel decided not to argue.

Instead, he said, "Limre has a heart of gold, and she's a beautiful girl. Lamanite features, yes, but beautiful."

"Sister to all, but wife to none," Ophera said sadly. Tears misted her eyes.

Samuel put an arm around her shoulder. "She'll be all right, Ophera. She'll always be happy."

"Oh, Samuel, I know that," Ophera said, her voice full of emotion. "I wasn't crying for her. I was crying for our son. I wish he would return soon."

"Jath will come, dear. Limre just told me so," Samuel said comfortingly. "And she has such great faith."

"Then he will come," she agreed. "But I still worry so much about him, Samuel."

So did Samuel.

* * *

So did Jath! He worried and he prayed and he rowed until his arms were numb and his shoulders were aching unbearably. The island, by mid-morning, was still not in sight. He glanced across the deck at Lariah. Her strength was obviously spent.

"Lariah," he called. "Let me do it alone. Don't you try anymore. You need rest." His voice, like his throat, was cracked and dry.

Lariah shook her head. "There's no breeze at all. I know I'm not much good at this, but you can't do it alone."

If we just had some water and a little more food, Jath thought.

The sun was like fire on their faces, and the reflection it cast from the glassy surface of the sea burned their backs as well. Lariah's tender face would soon be covered with painful blisters.

"Shade your head, Lariah," Jath pleaded. "Go sit in the shadow of the sail, please."

"For just a little while, maybe," she agreed reluctantly. "Then I can help you again."

Lariah stumbled as she climbed from the canoe to the deck it was bound to. Jath pulled his own oar from the water and began to get up. "Wait. Let me help you," he called over to her.

"No, Jath. I'll make it."

He sat back and picked up his oar. His hands still hurt from the tears they had received when Pagros and Shecum had tried to shove him into the crater. It seemed as if it had been weeks ago, Jath thought, but it had been only a few days. It felt like weeks since he had tasted water, but it had been less than a day. His mouth was sore, and his tongue was swollen. Had it not been for the little bit of moist fruit that they had eaten, they would be in even worse shape than they were. But the fruit was gone now.

"I'm hungry!" Shecum called out. "How about some fruit?"

It were as if he had read Jath's mind. His request angered Jath, for it was Shecum who had gorged himself and drank the last of the water. "Sorry," Jath said. "It is gone. You had your share last night."

"What did you say?" Shecum demanded, reminding Jath that his voice was nearly gone. He could not speak loudly.

"No!" Jath tried to shout.

"No!" Amoz mimicked.

Shecum heard the parrot. "When I get loose, I'll wring your neck, you ugly bird," Shecum threatened.

"No you won't," Lariah called to Shecum from her resting place in the shadow of the sail.

"You better get back to rowing, Lariah," Shecum said.

"Jath told me to rest," she said loftily.

"I'll row," Migroni offered. It was the first he had spoken all morning long.

Jath again pulled his oar from the water and crawled slowly onto the deck. He walked past Lariah, past the sail that shaded her, and knelt beside Migroni. "You want to row?" he asked the securely bound Lamanite.

"Someone better, or we'll all die out here," Migroni said. "I can help, if you'll allow me."

Without another word, Jath pulled his knife and cut Migroni free. "Let me loose, too," Shecum said in a taunting voice. "I'll help row."

Jath ignored him. "Which side do you want?" he asked Migroni.

Migroni nodded toward the left side and took a position there. Jath was wary, but he needed help—they all needed help if they were to survive. Lariah was wary, too, and she fingered her blow-tube.

Another hour of slow, laborious rowing finally brought the island into sight on the horizon. The first thing Jath saw was the smoking cone of the volcano, easily the tallest peak on the island. It even poked into the blue of the cloudless sky much higher than the towering mountain-tops to the south.

Jath was so intent on forcing his tired muscles to keep rowing he had not noticed the breeze which picked up behind them. It was Lariah who finally observed that the sail had filled out and the smooth surface of the sea had begun to ripple.

"Jath," she called back to him. "There is a breeze again. It is moving us along now. You can quit rowing and just steer."

Jath was so tired that the importance of her words took a moment to register. So grateful was he that tears began to fill his eyes, and happily he leaned back and rested.

The breeze picked up a little over the next few minutes and remained steady, rushing the craft directly toward the distant island. Very little steering was necessary after that, and by early in the afternoon, they approached a sandy stretch of beach several miles south of the volcano and far from their homes. Jath and Migroni allowed the craft to run straight in, nosing solidly into the sand.

Too weak to move, Jath did not move from his place in the rear of the boat. Longingly he thought of the cool drink of water he so desperately needed and which was now so close at hand. Ontius sat hunched forward as he had been for hours. If Jath hadn't seen the even rise and fall of his head as he breathed, he would have feared that Ontius was dead.

Shecum, though still bound tightly, was in the best shape of anyone. He struggled with the cords to no avail and resorted to raspy cursing.

Migroni wearily laid his oar aside and clambered onto the deck. Without a glance at Jath, he walked past the sail where Lariah leaned tiredly against the mast. At Migroni's approach, Shecum called out, "Help me get loose."

Migroni paused and stared at his fellow invader for a moment before continuing forward. At the bow of the boat, he hesitated.

"Look out!" Shecum called. "Lariah has her blow-tube!"

Migroni turned his head and saw Lariah raise the tube to her lips as if in answer to his challenge.

"Don't do it, Lariah," Jath said softly. "He saved my life. Let him go."

As she lowered her weapon, Migroni shifted his gaze to Jath. "We are even now," he said solemnly. Then he leaped to the sandy shore, made his way up the beach, and disappeared into the trees.

"What about me, Migroni?" Shecum yelled after him. And then he began to curse again.

"Oh, be quiet!" Lariah said.

"Be quiet!" Amoz mimicked just as sternly. Then the brightly colored parrot flew from the shoulder of his mistress and into the trees that bordered the seashore in search of water.

Jath forced himself to move and struggled from his cramped position in the rear of the right canoe and staggered onto the deck.

"Should we have let Migroni go free?" Lariah asked doubtfully.

"He isn't a killer, Lariah," he answered. "Come on, if I don't keep moving now I never will. We need to find some fresh water." He picked up Shecum's quiver full of arrows, and Ontius' big bow.

After locating an empty water-gourd, Jath helped Lariah to the ground. Together, they staggered wearily into the trees in search of water. Amoz called, "Lariah!" from a mango tree.

"Amoz, have you had a drink already?" she asked cheerfully as she picked several mangoes.

He flew down and perched on her shoulder. Then, as she started away from the tree, he again took to the air and flew to the east, circling back and going east again. "He wants us to follow him," Lariah said. "He'll lead us to water."

Lariah was right. Amoz did fly directly to a small stream a few hundred paces away. There they wet their parched lips, drank sparingly, rested, then drank a little more. They ate some of the mangoes, filled the gourd with cool water, and slowly made their way back to the vessels.

Their strength slowly returned as they walked. "We must get a drink to your father and then get him out of the boat and out of sight," Jath said. "We will have to find a place to hide until he gets stronger."

Lariah stopped and took hold of Jath's arm. "Father hates you, Jath," she warned him. "I don't know why, but he does."

Jath shrugged. "I hope we can change that. I don't intend to lose you, Lariah," he said huskily.

She put down her bananas and gourd of water and stepped close to him, dropping her head against his chest. "You will never lose me, Jath," she whispered softly. "Not ever."

Dropping the bow he still carried in his hand, Jath put his arms around her. For several minutes, they both forgot about Ontius, Shecum, and all their troubles. She lifted her head and Jath gazed into her eyes. The sparkle was back. Even with her face badly burned and her lips cracked, the beauty of her face thrilled him.

"I love you, Lariah," he said, surprising himself with his boldness.

"I love you, Lariah," Amoz teased from a nearby branch.

Jath laughed. Lariah giggled. "And I love both of you," she cried in delight. "Now, we better get this water to Father."

An unpleasant surprise awaited them as they stepped from the shade of the forest a few minutes later and stared at the vessel where they had left Ontius and Shecum.

Migroni had returned!

He was busily recovering his arrows, bow, and sword. Jath tugged at Lariah's arm and pulled her back into the safety of the trees where they could watch without being seen, for Migroni had not glanced their way yet.

After strapping on his sword, Migroni approached Shecum, who was still securely bound and lying on the deck in the hot sun. "Cut me loose," he ordered.

Jath struggled with the large bow, finally managing to pull the string back and slip it into a notch on the cross-piece. He inserted an arrow into the bamboo rings and brought the weapon to his shoulder. Then he waited.

Migroni appeared to be unsure about Shecum, but at length, he drew his sword and cut the cords that held him bound. The moment he had freed his fellow invader, Migroni turned and leaped from the grounded craft and trotted into the trees. He passed very close by Jath and Lariah but did not see them.

"Wait for me!" Shecum shouted angrily.

It took the wiry invader a moment to stagger to his feet. Then he searched for and found his bow, cursed over his missing arrows, strapped on his sword, and climbed down to the sand. He then trudged wearily after Migroni.

Lariah looked at Jath with a question in her green eyes. He lowered his bow. "I won't shoot him, Lariah," he whispered. "I can't when he's not threatening me directly. But unlike Migroni, he is a killer."

She raised her blow-tube. Jath nodded his approval. She waited until Shecum was closer. Finally, she blew a short, hard puff of air into the tube. Shecum yelped as the dart struck his cheek and buried itself in his soft flesh. He grabbed it and pulled it out, but the dart had already done its work. Shecum staggered a couple of steps and then he fell, cursing, to the hot sand.

"I'll bind him again," Jath said. "You better get your father to drink some water."

Lariah ran for the boat while Jath grabbed Shecum by one arm and pulled him back across the sand. But he gave up after a few steps. He was still weak, and even though Shecum was small, it was hard work pulling him. Instead, Jath picked up the bows of Ontius and Shecum, returned to the boat, climbed aboard, and gathered up a handful of cords, all of which had been used before and cut. He hurried back to Shecum, tying several of the short cords together as he went. After binding Shecum the best he could, he returned to the boat.

Ontius was conscious and sipping water from the gourd. After Jath cut him free, he coaxed him to eat a banana. Ontius complied, chewing slowly while glaring at Jath with green eyes that emitted scorn and hatred. But Jath found that he was not afraid of Ontius in his weakened condition.

Lariah had recovered her bag of precious things from her father's canoe and had dragged it onto the deck. As she returned for her father's bag, Amoz, from his perch on the top of the mast, suddenly called out, "Lariah!"

Jath and Lariah both looked up and across the beach as several men stepped from the trees. Seeing Lariah and Jath, they shouted and pointed in their direction.

"Hurry, Lariah. It is the men of Antium!" Jath shouted. "Get in my canoe. I'll bring Ontius."

She threw her father's sack into Jath's canoe, jumped onto the deck, and threw hers in with it. Jath struggled with Ontius, who was stubbornly resisting. In desperation, Jath doubled his fist and planted it squarely on Ontius' whiskered chin. The older man folded easily and Jath, with strength that came from fear, picked him up and carried him to the back of the boat where Lariah helped him load Ontius into the canoe.

Jath ran back for the bows, bananas, and the water-filled gourd. He handed all but the bow of Ontius to Lariah. "Put the sail up," he said as he pulled back the string on the heavy bow. He inserted an arrow from the quiver on his back, threw the bow to his shoulder, and faced the band of invaders. They were quite a long distance off, but coming quickly. They stopped when he faced them.

The lead invader was a big man, far bigger than any of the others.

"Antium," Jath gasped.

One of the men drew back a bow and let an arrow fly. It fell short of the boat. He prepared to repeat his act, but the voice of Antium carried clearly up the shore as he yelled, "No! You might hit the girl. I want her alive."

The other man hesitated, but then he drew the string back. Jath decided not to take any chances and released the string on Ontius' bow. The distance was much too great for an ordinary bow, but Jath was not using an ordinary bow. His arrow struck the invader, dropping him to the hot sand.

Jath then turned and jumped into the canoe, drawing his sword and cutting the cord that held them bound to the invader's large craft. Lariah had already begun rowing the heavily loaded boat, and when Jath added his efforts to hers, the canoe made rapid progress away from the shore.

Jath glanced back to see Antium swinging a whip with great force over the invader Jath had shot. The rest of the men were cowering some distance from him, watching him whip their fallen comrade.

Lariah looked back, too. "He's whipping the man you injured," she said with a frown. "Why would he do that?"

"The poor man disobeyed, I guess," Jath said as he turned the canoe and adjusted the sail so it would take full advantage of the stiff breeze.

"But he's *already* hurt," she said. "Why do they follow a man like Antium?"

Jath shrugged. "Out of fear, I guess. Or maybe they are all like him."

"Migroni isn't."

Jath paused to think. "No, he doesn't seem like it," he agreed. "Strange how he got mixed up with them."

The wind had filled the sail, and they picked up speed. "You can quit rowing now," Jath said. "I'll steer when we need it."

She moved forward, adjusting her sack and that of Ontius. Then she knelt beside her still unconscious father. She began to gently stroke the graying hair of the difficult man she both loved and feared.

Amoz, who had saved them from the hands of Antium, proudly perched himself atop the little mast and watched the island as it passed to their left.

CHAPTER 14

Antium coiled his whip after wickedly beating the now dying man. "Cowards," he shouted at the rest of them. "How will we ever take this island if you crawl on your bellies in the sand?" Although the men were not on their bellies, several of them felt like crawling away.

"We can pursue them in our own vessel. Hurry!" he ordered. "You should have already been there instead of watching me punish this disobedient one."

His men, chastened and short yet another fighter, hurried like a pack of starving dogs after their cruel leader. To stop and render aid to the one who would die after the brutal beating by Antium was not even considered.

Near the vessel, one cried out, "There is Shecum over there! He is bound and cannot move."

Favored of Antium, the errant Shecum did not feel the sting of the long whip of Antium. But to protect himself he was quick to put the blame for his dilemma squarely on the shoulders of Migroni, since Migroni was not there to defend himself.

As they cut the cords that bound his wrists and ankles, Shecum said, "Migroni is a traitor to our cause. I had three captives all tied up and ready to deliver to you, Antium. Then he hit me with an oar from behind!"

Antium's dark, beady eyes were narrowed in anger. "Did Migroni cut them loose?" he asked.

"Yes, then he helped them tie me up!" Shecum whined with self-pity.

"Where is he now?" Antium asked. "I didn't notice him with them when they put to sea."

Shecum said hastily, "He went in search of some food for them— that way." He pointed into the trees where he had last seen Migroni.

"Then he will be back," Antium said, pulling thoughtfully on his dirty beard.

"He is probably watching us at this very moment," Shecum said. "He will know that I told you of his treachery. He will hide like the coward that he is, and when we catch him, he will lie like the liar that he is."

Antium nodded and said, "And his brown skin will bleed with very red blood." Once again, he stroked his whip absently.

Shecum shook off the last of the cords and rubbed his raw wrists. "I would like to give him some of—"

"I will administer the punishment!" Antium said with fire in his little eyes. "Tell me, Shecum, who were the three you captured?"

"Ontius and his pretty daughter, Lariah. They were the ones Pagros and I were after before the mountain erupted."

"And the third?" Antium pressed.

"Jath, the son of Samuel," Shecum answered smugly.

"You had the son of the man who killed my father, and you let him go!?" Antium screamed in outrage.

"Not me," Shecum said, raising his hands in denial as he backed away. "Migroni did it."

"Then Migroni will pay dearly for his treachery!" Antium cried. "He will pay with his life: the whip to the death!"

Raising a brawny, hairy arm, Antium pointed toward his vessel. "To the sea with us, men. I want the son of Samuel!" His men were poised to run for the boat but awaited his final signal. He added with a snicker, "And I want the pretty girl, Lariah."

Antium did not see the look of intense hatred that Shecum cast his way, for his back was to the young invader. If he had, Shecum would, for the first time, have felt the sting of the whip. But both Shecum's fear and his cunning prevented him from revealing his innermost thoughts. He would bide his time. He had claimed Lariah to be his wife, and he would stop at nothing to prevent anyone else from having her, even Antium!

* * *

Later that day Shecum learned why Antium and his men were so far south on the island. He had wondered, for when he left them they were at the settlement that lay on the north side of the volcano, several miles from where they found Shecum.

Zermanah, who was still weak but had largely recovered from his wounds, told Shecum in a quiet and secretive voice, "We were headed south with the hope that you and Migroni would see us on the shore and share this vessel with us."

They were now at sea, sailing with a full sail in pursuit of Jath, Lariah, and Ontius. The two men were sitting on the deck near the bow of the craft. "What about the other islanders?" Shecum asked.

"Antium thinks they have crossed the island on foot, fleeing in fear of their lives," Zermanah reported. Then he added, "Antium has been in a foul mood. You are a lucky one, or highly favored, for we thought he would whip you to within a breath of your life when he found you."

"I did nothing wrong," Shecum said, acting surprised. "I see you are feeling much better. Where is the other wounded man?"

"We left him in our cove," Zermanah said. He glanced back at Antium, who was sitting near the rear of the boat. "He is the lucky one, I fear," he added darkly.

"Lucky? How come he is lucky?"

Zermanah shook his head. "I've said too much already."

"You must fear another battle. Are you afraid I will tell Antium?" Shecum quizzed with a mocking smile.

"You told quite a tale on Migroni," Zermanah pointed out.

"I had to!" Shecum hissed. "Migroni put me in great danger of Antium's wrath. But we are friends, you and me."

"And you want the girl, Lariah," Zermanah added. "Antium would not like that if he knew." He was silent as he gazed over the sea.

Shecum watched him. Zermanah knew too much, or at least thought he knew too much. Shecum must gain his trust, for he did not need an enemy in the badly reduced ranks of Antium's force. And he would need a friend. He was quite sure that Zermanah hated Antium, even as he himself did. Yes, Zermanah would be a bad one to have as an enemy, but he was just the one to be that needed friend. Shecum would be patient. He would find a way to enlist the aid of the lanky invader when he needed it.

* * *

Jath watched the island as the little canoe, heavily laden though it was, skimmed across the waves. He worriedly glanced back. There was still no sign of Antium and his men, but Jath was sure that they were not far behind.

His frequent glances over his shoulder had not gone unnoticed by Lariah. "Will Antium catch us?" she asked.

"No. We have the fastest vessel," he replied with a confidence that exceeded his true feelings.

Lariah wrinkled her sunburned nose. "We need some variety in our diet." She grinned and added, "These few bananas are not enough."

Jath thought carefully. "We might be able to go ashore just before it grows dark. Maybe when we do, Antium will go on by."

The crooked shoreline jutted out into the sea in some places for well over a mile. When it was nearly dark and the invaders' vessel still had not come into sight, Jath guided his canoe through a narrow passage near the base of a long peninsula. A coral reef surrounded the peninsula, but within the ring, the water was smooth and the shore sandy. The forest came nearly to the water.

The young couple helped Lariah's stubborn and surly father into the trees where they left him bound and spewing threats at Jath. Then they returned to the canoe and pushed it from the sea and into the dense foliage. Leaving Lariah to keep watch, Jath went in search of food. He caught several small reef fish and two skipjack tuna, and dug some yams that grew wild in the area. For dessert, he picked a large breadfruit.

Jath was careful to build their small fire far enough back in the trees so it would not be seen from the sea. Fortunately, the breeze that blew off the ocean blew the smoke inland rather than out across the ocean where Antium's men would have seen it. Lariah baked the breadfruit and yams, and roasted the fish. With this meal, they drank coconut milk. It was the first good meal they had eaten in days.

Even Ontius was in better spirits after eating, although he continued to glare at Jath in the light of the small fire. To escape his embittered stare, Jath slipped down to the edge of the forest where he listened as he peered into the darkness.

The chance of Antium and his men picking the same place to camp for the night as he had was a slim one. And even more remote was the possibility of them finding the opening through the dangerous reef in the darkness. They were really quite safe now that it was dark, but still Jath worried. Ontius and Lariah had long been asleep when Jath finally made himself a small bed of leaves and gave in to his fatigue.

* * *

Several miles away and several hours later, Migroni stirred in his sleep. A few minutes later he became fully awake. He had eaten with the setting sun and gone to sleep when the last shade of pink light had faded from the sky. He could not recall a time when he had been so utterly exhausted, but he was feeling better now. Getting to his feet, he gathered up his bow and quiver of arrows and began to prowl nervously about his dead campfire.

Migroni was all alone. In a way, he had been alone for many years. Growing up in a family of Lamanites among a colony of Nephites, he had always shied away from close friendships. He looked different and felt different when he was around his Nephite neighbors.

Even after falling in with Antium and his renegade band that plundered and stole from the colonizers, the young Lamanite had been alone. He was again the only Lamanite of the lot. He was also the only one who was not a bloodthirsty killer. When Antium and the others were finally banished from the island, Migroni was given the chance to stay and redeem himself. His mother and sisters begged with their tears, but he had refused.

He reflected now on the reasons that he had chosen to leave with Antium. There were several. First, he had never accepted the Nephite God as his family had done. He stubbornly held to the pagan teachings of his young childhood before his father and mother had been baptized and sailed with Hagoth and his group of Nephites. Migroni still saw his gods in the sun, the moon, the stars, the fire, and the wind.

For that reason, he had feared the volcano—and still feared it. Nevertheless, deep in his soul, he felt a strange yearning to believe as his father had before his untimely death on Hagoth's island shortly after his family had arrived there. Perhaps if his father had lived longer and not left him a lone Lamanite male with only a mother and three little sisters . . .

Then Migroni recalled another reason he had chosen to sail with Antium and his rebellious band. He had been intrigued by Antium's tale of Samuel and Gadoni. He longed for the companionship of another Lamanite man. He had wondered what would make a man like Gadoni hold to a friendship with a Nephite. And he wondered why that Lamanite man had married a Nephite girl. Those questions begged for answers, and by coming to this place, Migroni had secretly hoped to somehow find an opportunity to talk with Gadoni and learn the answers.

Despite the vicious things Antium had said about Gadoni and his Nephite friend, Samuel, Migroni did not believe Gadoni was a bad person—certainly not a murderer! Gadoni had probably even accepted the Nephite God, even as his own father had. Now, as an adult, Migroni wanted to ask Gadoni why. He had never had that chance with his father.

As he reflected on these things in the still darkness of the hour before dawn, Migroni wondered if he might have come here to, in some way, protect a fellow Lamanite from the evil hatred of Antium. He felt sheepish at the thought, but he could not drive it away.

Migroni had told Shecum that he came because he feared Antium. That was partly true, for he had been afraid of Antium after a few months of association with him. But the other thing that he had told Shecum had been one of the compelling reasons he had sailed with Antium; Migroni very much wanted a new place to live—new beginning.

Now, here he was, alone in a new place, a strange and distant island, and he was an enemy to everyone on it, including the invaders that had brought him here. Jath had extended a hand of trust and friendship, but he was a Nephite, and Migroni had, almost from old habit, rejected it. He felt a pang of regret now, for Jath, the son of Samuel, could have told him much of Gadoni, and perhaps he could have even led Migroni to him. Yes, he regretted his rejection of Jath.

Still, here he was on this island, alone and hated, but his desire to meet Gadoni had not diminished. He must be very cautious, for he was a marked man, but he would search for the islanders, spy on them, and perhaps learn more of this Lamanite called Gadoni.

Migroni had traveled south until late in the evening of the preceding day. He had gone that direction because Jath had sailed that way, followed by Antium. He knew that, because he had watched them from the trees, just as Shecum, that liar Shecum, had suspected. He had also witnessed the incredible shot Jath had made with the strange bow of Ontius. And he had witnessed the brutal whipping Antium had given the man after Jath had injured him. Although his efforts had been futile, he had tried to give the dying man aid after Antium and the others had sailed south. But the only service he could render the man was to bury his body after he had died.

Of one thing Migroni was now certain. He despised Antium in a way he had never despised anyone in his life. Yes, he hated him. He swore that Antium would never again touch him with his cruel whip. Never!

Daylight finally filtered in golden splendor through the leafy tree-tops, and Migroni resumed his lonely journey southward. He had no plan; he had no definable destination. He had only the desire to speak with Gadoni, and his loneliness.

* * *

Good food, a soft bed of leaves, and a long night of undisturbed rest had worked a bit of a miracle on Ontius. He awoke in a reasonably good mood, and in exchange for the removal of the cords that bound him, he promised Jath he would make no attack on him.

It was an uneasy truce, however, as Jath was not inclined to trust Ontius fully. Ontius, for his part, cast frequent hateful glances at Jath, glances that did not go unobserved by his daughter. However, despite the mutual mistrust, Jath and Ontius made a good team as they launched their canoe, rowed through the narrow gap in the coral reef, adjusted the sail, and took to the open sea.

There was no sign of Antium and his band of six bloodthirsty warriors. Jath was sure that was all of them, for he had counted. Of course, if Migroni had joined them, there would be one more, but somehow, he was certain Migroni would not have done that.

"They could be ahead of us or still behind," Jath said uneasily as he scanned the sea to their rear. "If they get close, Ontius, a long shot with that magnificent bow of yours would probably convince them to keep their distance."

Ontius smiled briefly at the compliment paid to his weapon.

The breeze was stiff, carrying the canoe swiftly south as it blew. They had sufficient food and water to last for two days, although Jath hoped they would find a place to land where they could hide out in safety somewhere along the miles of rugged southern shoreline before they used up their supplies.

Ontius seemed distant and preoccupied as they sailed, and Jath watched the strange man's back with concern. Despite his love for her, Ontius had twice endangered Lariah's life. Unless Jath prevented it, Ontius would probably lead his daughter into danger again. Jath wondered how he could prevent it.

Their boat rounded a rocky point that jutted hundreds of paces into the sea and began to sail east along the southern coastline. Jath looked up at the towering, jagged ledges that rose from the sea to the summit far above. They were green with vines and crawling plants of a hundred varieties that clung in matted masses across the face of the mountain. Anywhere there was a handful of soil, a clump of grass, a shrub, or even a tree clung to life, adding further to the fantastic beauty of the impossibly steep slopes.

Several silvery ribbons of water cut like gigantic knives though the greenery as the water from high above responded to the relentless call of the sea and plunged downward. Lariah stared at the sight, and even Ontius was impressed with the rugged beauty of the mountains that towered like a gigantic, veiled fortress above them.

"I wish we were up there somewhere," Lariah said with a sigh. "Maybe then we'd be safe."

Jath nodded in agreement and adjusted his sail to more fully utilize the wind that swept eastward along the southern shoreline. The canoe shot ahead like a bird in the wind, and Amoz was forced to cling more tightly to his perch on the mast.

A few minutes later, they could see where a deep canyon cut a jagged gash into the mountain. Where it met the sea, Jath spotted a narrow stretch of sandy beach, guarded jealously by huge rocks that jutted southward into the sea, creating a formidable passageway where the water crashed against the rocks, shooting upward in a continuous sheet of white foam.

"There is a place where we can stop for the night," Jath said as he pointed to the strip of glistening black sand just visible through the narrow, foaming passage. "It's the only place I've seen along this shoreline where we wouldn't be dashed to pieces against the rocks if we tried to land our canoe."

Lariah looked nervous. "It looks very dangerous, Jath. Are you sure we can make it through that narrow channel?"

Jath glanced at Ontius, then said, "Your father is an experienced oarsman. With his help, we can make it."

Lariah looked at her father, then back at Jath. "Then let's do it," she said. "Antium would never see our canoe back in there. Anyway, it may be hours before we find another spot, and by then it will be dark. What do you think, Father?"

Ontius grunted sullenly, but he nodded his head. Jath took that as agreement, and he lowered the sail. "You two help me row, and we'll shoot past those rocks in the very center of that opening and glide onto that sandy little beach," he said as he dipped his own oar into the water, turning the canoe on the choppy sea until it faced the deep gorge.

* * *

Samuel heard a shout. "There is a boat down there," Limre called. While the other islanders had spent the day making the plateau a safe haven for the women and children, Limre had been standing at the southernmost edge of the small plateau watching the sunset. Slowly the blazing sun had settled toward the waiting sea, swathing it with a soft, golden radiance.

Samuel responded to Limre's urgent cry, as did her father, Gadoni. "Can you see it?" she asked them, pointing her finger.

Samuel and Gadoni both squinted. "I can't see anything," Samuel said after a moment of unsuccessful searching.

"Nor can I . . . Wait . . . yes, there is something. It does look like a canoe," Gadoni agreed. "It appears to be heading from the open sea toward the rocky channel that is straight out from the mouth of this gorge below us," he explained to Samuel. "It must be headed for that little spot of sandy beach you can just barely see from here. I wonder if it could be some of the invaders."

"Maybe," Samuel muttered. "Oh, now I see it. Yes, it is heading for the shore in the only place a vessel can land for quite some distance. That is a dangerous channel it must come through. Perhaps they won't make it."

"But what if it is Jath?" Limre asked, her dark eyes looking at him hopefully.

"That may be," Samuel said slowly. The thought had occurred to him, but he was afraid it was too good to be true.

As they watched, silently now, the canoe became more distinct as it approached the turbulent waters of the narrow passage. When it finally reached the channel, it kept coming straight on. It was thrown about like a piece of driftwood, and the occupants could be seen paddling furiously to maintain their course and avoid being thrown into the rocks to their left or their right.

"What are you all watching, Samuel?"

Samuel turned his head at the sound of his wife's concerned voice. "A canoe. Limre spotted it. It is trying to make the shore."

Ophera had the same thought as Limre. "Oh, Samuel! Could it be Jath?" she cried.

"Maybe. Or it could be—" he began.

"He can't know that we are here," she interrupted urgently. "We must send someone down to him."

Limre sided with Ophera as other islanders gathered around and watched the distant drama. "We must let him know we are here, Samuel. He'll be safe with us. And maybe Lariah is with him. Then she will be safe, too."

"If she is with him, then Ontius will be with them," Samuel said with a scowl. He was angry and upset at the trouble Ontius had caused with his stubborn, selfish behavior.

"We must send someone to lead them up here," Ophera insisted. Uri, Kim, and Kib eagerly volunteered to go.

"It could be some of the enemy," Samuel warned.

"Then we'll fight them," Uri insisted as Kim and Kib nodded in silent agreement.

"It will be dark soon," Samuel warned. "Descending the hill will be difficult."

Gadoni spoke up. "But if we wait until morning to send someone, Jath—if it is him—will probably sail back out to sea and be gone long before anyone can reach him."

"We will leave now," Kib spoke up. "We can do it."

Josh, the younger brother of Ophera, also spoke up. "Let me and Nemti go with them."

Samuel looked at the young men. He was afraid to hope that it was his son down there battling the turbulent water of the narrow channel. "But we were to leave in search of Antium and his men in the morning," he said. "We won't have enough men left to do that. And it might be noon or later before you can get back here—if everything goes well, that is," he added.

"We can go after Antium the next day," Gadoni said sensibly. "What is another day, or even two or three for that matter?"

"And if it turns out to be a few of the invaders, the five of us can defeat them very readily," Nemti said confidently. "The advantage of surprise would be ours."

"Please, Samuel," Josh begged again. "Let us go. Nemti and I are experienced soldiers. We have not lost our skills in the years of peace we have enjoyed on the island."

"And there are none better to aid them than Kim, Kib, and Uri," Samuel's brother, Oreb, added. "Let them go."

Samuel nodded his assent. "May God go with you," he said, and he looked out across the distant sea to hide the mist that clouded his vision.

"It must be Jath," Limre said confidently, lifting Samuel's spirits, as he rubbed his eyes and watched with mounting suspense as the little canoe was tossed about. Silently, as his wife held his arm tightly, he prayed that if it were Jath, he would come through the treacherous waters of the channel in safety. Oh, how he wanted his son back.

CHAPTER 15

The approach to the strip of sandy beach was proving to be more difficult than Jath had anticipated. For several minutes, he feared that the current would drag them into the rocks on either side of the passage and toss them to their deaths.

Ontius and Lariah both paddled furiously. Their fight to stay in the very center of the channel took every ounce of strength they had. Without their efforts, the canoe would no doubt have been dashed to slivers on the rocks, for it was heavy and hard to guide with the load it bore. The trio finally managed to shoot past the last of the dangerous rocks, and the canoe coasted safely across the smooth water of the little lagoon and nosed gently into the black sand of the beach.

For several minutes, they sat silently in the canoe, catching their breaths and calming their rapidly beating hearts. Jath prayed silently, certain that Lariah was doing the same.

He asked the Lord for nothing; rather, his entire prayer was one of thanks, for he knew that God had led them through the narrow stretch of water that guarded this peaceful little beach.

When Jath had finished, he and Ontius pulled the little canoe out of the water and beneath the leafy trees that grew dense at the base of the mountain. As darkness settled in, Jath helped Lariah fix a meal. They talked as they worked, but Ontius sat sullenly a short distance from them, his back against a mossy rock. Jath attempted to ignore him and was grateful that at least Ontius was not threatening him in some way.

"What will we do in the morning, Jath?" Lariah asked, her gaze drawn to the darkness where the waters of the narrow passage churned and roared. "I don't want to go through there again. It was horrible."

Jath nodded in agreement. "It was bad, I know. But we made it, didn't we? I'm sure we'll be able to do it again when we've rested, but I'm wondering if we should just wait here for a day or two while Antium searches for us."

Lariah paused to consider the idea. "What if he finds us here?"

Jath smiled. "He can't get his boat in here. It is too big and it would be hard to steer. It would almost certainly be smashed into the rocks if they tried to enter the channel. No, you don't need to worry. Nothing can happen to us here."

"Someone could come from that way," she said pointing toward the steep, tree-choked canyon at their backs. "I know it's a rugged place behind us, but a person could get to us from that direction."

Jath chuckled. "You worry too much, Lariah. Antium and his men are on the sea."

"They could land somewhere and climb the mountain and come down," she reasoned stubbornly.

"I suppose they could," Jath said slowly, "but it would take them awhile. Anyway, we—"

Lariah interrupted him. "There are seven men on Antium's boat. Isn't that what you counted?"

"Yes."

"Then where are the rest?" she demanded.

"Well . . . I suppose that . . . well . . ." Jath stammered. The truth was, he didn't know about the rest. Some were dead, of that he was certain, but he had no idea how many. There could be other invaders anywhere.

"What if some of them came down that canyon?" she insisted.

Jath put a hand on one of hers and looked earnestly at her. The light of their small fire frolicked in her eyes and cast a dancing yellow glow across her face. "I will protect you, Lariah. Now, please, quit worrying."

"Is that a promise?" she asked, her eyes meeting his, sending an urgent plea of their own.

She seemed to like to extract promises from him, Jath thought, but he liked to give them. It made him feel needed. "It's a promise, Lariah. I won't let anyone hurt you or take you away. Now, please quit worrying."

"Thanks, Jath. I'll quit fussing," she promised in return, and her face lit into a smile that melted Jath's heart with its warmth.

The pounding of the surf against the rocks lulled Jath to sleep that night. Ontius had been very quiet as they ate and later as they lounged beside their fire. But Lariah had been cheerful and filled the night air with her lighthearted chatter. Once she had obtained from Jath his promise to protect her, she put her trust in him and was her old self again.

Jath awoke to the sound of a familiar voice calling out, "Jath, wake up."

He rubbed his eyes, trying to recall where he was. Then it came flooding back to him, and the friendly voice in the dark did not fit here. "Jath!"

Jath sat up with a jolt. "Uri?" he said. "What are you doing here? Where did you come from?" He scrambled to his feet and embraced Uri as a great surge of relief and love almost overpowered him.

Uri grinned as he explained, "Samuel sent us for you."

"How did Father know we were here?" Jath asked in bewilderment.

"All of the people are on a little plateau far above this canyon, near its west rim. We saw your canoe in that passage you came through. It's taken several hours to get down here."

Jath was equally pleased to see his uncle Josh. "We weren't completely sure it was even you down here," Josh said. "We can't start back in the dark, so we may as well get a few hours sleep now. Then we can start back to rejoin the others when it's light."

Jath had never felt such relief. It felt good to have someone to share the burden of caring for Lariah and worrying about her strange father. He felt as if a great weight had just been lifted from his shoulders.

Nemti asked, "Wasn't there someone else with you?"

Jath was surprised at the question. "Ontius and Lariah," he replied.

"Where are they now?" Nemti asked. "I don't see anyone."

"They're right over here," Jath said confidently as he stepped lightly to where he had helped Lariah pile leaves and twigs for her bed.

She was gone!

He gasped. "Lariah! Where could she be? She was right here!"

"You were alone when we got here, Jath," Uri said. "We searched carefully before I awoke you since we weren't sure at first who you were."

Jath's heart pounded in his ears. He felt weak and sick. "But they were right here," he insisted. "I didn't go to sleep until after they did."

Kib and Kim had been working on the coals of Jath's fire and had finally coaxed it to life in a burst of orange light.

"Their sacks are in the canoe with our bows and arrows," Jath said. "Maybe they moved over there."

"The canoe is empty, Jath, except for this bow," Josh said, holding out Shecum's bow.

"Empty?" Jath said hoarsely as he took the bow.

Josh gave a wry grin. "They left you without so much as an arrow."

Jath was silent, remembering how quiet Ontius had been as he and Lariah had chatted beside the fire. And he remembered his promise to protect her . . . and not to let anyone take her! He sighed heavily. He had failed Lariah again.

"Ontius!" he yelled into the darkness. "You fool! You crazy, mean, stupid fool!"

Uri put an arm around Jath's shoulders. "Ontius is indeed a fool," he agreed quietly. "We'll find her again, Jath. But first we need to deal with Antium and what's left of his band of invaders. Then we'll find Lariah and her father."

"Her father is crazy, Uri. He's out of his mind! I've got to go in search of her—now!" Jath said urgently.

Uri took hold of Jath's arm. "It's dark, Jath. You must wait. And when you do go, you must not go alone again."

Uri was right, and Jath knew it. He must accept help if he were to provide help to her again. He could not do it himself. Her absence now and his broken promise were proof of that. With an effort, he pulled himself together and asked about his family.

For the next hour, Jath listened as his five friends told him of the battles they had fought and the other events that had occurred after he had gone in search of Lariah. Then he told them his story. When he mentioned Ontius' attempt to kill him, Josh broke in angrily. "Jath, you must give us your word that you will not go after Lariah again until some of us can go with you. Ontius is a dangerous man."

Jath gave his word reluctantly, then finished his story briefly. Nemti whistled and said, "So Antium is on the sea. That will certainly change Samuel's plans."

Jath lay awake long after his companions had fallen asleep. He scowled, he tossed, he prayed, and he cried.

He awoke to the throaty sound of Lariah's parrot, Amoz, crying, "Lariah" over and over. "Looks like we were both sleeping when Ontius left with Lariah," Jath commiserated with the bird. "Come over here, Amoz."

The bird ignored him, so Jath called again. It took several minutes and he awoke the whole camp in the process, but Amoz finally flew from the tree limb where he had stationed himself and accepted Jath's shoulder as a substitute for Lariah's.

"We'll find her, Amoz. We'll find her and tie old Ontius up so tight he'll never get loose again!" Jath vowed fiercely.

The other young men chuckled at Amoz, but Jath just smiled and kept his thoughts to himself. He had plans for Amoz. Big plans. He just hoped it would work.

* * *

Lariah's eyes were red from crying, but all her tears and pleas had been wasted on her father. Ontius drove her relentlessly up the canyon. A few times her father had even called her by her mother's name. The look in his eye at those times was distant and hollow, as if he did not recognize her.

As the day wore on and the heat grew intense, he led her to the east rim of the canyon and then continued east. These were incredibly rugged mountains, she thought, but also they were incredibly beautiful.

Her father's ravings as they trudged along, lugging their sacks and weapons, became increasingly disturbing. Lariah feared that her father had lost his mind. Remembering his murderous attack on Jath in the canoe when he was like this before, she was careful to not rile him if she could help it. But once she slipped, bruising her knees and dropping her sack. "Oh, Jath," she sighed. "If only you were here . . ."

"Him again?" Ontius scowled. "Forget him!" Then he slapped her, hard, across her face.

Lariah knew something was terribly wrong. Her father had never done that before. Even though he had been a strange and moody man since the death of her mother and sister, he had always been kind to her. She took a deep breath and resolved not to mention Jath's name again, but she would not, could not, forget him, for she loved him.

Even as she thought of him now, she choked up in grief. She knew he would be blaming himself for letting her father take her away, and that hurt her, for she had made him promise to protect her. A promise to him, she knew, was as good as his honor.

Shortly before sunset, Ontius dropped his sack with a groan. "This is where we will build our new home, Lariah," he announced.

She laid her own sack down and looked around her. They had been following a stream that led from higher slopes for over an hour. It had wound its way southward through a forest of fragrant, flowering trees and bushes for a mile or more before breaking into this grassy, flower-choked clearing. Blossoms of a hundred varieties graced the spot Ontius had chosen, and thick, leafy vegetation almost hid the clear water of the stream from view.

The scent of the flowers, trees, and shrubs was rich and sweet. She bent and dug her fingers into the ground. The soil was moist and dark. Taros, yams, sugarcane, and sweet potatoes would grow well in this fertile little spot.

Away to the west a short distance, the mountain rose sharply, providing a break from the winds. There had been little damage from the recent storm, the one that had thundered across this island paradise the night the invaders had first made their presence known.

Ontius had indeed chosen well. Too well, Lariah thought sadly, for, though beautiful, their new home was a lonely, remote little spot on the island. Nevertheless, the pleasant sound of falling water caressed her ears, easing her sadness, and she moved instinctively toward its musical call.

"Where are you going?" Ontius demanded harshly after she had gone only a few steps.

"This is such a beautiful place," she said, trying her best to sound cheerful and reassuring. "If this is to be my new home, I want to know it well, and that includes everything that surrounds us. I'll be back in a minute, Father." Her muscles ached and her feet were blistered, but Lariah needed a few moments away from her father.

"Of course, my dear," he replied, smiling.

Lariah followed the stream, guided by the lyrical call of falling water. As she walked, it gradually became louder, beckoning her onward.

Suddenly, she emerged from the trees and found herself on an outcropping of solid rock. To her left, the water plunged over the edge, out of sight. She could only guess how far it fell. She was sure it was an incredibly long distance because, from where she stood, she could see the ocean about a mile away and far, far below as it stretched interminably to the south, east, and west.

On an impulse, she dropped to her stomach and crawled forward until her head hung over the edge. The mountain and the stream fell straight down for hundreds of paces. Both were swallowed up below by the dark green jungle that stretched like a velvet carpet to where it ended abruptly at another giant overhang, directly overlooking the frothing seashore.

She watched for several minutes, spellbound by the breathtaking beauty of the scene God had sculpted for her. Finally, promising herself that she would visit this lovely place often, she eased her way back and stood up.

"Lariah!"

She whirled in fright. "Oh, Father," she scolded. "It's you. You frightened me."

"You've been gone far too long," he said forlornly.

"I'm sorry, Father. Come look. The view is magnificent. I love it."

Ontius stepped beside her, giving the scene only a cursory glance before taking her arm tightly and leading her away. "Be careful, Lariah," he cautioned gruffly. "It is dangerous here. Come, it is past time for you to prepare my supper."

Lariah was astonished. He had always loved the beauty offered by this island. Now, however, he seemed not to even notice a view so wild and exquisite that it took her breath away. He definitely was not himself!

She took one last look. *How wonderful it would be to share this place with Jath,* she sighed to herself. Then she allowed her father to pull her away and back into the forest.

* * *

Antium the Younger was furious, a state he was in more and more frequently since the invasion, Shecum thought wryly. His current rampage was directed at all six of his men for their inability to locate the son of Samuel and his two passengers. As usual, Antium accepted none of the blame himself, even though his men only did as he ordered and searched where he directed.

They had stopped at every one of the few places it was possible to safely land a boat along the rugged southern coast of the island. No sign of Jath's canoe or its occupants could be found anywhere. Shecum finally took courage. "They probably sailed right around this island and back to the other side," he suggested.

As Antium thought about that possibility, Shecum watched him, his hatred festering inside him like a giant boil. Shecum had once admired this renegade leader, but he admired him no longer. Frustrated by their lack of success, Antium and his men had camped beside one of the few strips of sandy beach this southern coast offered. Antium stood leaning against an ancient coconut palm, alternately stroking his beard and his ever-present whip as he mulled over Shecum's words.

Finally, he spoke. "We will sail west at dawn. Unless we meet Jath and my beautiful Lariah, we will return to our cove. Perhaps our lazy comrade will be ready to join us by then."

Shecum bit his tongue, not because he cared about the man who had been injured fighting Antium's battles, but because Antium had mentioned Lariah. Shecum had revealed her name to him, but he had no intention of relinquishing his claim on her to Antium. He knew he had to be very careful not to let Antium have any idea of the mutinous thoughts he harbored in his heart.

* * *

After welcoming Jath back with tears of gratitude and love, Samuel canceled the plan to go in search of Antium. Instead, he placed a lookout at the very place from where Limre had spotted Jath's canoe as it approached the narrow passageway far below.

"Watch for Antium's craft on the ocean," Samuel warned Uri. "If it passes this way, let me know immediately."

Uri was getting quite bored as the noon hour approached, but his boredom vanished the instant he spotted a tiny dot on the sea far to the east of Jath's channel. In a short while, the dot grew bigger. Finally, as it passed to the south, he was sure it was the boat he sought, and he called out to Samuel. All the men came running at his call.

"Out there," Uri said. "It is sailing a little farther from shore than Jath did."

After watching the bobbing vessel for a moment, Jath was certain. "It's Antium," he said, looking at the other men around him.

"And he is heading back around the island," Samuel observed thoughtfully.

Oreb pounded a clenched fist against a large boulder. "If we were just down there in our canoes right now," he said angrily, "we could finish this thing for good."

The women joined the men as they watched the boat of their enemy. It was Limre who first detected a slight change in course of the boat.

"They are going to turn. Do you think they are going to try to come through Jath's channel?" she asked of no one in particular.

Indeed, the boat did turn, and it sailed north toward the channel Jath had used to reach the black sands of the little beach. "They can't make it in that big boat," he gloated. "But I hope they try!"

They did not.

They did, however, spend an unusual amount of time in the vicinity before going on at last to the west.

"They must have decided it was too hazardous," Samuel said.

"They might also have realized that a small canoe could do it," Oreb mused. "I wonder if they suspect that Jath came in through there."

"Perhaps they have figured out how they lost him," Gadoni said. "If so, they will almost certainly land somewhere on the west coastline and come back in search of him on foot. We must prepare for that."

"Yes, we must," Samuel agreed. "Let us pray for direction, and then plan, and plan quickly."

Within an hour, a course of action had been agreed upon. Uri and Jath, armed with two of the strongest bows the islanders possessed and lugging several days worth of provisions, departed first. Amoz, Lariah's parrot, accompanied them. Jath had tried to get him to stay, but Amoz would have no part of that.

After Samuel had assigned two men and three boys of under seventeen to stay with Captain Baronihah, who insisted that he was strong enough to mount a defense if necessary, he led the rest of the men and older boys off the mountain, retracing the route they had used when they arrived here.

Jath and Uri made good time down the rugged canyon to the sandy beach. They arrived there with a couple of hours of daylight still remaining. "We have time to get onto the sea," Jath said as they emerged from the forest at the base of the mountain.

"Then let's get the canoe in the water," Uri said with mounting excitement.

Both young men were rested and strong. The channel, although it remained as rough and threatening as it had been when Jath entered before, was no great challenge for the pair of them. After safely scooting through, they raised the sail, providing a perch for Amoz. They adjusted it so that the winds would move their craft westward, then paddled with all their strength to add speed to the little craft.

They rounded the rocky ridge that marked the southwestern point of the island just as the sun, in a gigantic splash of red and pink, plunged into the western sea. Readjusting the sail, they next headed north. They sailed as far as they dared, trying to calculate the distance Antium might have come before darkness sent him in search of land for the night. While they did not know for certain that Antium and his men would spend the night on the beach somewhere, they knew they must expect it, so they did not risk getting ahead of them.

Jath knew this coastline well, as did Uri. Even in the darkness, they were able to select a beach where they could safely guide their little canoe to shore. They ate quickly and went to sleep, hoping to be awake at dawn and back on the sea.

* * *

Migroni was awake before the sun came up. He had smelled the smoke of a fire the night before. He had gone toward it for an hour or so, but the smell had eventually dwindled until he was forced to camp for the night. He supposed it could be Antium and his men, but he doubted it. He hoped that he had found the place where the people of Samuel were hiding.

He climbed to a high ridge with a rocky, barren point. From there he surveyed the surrounding forest as the sun came up. He spotted what he searched for almost immediately. A thin column of smoke rose from the trees less than a mile to the west, toward the coast.

Migroni hurried from his ridge and trekked as rapidly as he could toward the source of the smoke. By the time he arrived, there was only a dying fire, but he could see that the men he sought had not been gone long, and the route they had taken was easy to follow. He knew at once that he had not found the place where anyone had spent more than a few hours. He also figured that men, and only men, had been there.

By noon Migroni had caught up with the men he trailed, and he followed them until they stopped for lunch. Then he moved stealthily toward them. It was obvious that they did not expect to find Antium up here, for they were making no attempt to keep their voices down, nor had they provided a guard to surround them while they ate.

Migroni crept very close and peered from the bushes. He realized at a glance that most of the men of the island must be here, and they were all heavily armed. He also knew immediately which one was Gadoni, for there was only one Lamanite in their midst.

Gadoni was about the same height and build as Migroni himself. In fact, he reminded him a lot of his own father, and he was instantly drawn to him. Gadoni was speaking to his men.

"We must make this the last battle," he said. "We came here seeking peace, and we found it. This madman, this Antium the Younger, has stolen it away from us, even as his father did many years ago. It must be restored at once. Our families have suffered enough. I will gladly give my life if that is what it takes to restore peace to our people."

His words struck Migroni with such force that he did not hear the response from the one who must be Samuel. Migroni was right. He had been right all along. Gadoni was not a bad man as Antium would have him believe. He was a good man who had come here seeking peace for himself and his loved ones. Migroni recalled that his own father had said that same thing many years ago when they had sailed with Hagoth. He too had sought peace.

Now he, Migroni, had helped to destroy it! He felt a great wave of shame wash over him for what he had done in following Antium.

He listened again as the voice of Gadoni once more caught his attention. "There was a Lamanite man with them. Jath said that he does not believe he would have sailed with Antium, even though he did free the wiry one called Shecum. I wonder where he is. We must watch for him, although if Jath is right, he should not be a danger to us, for Jath said he is not a killer. In fact, he saved Jath's life from Shecum."

"Then why did he come to our island with Antium?" one of the other men asked harshly. He was a broad-shouldered man with an angry look on his face who stood out in contrast to the other men. He rose to his feet, glared for a moment in Gadoni's direction, then added, "I say we must deal with him if we come across him the same as with the others."

Samuel spoke, and Migroni listened to him this time. "We will not hurt anyone who is not a threat to us, Jarium. This Migroni is not a threat, at least not while he is apart from Antium."

Despite this Jarium, Migroni's heart took courage. He could see why Gadoni liked Samuel. He was a fair and just man, and the color of one's skin did not matter to him. Migroni almost rose to his feet, tempted to step into the midst of these men and offer to help them defeat Antium. But he did not, for despite the words of trust from Samuel and Gadoni, the others, particularly the one Samuel had called by the name of Jarium, might not feel the same, and even if they didn't slay him, they would probably take him captive.

Instead he lay still, listening as his heart pounded like an ax in his chest. He wondered where Jath was. It was clear that he had somehow met with these men since Migroni had last seen him sailing south in his canoe with Lariah and that crazy man, Ontius. It was also clear that Samuel and Gadoni and the others must have some idea where Antium, Shecum, and the others were.

Perhaps he would follow them, he decided. Maybe he could aid them in the coming conflict with Antium without their knowing it and repay, in some way, the trust Jath had shown him and instilled in Samuel and Gadoni. In so doing, he could also repay Antium for his cruelty with the whip and Shecum for his lies.

CHAPTER 16

The horrid stench of death greeted Antium when he and his men entered the cove that had served as their island hideout. Left without food or water, his wounded man had died.

Antium blamed Shecum. "Had you been here to care for him when he was wounded, he would be alive and ready to fight. Now, thanks to you, he is dead and there are only seven of us left."

Shecum began to lodge a protest, but a sharp look from his new ally, Zermanah, caused him to snap his mouth shut and remain silent.

Silence was not what Antium wanted from the favorite of his band of invaders. "Are you prepared to fight as three men?" Antium asked him mockingly.

"I will do my best," Shecum responded, feigning humility.

"Well, you better!" Antium snapped. He cracked his whip, startling a flock of bright yellow birds in the branches overhead and sending them chirping into flight.

Shecum winced, afraid that the next crack of the whip would descend upon him. However, still favored of Antium, he was spared yet again. Antium neatly coiled his whip and spoke again, "It will be dark soon. Gather food and water and store it on the boat. We will leave at daylight."

"Where are we going?" Shecum asked.

Antium scowled at him but replied gruffly, "We are going to sail a few miles, beach our boat where it cannot be found, and go over the mountain to find Jath, Lariah, and Ontius. They will lead us to the others, wherever they are hiding."

"What if they don't know where the other islanders are?" one of the men foolishly asked.

The whip shot out, cutting a nasty gash across the man's shoulder. "They will know," he shouted unreasonably, and no one else attempted to question his judgment. "I will avenge my father, and we will have our island soon."

Shecum doubted that, but he didn't care anymore. He intended, with the help of Zermanah, to find Lariah. *Antium had better not stand in my way,* he thought bitterly. After he found her, then . . . well, he didn't actually know what he'd do then, but he would face that when he came to it. At any rate, he had no intention of dying for Antium's cause. For the present, however, he would play along with Antium, as long as it suited his own purposes.

The surviving invaders welcomed a good night's rest. They had been sailing for the entire previous day and all night the night before, taking short catnaps on the deck whenever they could, but never really resting. By the time the full light of morning had arrived, they were rested and already sailing south upon the sea.

* * *

Jath and Uri were also up early. They had rejoined Samuel and the others the evening before and reported that they had not seen the big boat of Antium.

"Go in search of them again," Samuel directed them. "If you find them, lead them here. We'll be quite a distance back in the forest waiting. I want them far enough from their boat that they cannot retreat to the boat when we attack. If you fail to find them today, then meet us here again tonight."

After giving his instructions, Samuel led Jath and Uri back to where he and the others would be waiting to surprise the invaders and in this way, they hoped, end the invasion and restore peace to the island.

As the sun broke over the mountains, the two young men returned to the sea with Samuel's blessing and a stern admonition to be careful. They rowed away from shore, leaving the others to set their trap and wait. "We'll sail north," Jath said as they paddled away from the beach and adjusted their sail. "I don't think they went south in the darkness."

A few hours of sailing proved Jath right. He spotted Antium's sail over the top of the waves in a moderately choppy sea. His chest tightened and his hands gripped his oar until his knuckles were white. "I wish we had Ontius' bow," he murmured to Uri as the two vessels approached one another. "We could torment them with arrows and still be out of range of their bows."

"We have good bows. Ours are the best on the island," Uri said.

"You have not seen or handled the bow Ontius made," Jath responded. "I'll show you what it can do when we find Ontius and Lariah. It is amazing."

"Fine, but we don't have it," Uri said sharply. "We better turn south now. They see us, I think."

The young men quickly spun their little vessel in the water and lowered the sail. "They are coming fast," Uri said a moment later. "A little closer, and we better raise our sail and get out of here."

Uri held his bow while Jath kept a hand on the little mast, ready to raise the sail and scoot with the wind. Soon they heard Antium's raspy voice as he began to scream threats at them across the waves.

Still they waited. Antium shouted, "Throw down your weapons and you won't be hurt."

"Sure," Jath mumbled sarcastically. "We can trust Antium. He would never hurt the brother or the son of Samuel."

"Okay," Uri said with a smile. "They're almost as close as we dare let them get. Okay . . . ready . . . raise the sail!" he shouted, and he shot an arrow at the oncoming vessel with all his strength.

Jath swiftly raised the sail and the canoe darted southward. Uri's arrow struck the water several paces short of the boat of Antium, causing the invader's leader to throw a volley of curses toward them. Then Jath distinctly heard him shout, "After them, men! Don't let them get away!"

Jath and Uri used their paddles to steer and even rowed backwards to slow the craft down when they began to gain too great a lead over the invaders. They wanted to stay well out of the range of their arrows but remain close enough to keep them coming after them with all the speed they could muster. And the invaders were trying hard to catch up. Six men could be seen bent to their oars, doing their best to assist the wind that filled the sail of Antium's boat.

For several hours, Antium urged his men on, never once taking an oar himself as Jath and Uri fled in front of them. Jath and Uri turned toward the beach when they neared the spot where Samuel and his men waited several hundred paces inland to make the attack. Riding on a curling wave, the canoe hit the beach so abruptly when the wave let it down that it threw the two young men forward and sent Amoz flying in a panic from the mast. Jath and Uri both tumbled swiftly from the boat, rushed across the sand, and fled into the trees just as Antium's boat slid to a stop. At Antium's order, his men jumped out onto the sand and ran after Jath and Uri.

The last two men off the boat, Shecum and Zermanah, looked at each other. "Don't go!" Shecum whispered urgently. "It may be a trap! Let's take the little boat and leave. I don't want to die here."

"Nor do I," Zermanah said as he quickly assessed the situation and decided that Shecum was probably right.

Antium drove the other four men ahead of him all the way to the trees. He looked back just as Shecum and Zermanah were scrambling into Jath's canoe.

With a cry of rage, he turned back. His other men, upon hearing his cry, stopped in confusion and began to run toward the boats. By the time they reached the shore, Shecum and Zermanah were already skipping southward across the waves in their stolen canoe.

"Antium is coming after us!" Zermanah cried. "It was not a trap after all. There has been no attack."

Shecum had no response. He had been so sure that Jath and the other young man were leading them into an ambush of some sort that he had given no thought to the consequences of being wrong.

Zermanah was angry, for now they had invoked the wrath of Antium. "You said that there was no way Jath could have known where the other islanders were! That was a young man with him, not Ontius, like you said," he accused.

Shecum was indeed puzzled. He had been sure it was Ontius with Jath. "I guess I was wrong," he responded.

Zermanah wasn't satisfied with a simple apology. "I trusted you, Shecum!" he shouted.

"Well, keep trusting me. They can't catch us, Zermanah. We are in a much faster boat," Shecum reasoned.

"But Jath couldn't get away from us a few minutes ago. What makes this boat faster now?" Zermanah argued.

"It appeared that way," Shecum said slowly. It didn't make sense. He knew the speed of this canoe. Jath had to have been holding his speed down and gone to shore where he did for a purpose. He looked back.

Antium's boat was already leaving the shore with four men paddling for all they were worth. Beneath him he could feel the incredible speed of this light canoe as it cut through the water, and his confidence grew.

"Antium will whip us to death!" Zermanah cried in terror.

"We'll be safe, Zermanah," Shecum said almost gleefully, for he had just thought of something that pleased him immensely. "In this little craft we can enter the channel on the south shoreline where Jath went with Lariah and her father."

"Are you crazy, Shecum?" Zermanah asked in horror. "That is where Samuel and the other islanders must be."

Shecum hadn't considered that. Before he could think of a response, he looked back. Men were pouring from the trees! "It was an ambush!" he cried. "Samuel's men were back there hiding. If we had followed Antium we would be dead by now."

Zermanah stopped his babbling and looked back, shocked.

Shecum gloated. "And that means they will have left Lariah and the other women and children behind. We must hurry, while they are yet defenseless."

"You are right!" Zermanah exclaimed. Then he frowned again. "How will we explain to Antium why we did not warn him that we thought it was an ambush?"

"I will think of something. Don't worry, Zermanah. We are going after Lariah now." Shecum laughed, then added, "And we will find a wife for you, too, if you want one."

* * *

As the boats sailed away from the shore, Samuel and his men watched in gloomy silence.

"It should have worked," Oreb said at last, breaking the grim stillness. "Our ambush should have worked."

"It would have worked if Shecum and that other man hadn't deserted Antium and taken my canoe," Jath said bitterly.

"Yes, our plan was a good one," Samuel agreed glumly. "But I overlooked one thing; there is never honor among evil ones. We came so close to ending this thing. So very close."

"What do we do now?" Uri asked. "It is many miles back to where our other boats and canoes are docked."

Gadoni was squatting and idly drawing lines in the sand with his fingers. Suddenly, he leaped to his feet. "With the small canoe, they can enter Jath's passageway!" he exclaimed.

"Hurry men! Gadoni is right. We must return. Maybe we can catch them on our mountain and finish this fight yet," Samuel said urgently.

At a quick trot, the islanders started south, hopeful again of putting an end to the trouble Antium had brought with him.

* * *

Migroni, determined to help the islanders in some way, was equally frustrated. He had heard every word of Samuel's plan to ambush Antium and the invaders. He thought, as Samuel had done, that it would end the conflict. But he had not counted on two of the men deserting Antium at the crucial moment.

Oh, he should have guessed, he scolded himself, for Shecum's hatred and jealousy was no secret to Migroni. Migroni allowed himself a wry smile at the thought of what Antium would do when he caught up with Shecum—if he did. Surely, for this offense, Antium would not spare Shecum from the sting of his whip, Migroni reasoned.

From where he now stood far to the south of the islanders on a ridge overlooking the beach and the sea, Migroni watched the racing boats. For a moment he just stared, but an idea suddenly sprang into his head. "I can still do something to assist Gadoni and Samuel!" he said aloud with building excitement.

The jagged coastline below him might provide just the help he needed. The ridge on which he now stood jutted into the sea for almost a mile to the west. The canoe and the boat of Antium would have to sail around that point and then come back to the southeast to avoid sailing far into the open sea. He was quite sure that Shecum, if it was he, would not want to be too far from shore after his last experience at navigation.

By running hard, Migroni could probably get to the beach on the other side of the ridge before the canoe arrived there. It was not all that far across the ridge. *Yes,* he thought, *it just might work.* He headed over the barren ridge at a run.

* * *

"Look! Is that someone running over that ridge?" one of the islanders shouted.

"Who could it be?" another asked. "There are none of us missing."

"Maybe it is Ontius or his daughter," another suggested.

"Or maybe it is Migroni," Jath said calmly, for he was sure that neither Ontius nor Lariah would be alone. And he was equally sure that they would not be this far north. Lariah had told him of Ontius' plan to build a new home on the south side of the island.

"Migroni? The invader that saved your life?" Uri asked.

"Yes, it could be him."

"I wonder if he's seen us," Uri mused.

Jarium suddenly shouted, "By crossing that ridge, he could catch up with and meet Antium and his men."

Jath shook his head fiercely. "Migroni would not want to do that," he said. "And Ontius certainly wouldn't if it were him. He's not that crazy yet, I don't think."

"I think Migroni would," Jarium countered angrily.

"Never!" Jath insisted, surprised at the strength of his feelings.

"We may never know," Uri broke in. "I wish we were closer. By the time we could get over that ridge ourselves, whoever it is will be long gone."

"We can't worry about that now, anyway," Samuel said sternly. "We need to get back and help Baronihah when the invaders reach our mountain."

* * *

Shecum and Zermanah rounded the point and sped southeast. As they neared the beach, Zermanah shouted, "Look, Shecum. Someone just came onto the beach. He is waving at us."

Shecum threw his head back in laughter. "It must be Migroni. He wants a ride." He looked over his shoulder. The larger craft of Antium was coming. There was a way out of this dilemma they were in with Antium. Indeed there was.

"Zermanah, let's stop and pick Migroni up. Then we can turn him over to Antium. We will tell Antium that we spotted Migroni and only hurried away in this canoe so we could catch him over here. He will believe us, and his anger will descend on Migroni instead of us."

Zermanah did not harbor any particularly bad feelings toward Migroni, but if turning him over to Antium would save him from punishment for the blunder he and Shecum had pulled, then he would certainly lie. Let Migroni take the whipping if need be, as long as he himself was spared.

"That's a good idea," he agreed. "Let's get him."

Migroni waved again as they sailed closer, signaling them to come to him. But when the canoe was almost to the beach, he suddenly seemed to have a change of heart, for he began to run toward the forest. "He's changed his mind," Zermanah cried.

"Too bad!" Shecum retorted. "We must get him now and return him to Antium, even if he's dead or wounded. If we don't, we may not be able to make peace with Antium."

A glance back indicated that Antium had seen Migroni, too. Shecum and Zermanah paddled fiercely, and the canoe ran swiftly onto the beach. Both men grabbed their bows, jumped out of the canoe, and splashed to the sandy shore.

Zermanah was worried. "What about the islanders?" he shouted as they pursued Migroni.

"Even if they are coming this way, they won't be here for a long time yet," Shecum yelled. "We'll catch Migroni and be back to our boats and gone long before they show up on the ridge."

Migroni stopped for a moment before he reached the forest, leaning over with his hands on his knees.

Shecum wanted to laugh. "He's very tired," he called out over his shoulder. "We have him now!"

But Migroni took off again, ran a short distance, and stopped again at the very edge of the trees. Shecum fit an arrow to his bow as he ran, and then he stopped and took aim. He let the arrow sail. Migroni dropped to his knees, then rose again and limped into the trees.

"I hit him! He's hurt now! Hurry, Zermanah!" he shouted.

"I'm hurrying," Zermanah cried. In reality he was not feeling so well. His old injuries had flared up as he began running, and now pain shot through him like fire. He stumbled and nearly fell, but he struggled on.

Shecum looked back and realized that Zermanah was not feeling very well. He also saw Antium's boat closing in on the shore. He had no time to waste. He had to get Migroni, now! Furiously, he plunged into the woods after the young Lamanite.

* * *

Shecum's arrow had come dangerously close, but Migroni had faked his injury in hopes of encouraging Shecum to continue after him. It worked, for Shecum kept running toward him. Migroni hoped that now the rest of the men of Antium would do the same.

For a while, Migroni led Shecum through the thick forest, and then he gradually turned back toward the beach. A few minutes later he again reached the edge of the trees. Antium's boat was beside Shecum's. It was empty! There was not a single man left in sight on the beach.

Perfect! he thought.

Moving silently now, Migroni doubled back. He could hear Shecum as he passed by in the thick forest. A little later, he heard several others. Finally, he caught a glimpse of Zermanah. He was moving very slowly and was in obvious pain.

Migroni had no time to waste now, for Shecum would soon realize that he had been tricked and come after him again. Migroni's lungs burned and his legs ached, but he courageously summoned all his strength and burst out of the trees like a wild boar. He ran straight for the deserted boats.

Not until he reached them did he look behind him again. He had no time to rest, for Shecum was already on his way back. Migroni pushed the bow of Antium's boat off the sand. Then he did the same with Jath's canoe before tying it to the rear of Antium's as he had done when they had captured Jath before. Then he scrambled onto Antium's big vessel and began to row as hard as he could. He was in deep water by the time Shecum reached the shore. Screaming threats, Shecum began to shoot arrows at him, but he was weary from running and his aim was off. Migroni bent over, making himself as small a target as possible, and continued to row.

More invaders joined Shecum, but they were all too tired to shoot straight. By the time they had recovered enough to hold their bows without trembling, Migroni was out of range. Migroni then adjusted the large sail on Antium's vessel until the breeze was pushing him in a southerly direction, and gradually away from the island. After satisfying himself that Antium's boat would drift away on its own and become lost in the large expanse of the ocean, he jumped into Jath's canoe, cut it loose, adjusted the sail, and headed northward in it. Looking back, he saw the last of his old comrades fading into the forest.

* * *

Samuel's men topped the barren, rocky ridge and gazed down upon an empty beach, distorted slightly by gyrating heat-waves.

"Migroni isn't loitering on the beach," Oreb said dryly. "If it was him."

"But there go Antium and his men," Uri said as he pointed to the boat which was now far to the southwest.

"That's strange," Samuel mused. "I wonder why they are moving so far from the island."

"Shecum must be ahead of them, out of our view. They're probably still trying to catch up with him," Jath added as Amoz landed on his shoulder and perched there comfortably.

"He must be way out there, because I can't even see a speck," Uri said as he squinted and shaded his eyes from the sun which was now lying quite low over the sea.

"There's why you don't see it," Kib shouted. "Shecum's out by the point. He's going the other way!"

The men all began to chatter in confusion until Samuel raised his arms to silence them. "Anyone on the big boat, unless they land somewhere and go by foot, will not soon arrive at the base of our mountain. We could sure use a canoe." He looked around. "Jath? Uri?" he asked them.

"Yes," they responded in unison.

"I want the two of you to go north and get a canoe. Then . . ."

Oreb interrupted with a shout. "Samuel. Look! The canoe is coming back."

Samuel squinted along the ridge. Oreb was right. He shook his head and said, "I don't know what's happening, but don't leave yet, Jath and Uri. Let's get down to the beach."

Jath walked beside his father as they descended from the barren ridge. They watched the canoe closely. It continued to come toward the beach. Jath was surprised when it finally nosed onto the shore. There was only one person aboard, not two like there had been when Shecum and Zermanah had stolen it. That one person climbed out, waved at them, and started toward the trees. They were too far away to ever stop him but close enough that Jath could identify him.

"Father, that's Migroni. He got our canoe back for us."

"I wonder why?" Samuel asked thoughtfully. "There must be a reason."

No sooner had Migroni disappeared into the trees than the reason made itself manifest. A half-dozen men appeared from the forest farther to the south and began running toward the canoe.

"Antium!" was the cry from a dozen of the island men. "The canoe!" they cried in the next breath.

"Stop them, men!" Samuel ordered, and the defenders of the island entered the race for the canoe.

Four of the invaders reached the boat first. The other two, who had lagged behind, apparently saw that there would be no room for them. They turned and fled back into the trees.

The four men at the canoe stumbled over each other in their haste to get aboard and launch the craft. They had made no significant progress before the fastest of the islanders began to launch arrows at them in a fierce attack. The invaders turned to fight, using the canoe as a shield, but in the short battle that followed, they failed to inflict a single injury on any of the islanders. They didn't have a chance, and their blood turned the frothing water where the sea met the sand a pale red color.

Antium was not among the four invaders who died beside Jath's canoe. Nor was Shecum.

While some of the men buried the dead invaders, Jath overheard Samuel say to Gadoni, "Trust Antium the Younger to run out on his men just like his father used to do."

Gadoni nodded grimly and replied, "He's down to four men, I'd guess. And I don't believe Migroni counts anymore. So that is three. But one of them is Antium himself, and that is not good."

Samuel nodded. "He is proving to be as hard to stop as his father was."

Gadoni met his eyes soberly. "This fight is not over yet, Samuel," he said. "In fact, it is a long way from being finished. A very long way."

CHAPTER 17

Antium, the hunter, had become the hunted. It was a difficult thing for Antium to be so enraged when at the same time he found it necessary to refrain from giving his position away to the islanders. As a result, his small black eyes bugged out from a face that was red and swollen. He clenched his whip in his hand helplessly. Several times, Shecum flinched, fearing that Antium would lash out at him, but Antium knew that any sound would lead the islanders to them.

Zermanah, who was stretched out on the ground beside him, groaned in agony. When Migroni had abandoned the canoe on the beach, Zermanah had begged Shecum not to leave him. Shecum had ignored him. However, when he and Antium had realized the danger they were in and retreated hastily, he again passed Zermanah and had a change of heart. Not that he had any compassion for Zermanah, for he didn't. No, he was looking out for himself again. The dismal fate of the four invaders who made it to the canoe was sealed. That left only Antium for companionship, and Shecum did not relish the thought of being alone with him. Thinking quickly, Shecum had helped Zermanah to his feet and urged him to come along as quickly as he could.

That had been over an hour ago. The three men were now in a small clearing surrounded by thick trees that were growing black in the expanding darkness of evening. It was the first chance Antium had found to vent his anger since fleeing from the islanders. And he was furious!

After listening for several minutes for any sound that might be made by their pursuers and hearing none, Antium let some of his anger spill out in fairly subdued tones. "Fools! Fools! Fools!" he hissed. "They are probably all dead now. If they hadn't run for that canoe, they'd still be with us, and we could make a winning fight of this thing yet. Not that we won't still win, but with larger numbers, we could have won sooner. The fools! I have been surrounded with fools. They deserved to die for running as they did."

Antium seemed to have conveniently forgotten, as was always the case, that he had given the order to run to the boat. When he had turned to follow Shecum in his retreat, he had neglected to shout the order for his men to retreat as well.

Shecum nodded in agreement while keeping a sharp eye on the whip in Antium's hand. He knew better than to do otherwise.

Antium shook his head, stamped his feet, and said, "When we catch Migroni, he will beg for mercy, but he will receive none!"

That came as no surprise. Antium was not renowned for merciful acts.

"He left us without a boat! And even if we still had it, our best navigator is dead," he said, favoring Shecum with a dark look from his beady eyes.

The expert navigator had been Pagros, and Antium's dark stare at Shecum was proof that Antium held Shecum responsible. The thought of Pagros' death in the volcano brought bitter memories back to Shecum, and he thought of Jath, the cause of all his troubles. He swore under his breath that he would make Jath pay dearly someday soon.

In thinking of Jath, Shecum was reminded of Lariah, and visions of her pretty face swam before his eyes. In thinking of her, he missed something Antium had said to him. He had even, without thinking, turned his back on Antium as he dreamed of Lariah.

That was a mistake.

There was a hiss in the air, much like the sound of a striking snake, and then sharp pain leaped from Shecum's back, causing him to cry out in pain. As a natural reaction to the attack, but a foolish one, Shecum pulled his sword as he spun to face his tormentor. The whip hissed again, and the sword leaped from Shecum's fist, gripped tightly by the whip that coiled around it.

A heartbeat later, the sword clanged to the ground.

Antium spoke coldly. "Don't scream, Shecum. You will only bring Samuel's people after us. They have probably heard your cowardly howls already. Thanks to you, we have to move on tonight. We cannot spend the night here after all the noise you've made."

Shecum's eyes narrowed, and he watched Antium with hatred a hundred times stronger than it had been before. "Why did you strike me?" he asked in a voice tight with malice.

"I asked you a question, Shecum," Antium said angrily, "and you ignored me. Apparently you needed that single little lash to remind you who is the leader here."

Shecum had told his lie about pursuing Migroni, and Antium had believed him. He had even been convinced of his loyalty. Now, despite that, Antium had struck him. As the bleeding wound continued to shoot pain through Shecum's body, it was all Shecum could do to refrain from leaping upon Antium like a wild beast. He tensed, his eyes upon the hated whip.

Zermanah broke the bitter spell between the two men. "I feel better now," he said weakly. "I can go on. The rest has helped."

Shecum glanced at him and saw Zermanah shake his head ever so slightly. He took a deep breath and held it as he forced the anger to still itself in his heart. When he finally exhaled, he had gained control.

"All right, we'll go on for a while," he agreed. He stooped to recover his sword, then moved into the deep shadows of the trees. Zermanah followed him, and Antium, after pausing a moment to coil his whip around his hand, plunged into the darkness behind them.

The night became so black that they were forced to stop again after only about an hour. The pain of the wound on Shecum's back was so intense that when he stretched out on the ground he had to lay on his side. Zermanah collapsed on his back beside him, instantly falling asleep. Antium prowled about them in the darkness, muttering to himself.

They had no food or water, and it was too dark to find any now. That discomfort added fervor to the festering hatred that filled Shecum's soul.

He lay thinking about all the horrible things that he would like to do to Antium. But when Antium broke the stillness of the night by calling out, "Shecum!" he immediately responded.

"I am awake, Antium. What do you want?" he asked.

Even as he spoke, Shecum recognized the motivation that made him respond as though he were a slave.

Fear!

Yes, Shecum hated Antium, but even stronger than his hatred was his fear. Shecum despised himself for that fear, for it brought him down to the level of the other invaders. And their fear had brought them but one reward.

Death!

Antium spoke again. "Shecum, we must fight a different battle now that the rest of my men have laid down like sick dogs and died on me. We must hide for a few days. We'll let Samuel and Gadoni think something has happened to us. They will relax their guard after a while, and when they do, we will strike. Anyone we find alone will disappear," Antium said with a chuckle.

"Good plan," Shecum responded. *It's a stupid idea,* he thought to himself. The islanders would hunt them until they ran them into the ground.

"This is a big island, Shecum. There are plenty of places to hide and lots to eat wherever we are. Yes, my young friend, that is what we will do," Antium gloated. "We will wait, then we will strike. One at a time we will destroy our enemies."

"Yes, we will do that," Shecum responded quickly, for he did not want Antium to think he was ignoring him. The pain in his back made him resolve to never feel the excruciating bite of that whip again.

Antium rattled on for several minutes, his mood growing lighter as he did so. Finally, he stretched out on the ground several paces from Shecum and Zermanah, and in a few minutes, he was snoring.

With Antium asleep, the fear in Shecum's belly subsided enough that he could think. The chance of the three of them ever defeating the islanders, as Antium boasted, seemed remote, if not impossible. But getting rid of Ontius and Jath was possible. In fact, it was essential if he were to get Lariah—and nothing would stand in his way of that!

But the sting of the wound on his back made him think of Antium and the whip, and his fear returned to haunt him in the darkness as sleep eluded him.

* * *

After searching unsuccessfully for the three missing invaders, Samuel held a council of war with his men. They had trailed the three invaders for several hours before losing their tracks on a rocky mountainside. Samuel said, "Men, our greatest danger now is not an open confrontation. Antium knows he is badly outnumbered."

"What will he do?" Jarium asked.

"I think he will fight like a coward. He and the other two will probably become snipers. Anytime any of us are foolish enough to be caught alone somewhere, they'll shoot us from behind," he said.

"Does that mean we can't return to our homes?" Oreb asked.

"What do you think?" Samuel countered.

"I think that is what he would like us to do. Then he could make his attacks on us one family at a time and probably in the dark of night."

"Exactly, Oreb," Samuel agreed grimly. "Our safety will be found in sticking together in large enough numbers that he will be afraid to attack for fear of retaliation before he can safely retreat."

"Can't we hunt them down?" Nemti asked.

"We must try, but it will not be easy. There are a lot of places to hide on this island, and I expect them to use some of them."

Jath listened to the men talk as an increasing feeling of concern gnawed at his stomach. Finally, he said, "Father, we've got to find Lariah and Ontius."

"Do you think Antium will find them? He doesn't know they are not with us now, like you are," Samuel reasoned.

"But what if they just happened to come across them? Shecum will never let her go if he ever gets his hands on her again. He will leave the island with her, if he can."

Samuel looked at his son's earnest, youthful face. "Very well, son," he agreed. "If you are that concerned, we'll try to find them."

Jath looked at Uri, who nodded eagerly. "Father," he began. "Uri and I could—"

"No, Jath," Samuel said, cutting him off firmly. "We must remain in strong parties. Antium is a coward by nature—his kind usually are. He will only attack us if he is sure he can kill without being in danger himself. Two men alone will simply not do."

"We'll help Jath," Kim said, looking at his twin brother, Kib, who nodded in agreement.

Kim and Kib, at age twenty-three, were strong, dependable men. Samuel nodded thoughtfully at them. Then he turned to his brother, Oreb. "What do you think, Oreb? Can these four young men take care of themselves while looking for Ontius and Lariah?"

Oreb grinned. "If they can't, nobody can."

"It's settled then," Samuel said. "You four search for Ontius and Lariah. The rest of us will return to our families. From our place of security there, we'll plan how we are to go about eliminating our three enemies."

"Aren't you forgetting something, Samuel?" Jarium asked harshly. Samuel looked startled. "Am I?"

"Yes, you are. Migroni is still out there somewhere."

Gadoni broke in sharply. "He is not our enemy anymore."

"But he was one of them," Jarium stubbornly argued. "I think he must still be considered our enemy."

"He risked his life to help us," Gadoni reminded him. "If he hadn't done what he did, we'd still have seven invaders out there instead of just three."

Jarium scowled. "Well, maybe you trust him, because he's a Lamanite like you. But I don't!"

Gadoni shook his head, and Jath spoke up. "I trust him, too, Jarium. He saved my life when Shecum was about to kill me."

Samuel intervened at that point. "Unless Migroni does something to demonstrate that he intends to harm us, we will not worry about him."

His words were spoken with authority, and Jarium said no more. But his sullen look told Jath that he was not convinced that he could be wrong about Migroni.

Samuel turned to his son. "Do you have any idea where to start looking for Ontius?" he asked.

Jath tried to remember what Ontius had said about finding a new place to live. "He planned to build a new home on the south side of the island," Jath said, frowning in concentration. "He won't go north again, I'm sure of that. Especially since he does not know that you brought the others south. So he'll be somewhere along the southern coast."

Samuel nodded. "Then you four must get on your way. For speed and safety's sake, why don't you go back to the canoe and sail around to that passage you used before? You can start searching from there, since that is where you last saw Ontius and Lariah."

Having thought of that already, Jath quickly agreed. After a few words of caution and advice from his father, Jath signaled for the other three men to follow him. With Lariah's colorful parrot perched firmly on Jath's shoulder, the four young men separated themselves from the others.

* * *

From behind a shield of heavy foliage a few paces away, Migroni watched and listened in silence. He had almost mustered enough courage to stand up and make his presence known, but when Jarium had spoken up against him, Migroni had decided against it. He had hoped that by assisting as he did, that he would earn the complete trust of the islanders, but Migroni was learning a hard lesson. He was learning that trust, after having hurt people, was not easily earned.

When Jath, with Amoz perched on his shoulder, and the other three young men started back to the north after the canoe, Migroni debated what to do. He finally decided to trail behind the main party of men. His eyes would be another set of eyes watching for Antium and his two unsavory companions.

* * *

Late in the afternoon, Jath and his companions arrived at the beach where they had defeated the four invaders the day before. They walked north along the beach, then turned and re-entered the forest where they had hidden the canoe.

It was no longer there!

"I wonder if Migroni took it," Uri suggested as he looked around nervously.

Jath searched the ground and found the answer there. "It was not Migroni. Three men have been here," he announced grimly.

"Antium?" Kim said, although it was less a question than a statement.

Jath nodded. "Yes, along with Shecum and another."

"They must have doubled back shortly after they led us into the rocks where we lost their tracks," Uri suggested.

Jath glared into the forest. "Now they have the canoe and we are farther from the southern coastline, still on foot," he said unhappily.

"Where do you think they will go now?" Kim asked.

"I don't . . . Yes, I think I know!" Jath exclaimed. "They'll sail back to the little cove where they think I stopped. If not there, they will go somewhere nearby, since they must suspect that our people are there. They may hide and watch and wait for us. But . . ." Jath paused. "What if they accidentally find Lariah and Ontius?"

That question needed no reply. The young men were all very tired, but not one of them considered delaying their long hike southward by resting now. With Antium and Shecum roaming the southern coastline, Lariah, with no one to watch out for her but Ontius, was in danger.

* * *

The sun worked its way past the scattered clouds in the morning sky. Although Antium was in a surprisingly good mood the next morning, Shecum was not. The more Antium spoke of Lariah, the more difficult it was for Shecum to hide his feelings. Only fear of Antium made him keep his thoughts to himself.

After eluding the islanders and stealing Jath's canoe, they had speedily made their way southward along the western coastline. While Shecum and Zermanah worked furiously with their oars to steer it to shore in the increasingly choppy waters, Antium rode lazily in the rear of the canoe. The salty mist from the rough water sprayed Shecum's naked back as he rowed, and the wound Antium had inflicted burned. When it was completely safe to do so, he would repay Antium. But that would wait, for his fear was still strong, and he would make no move against Antium until he was absolutely sure of his success.

The three men glanced cautiously at the channel where Jath, they suspected, had gone ashore with Lariah and Ontius. None of the three intruders were anxious to meet up with the main body of the islanders just now.

"The islanders must be somewhere in that area," Antium speculated.

Assuming that Lariah and her father would have joined the other islanders by now, Shecum thought of the bow of Ontius. "The girl's father has a bow that sends arrows farther than any ordinary bow," he reminded the others. "We must go carefully."

The canoe finally nosed onto the shore. Shecum and Zermanah pulled it across the sand and hid it behind some scattered boulders. An hour later, they were toiling up the rugged incline that separated the ocean from the dense jungle above. After entering the jungle, Shecum occasionally caught a glimpse through a break in the trees of a silvery ribbon of falling water a couple of miles to the west.

It was Antium's plan to somehow reach the top of the towering cliffs and hide near the source of the falling water. But as they started up the steep mountain, it soon became clear to Shecum that Zermanah would not make it without help. And he had no intention of leaving him behind. Despite Zermanah's weakened condition, Shecum found a measure of comfort in the companionship of the lanky invader; Antium's rages, he realized, were not quite as fearsome as when he was the sole recipient of Antium's anger.

Having done none of the rowing, Antium had much more energy than Shecum, and he was able to scale the mountain quite rapidly. He waited several times for Shecum and Zermanah to catch up with him, but finally grew impatient. "You two old women are too slow for me," he called down to them. "I'll go on up alone and wait for you near the mouth of the waterfall."

After practically carrying Zermanah as far as they had climbed, Shecum was relieved. He had feared that Antium would order him to desert Zermanah and keep pace with him. He was too exhausted to shout a reply.

"Be there before dark, and don't get lost!" Antium shouted. Then he worked his way around a boulder and out of sight. Shecum recognized Antium's command as a threat. He had learned that he was no longer exempt from the bite of the whip, and he knew he had no choice but to follow after Antium.

To Zermanah, Shecum said, "We will rest here for a little while. We can take our time now, but we better not be too long."

Zermanah sighed heavily with relief. "Thanks, Shecum. And thanks for staying with me. I was afraid that Antium would make you go with him and leave me alone."

Shecum recognized the fear in his companion's voice, for it echoed his own. "We are friends, Zermanah," he said. "We must stick together." He grinned maliciously. "Anyway, I don't think Antium wants either of us dead. We are his last hope for bringing about his revenge."

By the time Zermanah was ready to go on, Shecum could neither see nor hear Antium. Wearily, he helped Zermanah to his feet, and together, they struggled up the mountain. A cloud passed over the hot sun, giving his sore back some relief from its searing rays.

A cool wind began to whip along the face of the mountain, and in a few minutes the two men felt the heat of the sun across their backs again. However, it was not long before the sun again disappeared, and Shecum glanced upward. The heavy bank of clouds rolling toward the island from the west would soon block the sun, he thought gratefully. And it would be for more than just a few minutes.

"A storm is building," Zermanah observed. "I'm glad we are not still on the sea."

Shecum had thought only of the relief he felt at having a thick shield between his bare back and the hot rays of the sun. "I hope it waits until we reach the top," he growled. "Just our luck to be in a barrage of lightning on this barren mountainside."

At Zermanah's worried look, Shecum laughed. "Oh, I suppose we'll be safe. I just don't want to be late meeting Antium at the waterfall. He doesn't like excuses, you know."

"I know," Zermanah acknowledged. Again Shecum heard in Zermanah's voice the fear he himself felt.

As the heavy black clouds continued to amass over the island, there was a sound of distant thunder. The wind blew with increasing intensity. Shecum and Zermanah toiled on, but they were barely halfway up the mountain when lightning began shooting from the dark clouds. Several times it hit jagged points of rock near them, and they huddled uncomfortably beneath a shallow ledge. The thunder crashed about them and echoed along the face of the mountain. The rain poured torrents of raging water down the mountain, bringing rocks rolling and crashing down with it.

It was a terrible storm and almost as frightening as the eruption of the volcano had been. However, it was not a long storm. When it had passed and the water had ceased its pouring down the mountain above them, Shecum and Zermanah again tackled the rugged slope. The rocks were slippery, making the climb much more difficult and dangerous than it had been before. Shecum realized with mounting apprehension that he and Zermanah would not be able to get to the top of the falls before night fell.

He briefly considered abandoning Zermanah, but he did not, for he was not sure which would anger Antium the most, showing up late or coming without Zermanah. With only three of them left to attack the islanders, he suspected that it would be better to be late than to arrive alone, so he pulled, pushed, and shoved Zermanah upward, cursing his own fear as he did so. The festering boil of hatred within him burned like a raging fire, nearly matching his fear.

* * *

Ontius and Lariah had spent the duration of the storm in a crude shelter. That was all Ontius had accomplished since announcing to Lariah that this was where they would build their new home.

The shelter was made of light branches, leaves, and palm fronds. If it had not been for the protection of the trees around it and the mountain slope that diverted the wind from the west, it would have been torn apart in the storm. Even so, it had leaked a little and the rain had come in upon them through the open front. Lariah did her best to keep her sack of precious belongings dry while she herself was completely soaked.

As soon as the rain stopped and the sun broke through the thick clouds with its golden rays of promise, she left the shelter. After stepping into the wet grass and flowers of the clearing, she kicked off her sandals and ran barefoot to the stream.

Ontius did not stir from his bed in the shelter. He was no doubt asleep, she thought, as he had slept so much lately. He had always been a hardworking, active man, but now he was different. He had done nothing since arriving at this beautiful spot except build the shelter. The only work had been the gathering of branches and leaves, and Lariah had done almost all of that herself. Lariah feared that he would never build the home he promised.

Lariah thought she could make it to the waterfall and still be back before he awoke and missed her. As she worked her way down the stream, she listened for his voice to call her back, but she heard nothing. She then ran barefoot and carefree down the gentle slope.

Beneath her soaked wrap-around skirt, she still wore her little knife in its sheath of soft leather. The bag of poison darts also reminded her of its presence as it pressed against her wet stomach. Although she had considered putting the knife and darts in her sack with the rest of her belongings, the feeling had come to her that she should not do that, so they stayed beneath her red and yellow clothing. She reached a hand within her skirt and felt the hilt of the little knife. It somehow reassured her.

She stepped onto the rocky point and gasped in awe at the sight of the wildly thrashing water of the sea and the rapidly moving clouds above it. She dropped to her knees and crawled to the edge of the precipice and cautiously peered over. A mist slowly lifted from the trees and spread a thin silver veil across the jungle below her. The wind had lessened, but it carried the fog slowly eastward. It was like a giant ghost as it floated, dimming the green sheen of the jungle it veiled.

As Lariah watched the beauty of nature as it unfolded its miracles over this beautiful island, a wave of loneliness swept over her like the veil of silver mist over the jungle. She shivered, and the wind picked up, scattering the mist below her and bringing a new bank of clouds over-head. She sat up and hugged her knees to her chest, silently watching the distant sea as it frothed and roiled.

After a while, her eyes became heavy, and she dozed off. Her chin lolled against her chest. Another storm gathered in darkening fury around her.

CHAPTER 18

Jath and his three companions had found the camp of Samuel's men sometime during the night.

"Who goes there?" called Oreb, who had been standing guard. The news he was given that Antium was back on the sea sent him scurrying to awaken Samuel and Gadoni.

A brief conference followed, resulting in the awakening of the entire camp. Migroni had been awakened by Oreb's challenge, and he witnessed the hurried departure of the men. He was planning to follow them until he discovered that Jath, Uri, Kim, and Kib were settling down for a rest of unknown duration. So he settled down and waited as well. When they departed in the darkness an hour or so later, he silently trailed them.

Shortly before dawn, sheer exhaustion forced another stop. Migroni was grateful, for they were not the only ones who were tired. He curled up in the bushes not too far from them and slept. When he awoke, the sun was up, and he was startled to find that the young Nephites had already gone on their way. He had panicked at first, fearing that he might lose them, but he was in luck. In their haste, they were making no effort to conceal their trail, and he soon was comfortably following them again.

The storm caught the young men as they were descending a rough and rocky pass. Lightning flashed about them, and the rain, when it came, nearly washed them off the mountain. Bruised knees and elbows afflicted all four young men and the sturdy Lamanite who followed them.

Amoz had disappeared during the storm, and Jath began to worry when he didn't show up again shortly after the downpour had ceased.

"I've got to go back," he said to the others after stewing silently for several minutes.

"After we bruise ourselves black and blue and nearly drown, you want to go back?" Uri demanded.

"Amoz is missing," Jath said, expecting that to explain everything.

It did not. "He's just a bird," Uri reminded him. "I know he's Lariah's, but isn't it more important that we continue to press on and find her and her father?"

"You don't understand, Uri," Jath said urgently. He explained his plan and then finished by asking, "So, now do you see why we need to go back for him? He probably just found a tree where he could get some protection from the rain."

Uri nodded. "Yes, we better find him. I see that he could be very important to us.

The four young men retraced their steps for close to half an hour before Amoz responded to Jath's urgent calls. None of them actually saw where he came from. He was just suddenly there. He perched on Jath's shoulder and said loudly in his ear, "Lariah."

"That's right, Amoz. We are looking for Lariah. And we've got to find her." Jath noted the looks the others were giving him. He grinned and said sheepishly, "It might seem strange to talk to a bird, but it almost seems like he understands. You do understand, don't you, Amoz? We're looking for Lariah."

"Lariah," Amoz agreed with an intelligent cock of his red head, and the young men chuckled. With light hearts, they started southward again.

"I don't think we've seen the last of the storm for today," Kim noted a few minutes later.

Jath glanced at the sky. Another bank of dark clouds was rolling across the peaks to the west, and already the lightning had begun to dance across the mountaintops while the thunder rolled across the sky.

* * *

A loud clap of thunder awoke Lariah with a start. "Oh!" she exclaimed as she lifted her head and realized how dangerously close to the edge she was when she had inadvertently fallen asleep. The ocean was more turbulent than ever, and the clouds were so thick above her that it felt more like dusk than mid-afternoon. The trees below were swaying with the wind, giving the jungle the appearance of a rippling, dark green sea.

Before rising to her feet, she carefully slid herself backward on the rocky ledge, to move a safe distance from the edge. Then she got to her knees and paused to look once more at the ocean as it heaved and tossed.

"Lariah," someone called from behind her in a raspy voice.

She rose to her feet and spun around in one fluid movement, expecting to see her father, for she knew of no one else who would be there, although it had not sounded like him.

It was not him!

Standing at the edge of the trees was a tall man with long dark hair and a scraggly beard. Two small dark eyes stared past the end of a long, crooked nose. One side of the hideous face bore a ghastly deep purple scar that ran from beside one eye clear down his cheek. The man gave an evil grin.

A scream rose in her throat, and she took an involuntary step backward.

"You shouldn't do that, Lariah," the dreadful man said in a voice she should never have mistaken for her father's. "You're very near the edge, and I don't want you to fall, my lovely one." He smiled again, exposing a row of uneven yellow teeth with numerous black gaps. "I have found you at last, and I have claimed you as my own. I would hate to lose you now."

He moved swiftly and confidently toward her, and Lariah could see what he held in his hand—a coiled strip of braided leather. A whip!

A wave of nausea swept over Lariah, burning her throat. It was accompanied by a dizziness that pulled her, threatening to dump her over backwards.

He noticed that her eyes had fastened onto his whip. "This is only intended for those who do not obey the orders of Antium the Younger," he said reassuringly as he stroked the whip with his left hand.

Upon hearing him speak her name and claim her as his own, Lariah sank to her knees as her legs refused to support her any longer. It was good she did, for the nausea that had threatened her suddenly erupted, and she was violently ill. An especially loud clap of thunder shook the ground, and for a terrible moment, Lariah actually thought the rocky ledge was being rent in two and that she was about to be sent plummeting to her death.

"Get up, woman! You're coming with me!" Antium commanded, and he cracked the whip near her left ear, shooting pain into her head and leaving her ear ringing.

"No . . . please . . . I can't," she wailed in terror.

Antium's whip cracked again, and Lariah attempted to rise to her feet as he commanded, but she had no strength in her legs.

He claims me? she thought in terror. *I would rather this rocky ledge split in two and drop me into the jungle below. It would be better to so die than to be in bondage to this terrible man.*

"Look at me!" he commanded again, punctuating his order with another dreadful crack of his whip. In fear, she forced her eyes to look up, and she saw first the sinewy muscles of his hairy forearms, and then . . .

Her father!

"Father!" she cried out hopefully. "Help me!"

From where he stood, several steps behind Antium, Ontius gazed at his daughter with a vacant stare.

"Please, God," she pleaded in a whispered prayer. "Please, help my father."

Then she cried aloud, "Father! Please help me!"

"I am not your father!" Antium shouted in a confused and angry protest.

"No, you are not, but I am," Ontius said distinctly.

Lariah looked at him again and her heart sang with hope. In her father's eyes was a new light, or an old one restored. "Save me, Father, from this terrible . . . beast," she pleaded, clasping her hands together in desperate supplication.

Antium turned slowly, dragging his horrid whip across the wet rock like a dying snake. Flashes of lightning lit the sky with blazing intensity. "Who are you?" Antium demanded.

"I am Lariah's father," Ontius said, and for the first time in days, he stood straight and tall, almost majestic. He was the man Lariah remembered and had revered from her early childhood, and she felt a warm rush of love fill her tormented soul.

Ontius pulled his sword from its sheath and pointed it with an angry thrust at Antium. "Step aside, I have come for my daughter."

Antium sneered. "I have come to claim your pretty daughter for myself, and no one will prevent me from taking what I want. Put your sword away, old man, and depart while you still can."

Ontius glared at him. "Lariah is my only living daughter, and I will never allow one who is unworthy to have her hand. And you are certainly the most unworthy one I have ever seen," Ontius said.

Antium snorted. "It is not yours to decide whom she belongs to."

"She will belong to no one, but she may be loved by the man she chooses," Ontius countered.

"You are wrong, old man," Antium shouted. "This island and everything on it is mine! I control life and death here. And I have chosen to let her live, but only as my wife. You see, I take what I want, and I want your daughter."

The lines in Ontius' face hardened, and his eyes narrowed. "Lariah has already chosen," he said slowly. "I have not always been the best father to her, but I believe I have reared her well and she is wise." He looked past Antium, as if talking more to Lariah than to their evil tormentor.

"You are irritating me, Ontius. It is a foolish thing to irritate Antium the Younger," Antium said in a low and evil voice. "Your daughter is beautiful, and she is mine."

"Lariah has chosen Jath, the son of Samuel. And she has my blessing in her choice," Ontius said, still gazing at his daughter.

As those words rang in Lariah's ears, Antium bellowed with fury, "How dare you mention the name of Samuel! I came to this place to watch him crawl on his belly and beg for mercy. But he will receive none, for he will die beneath the tip of my mighty whip!"

Lariah saw a flicker of movement in Antium's right hand. "Father!" she cried out in warning.

Antium's whip snaked out, and the tip curled around Ontius' outstretched sword, jerking it from his hand. For a moment, it seemed to poise directly over Lariah's head, and then the whip loosed its grasp and sent the sword sailing far beyond the edge of the cliff.

Ontius rushed at Antium with balled fists and Antium struck again with his whip, slashing a terrible bloody wound across Ontius' cheek. But he continued his charge and struck a blow to Antium's face that closed one eye and opened a gash in his eyebrow that bathed his face with blood.

The thunder crashed loudly overhead as streaks of lightning darted through the sky. Lariah was both terrified and deafened as she watched the fight from her knees. Rain began to fall in great drops, making the rocky ledge a slick and treacherous place.

The two men exchanged powerful blows, and they grappled with arms of steel as blood poured down their faces. Antium held onto the handle of his whip as he fought, as if it were a living part of him. His angry curses were drowned in the increasing clamor of the storm.

The two men moved farther away from the sharp drop-off as Antium, both younger and larger, began to wear Ontius down. Lariah, who had known only fear for herself, suddenly realized that her father, who was fighting for her, was losing the battle.

She had to help him!

She jumped to her feet with a surge of energy, not sure what she was going to do, but determined to do something. Then she remembered the knife that she wore hidden beneath her clothing.

As the rain pelted her and the wind blew her long hair about her face, she reached inside the folds of her skirt. Her right hand touched the hilt of the knife, but before she could draw it out, lightning struck a tall tree just a few paces into the forest, sending jagged chunks of wood flying with deadly speed in every direction. One chunk struck Lariah in the stomach, stinging the hand that was closing over the hilt of the little knife. She bent over in agony. When she attempted to stand upright, she slipped on the rain-slick rock. For a moment she was left stunned and breathless. As her father and Antium continued their deadly battle, she tried to rise, but she could not use her wounded right hand and she failed.

She heard her father cry out above the din of the storm, "Run, Lariah, run!"

Why should she run? she wondered. Her father needed her help.

He called out again, his voice desperate, "Run, Lariah. Get away while you can!"

She tried again to rise. When she tried to lift herself, pain shot through her wounded hand. Her knees had been badly bruised by her falls, and somehow she'd gained a nosebleed. Breathless and sobbing, she managed, with her left hand only, to push herself from the ground and pull her knees up beneath her. Then, slowly, she rose to her feet where she stood, swaying dangerously, very near the edge of the precipice.

"Run!" her father commanded.

Lariah ran. Awkwardly and painfully, her eyes blurred by rain and tears, she ran for the trees, then hesitated, reaching again beneath her skirt. She could feel the hilt of the knife with her right hand, but did not have the strength to grasp it.

Use the other hand, she told herself. *I must not let my father down.* But before she could react to her thoughts, Antium sent her father hurtling toward the very edge of the gigantic drop-off. Ontius scrambled to his feet, but Antium's whip cut a vicious arc through the rain, striking him on the shoulder. Ontius stumbled backward.

"Father!" Lariah cried, running forward.

Antium's whip cracked again, but this time it was not directed at Ontius. It struck Lariah's thigh, inflicting pain as she had never experienced in her life. Falling to the ground, she screamed in agony, and Antium laughed insanely, a raspy, hollow bay in concert with the roar of the raging storm.

Again Antium swung his whip, backing Ontius to less than one short pace from the edge of the rocky cliff. His eyes looked at Lariah, and she knew from the look on his face that the fight was over. He had lost. Over the storm, he called to her a final time. "I love you, Lariah!"

The whip cracked again. Ontius fell backward, his cry smothered by the fierce pounding of the rain. As her heart burst with agonizing grief, all Lariah could hear were her father's last words, a final assurance of his love for her. She lay on the cold, wet granite as the rain continued to wash over her. The last thing she heard before blackness enveloped her was Antium's laughter, mixing with the clamor that raged about her.

When she awoke, it was to the calm that followed the storm. Pain coursed from her head to her knees. As she opened her eyes, she was shocked to see the damp ceiling of the little shelter her father had built. Was it a dream? she wondered. No, her father was dead. He had to be dead, for nobody could survive a fall over the cliff where she had seen him vanish. As she remembered his last words, her eyes stung with tears.

He had said something else, she remembered. Before Antium had struck him. He had told her that he accepted her love for Jath. He had spoken clearly, and she knew that her father had been himself. He died in her defense, with his mind and love strong. He had given his life for her. A greater sacrifice could be offered by no man.

Lariah began to weep. Never had she loved her father as she loved him now—now that he had been slain by Antium.

Antium!

She sat up in terror. He must have carried her here and placed her in the shelter. The thought brought bitter bile to her throat. She was in his power now! She would rather have gone over the edge of the mountain with her father than to have to face life with one so evil and immoral.

In desperation, she prayed to be delivered from Antium. Then she stopped and thought about what she was asking. Her father had been sent to her rescue, and he had died. Is that what she wanted for someone else, someone she loved, such as Jath? No, it was not!

She prayed again, asking this time that she be given the strength to somehow deliver herself. She thanked God for her father, and she begged for forgiveness for failing him when he needed her. She also implored her God that He would forgive her for everything she had ever done that brought him pain.

For comfort, she turned toward her sack—the sack filled with her special, private things, for in it she might find a little comfort from her grief.

It was not where she had left it! Her father's sack was also gone. So was his powerful bow. She did not wonder who had taken them, but she did wonder what he had done with them.

One thing remained in the shelter with her. Her blow-tube. To Antium, it must have been nothing more than a useless bamboo stick. She reached for it, but her hand was swollen, and she could not close her fist on it. With only one good hand, it would be almost useless to her, for she must hold the tube steady to blow a dart with any accuracy.

Then she recalled her knife. It was still there beneath her skirt, and so was the bag of darts. She flexed her left hand. At least it was not bruised and swollen, and that thought gave her hope, a thin shred at best, but it was hope nevertheless.

Footsteps outside the shelter drew her eyes to the open front, but she could see no one. She could tell that it was very late in the day, for the light was fading despite a blue sky overhead. She sat watching and listening, but the footsteps had ceased. She closed her eyes and tried to rub away the ache that throbbed in them. Then she heard the footsteps again.

Lariah opened her eyes and gasped. Antium stood peering into the shelter with one beady eye. The other eye was swollen shut and caked with blood from a cut on his eyebrow. His face, hideous before the fight with Ontius, was much worse now. His bent nose had acquired another sharp bend. The long purple scar was split open, and his beard was matted with blood.

Antium smiled, or at least, he no doubt meant it to be a smile. His lip was split and bleeding, and he appeared to be lacking several more of his crooked yellow teeth. Ontius had left his marks upon Antium in his bold attempt to save his daughter from his clutches. Through her terror and grief, Lariah felt a newfound pride. She not only loved Ontius, but she was proud of him. He had done his best for her, and against most men, that would have been sufficient to save her.

But this man was Antium the Younger, and with a sinking heart, Lariah wondered if anyone could defeat him, especially her.

"I see you are awake, Lariah," he croaked in his raspy voice.

She said nothing, and his eye narrowed. "Have you nothing to say to the man who rescued you from that dangerous cliff during a terrible storm? Had I not come to your rescue, you might have fallen," he said.

"You killed my father!" she said with a bitterness that burned her lips and scorched her tongue.

"I did not!" he exclaimed in mock surprise. "He fell. He fell just like you might have done if I hadn't found you there. Come, girl. It will soon be dark, and Antium is hungry. I've been waiting for you to fix me something to eat," he finished with a growl.

Something in his voice told Lariah that she must not refuse, and despite her aching body, she rose to her feet and stepped out of the shelter.

Her sack of belongings lay on the wet ground in a bed of wild yellow flowers. Near it, broken and strewn carelessly about, were the remains of the things Ontius had chosen to carry from his old house. Nothing that had been her father's had been spared brutal destruction by Antium except his powerful bow and quiver of obsidian-tipped arrows. They lay propped against Lariah's sack.

"Get to work, girl," Antium rasped at her. "I am not a patient man."

Not until that moment had she noticed what he held in his hand, for her eyes had been drawn morbidly to the ghastly thing that was his face. She noticed it now. In his hand, almost as if it were an extension of it, Antium held his deadly whip!

CHAPTER 19

The dim glow of a dying fire greeted Shecum and Zermanah as they entered the flower-scented clearing. Darkness had preceded them by several hours to the cliff where the waterfall originated. Shecum called Antium's name, but when he received no answer, he turned upstream, saying, "He must be near, Zermanah. We had better try to find him as quickly as possible."

He had scarcely stepped beside the fading embers when the voice of Antium called out of the darkness.

"Shecum? Is that you?"

"Yes, Antium. It is me and Zermanah."

"You are late!"

"I'm sorry, Antium. The storm delayed us. We came as quickly as we could," Shecum said, angry at the trembling in his voice.

Shecum had not yet seen Antium but only heard his voice from the darkness. He heard his voice again, but Antium did not sound as angry as Shecum had expected. He grumbled at them, "I guess I can't expect men so young and weak as yourselves to do all the things I can do."

"Yes, like let someone else row all night," Shecum mumbled.

"What did you say, Shecum? Speak up," Antium called out. He sounded as cheerful as Shecum had ever heard him, which aroused Shecum's suspicions.

"I said we did our best," Shecum responded apprehensively.

"Very well, then. Get some rest now," Antium ordered as he moved into view, a tall and shadowy figure in the dark night.

"We need something to eat . . ." Shecum began cautiously.

"You're too late," Antium retorted. "You'll just have to wait until morning. Lariah fixed me a good meal, but there wouldn't have been enough for you two anyway."

"Lariah?" Shecum was stunned. "Did you say Lariah?"

"Yes, Shecum. She is mine now, for I found her and saved her," Antium gloated. "And what a lovely creature she is."

"Where is she?" Shecum demanded.

Well-satisfied with his capture, Antium missed the irritation in Shecum's voice. "She is resting. She had a difficult day. Her father had a very nasty accident, and she is in mourning. But she will cease to mourn for him in the morning." Antium chuckled at his witticism and added, "She has consented to be my wife, Shecum."

From farther back in the darkness, Shecum heard the soft sobs that served to verify Antium's words, although he knew that Antium had lied about Lariah consenting to marriage. His hatred for Antium at that moment almost overpowered his fear.

Almost.

But not quite. That was a fortunate thing for Shecum, for Antium, with his whip in his hand, would have had the advantage at that moment. Shecum backed away, aware of Zermanah beside him. After the darkness had hidden Antium's shadowy figure, he turned and walked across the meadow, stumbled through the stream, and entered the trees. A few moments later, Zermanah joined him, and the two young invaders lay down on the wet ground to spend the night.

Shecum was awakened by the angry voice of Antium the next morning. "Shecum! Where are you, Shecum?"

Once again, Shecum's fear and his hatred did battle in his heart. As before, his fear won a clear victory. He arose from his damp bed of wet, rotting leaves, glancing only briefly at Zermanah. "I am right here, Antium," he answered.

"You lazy dog, were you planning to sleep the whole day away?" Antium demanded angrily as Shecum stepped into the clearing.

"It was a difficult day I had yesterday," Shecum complained as he glanced around the multicolored and sweet-smelling meadow. "I practically had to carry Zermanah up the mountain."

"You've had plenty of rest now. You and Zermanah are to take turns standing guard today. We cannot take chances. Samuel and Gadoni could come snooping around, although I doubt they'll find this place.

Where is Zermanah, anyway?"

"He is still sleeping. He is very sick," Shecum answered as he continued his inspection of the picturesque area Antium had discovered for a hiding place from the islanders.

Antium was standing beside a crude shelter of leaves and branches. His broad back was to Shecum and had been since Shecum left the trees. From where Shecum was standing, he could not see into the shelter, but he suspected that Lariah was in there. Antium confirmed his suspicion when he said, "My pretty Lariah is also sleeping, but I will awaken her soon so she can fix some breakfast for us."

Hoping to see her, Shecum crossed the stream, brushing the bushes out of his way, and walked toward Antium. "I'm hungry," he said. "I hope she hurries."

Antium swung around with a roar. "She cooks only for me and herself, you fool! You and Zermanah can take care of yourselves."

Shecum was not surprised by Antium's reaction; rather, it was Antium's face that stunned him. "What happened to you?" he asked before he could stop himself.

Antium's fearsome cry sent Shecum fleeing in terror. Fortunately Antium stumbled and went rolling into the stream that Shecum had jumped with ease.

Zermanah was on his feet, his dark eyes wide with alarm as Shecum charged into the trees. "What is Antium screaming about?" he shouted.

"Let's go, Zermanah!" was all Shecum took time to say as Zermanah watched him pass. Then Zermanah turned and followed Shecum as he ran deeper into the thick forest.

Shecum ran for several minutes before finally pausing to look back for Antium. Zermanah stumbled up to him. "Let's stop," he panted as he sprawled headlong onto the ground. "I can't go on."

Shecum listened intently for a moment. When he could not detect any sound of Antium pursuing them, he sank to the ground beside his companion. After his breathing had returned to normal and his racing heart had slowed down, Shecum described Antium's battered face and his own thoughtless question. "That's what brought Antium raging after me," he concluded. "I wonder what happened to his face."

"Where was the girl?" Zermanah inquired.

"In a little shelter made of leaves and branches."

"Was she hurt, too?" Zermanah asked.

"I don't know," Shecum responded as he rose to his feet and began to pace nervously. "I didn't see her."

"She must have been hurt, or else she would have run away into the forest. No woman would ever stay with Antium," Zermanah reasoned.

"Unless he tied her up. But she was going to fix his breakfast. She could never do that if she was tied up," Shecum said thoughtfully. That reminded him of his own hunger, and he began to search for roots and fruits.

As he ate hungrily, Shecum thought only of Lariah, and by the time he and Zermanah had finished eating, he had built himself into a fury. Zermanah attempted to calm him down, but Shecum's festering hatred ballooned, for the first time exceeding fear, and he began to plot.

"We will return and free Lariah from Antium," Shecum announced as he favored Zermanah with a cold smile. "He'll not expect us to come back so soon, so we can surprise him. The punishment I have planned for him will make his voice ring through the forest in fear of me!"

Zermanah spoke fearfully. "Shecum, this is foolishness that you are thinking. Antium will kill us both if you try to do anything to him. I don't think we should confront Antium. Not just yet, anyway."

Shecum glared at his companion. "I am sorry that you have no courage, Zermanah, but I do not fear Antium. I chose Lariah before Antium had ever seen her or even heard of her beauty. Now he has stolen her away from me," Shecum hissed, then added, "he'll be sorry he used his whip on me!"

With his mind set, a strange and purposeful calm settled over Shecum. "Come, Zermanah. Control your fear, my friend. Trust me. You deserve to share in the triumph as I bring Antium down," he said.

"I . . . I . . . don't know if you . . . if we . . . should do this thing," Zermanah stuttered.

"I will do it!" Shecum said coldly. "You can help or not, as you please. But if you wish to ever leave this island alive, you will join me."

Zermanah went with Shecum, but he went with fearful reluctance, fearful not only of Antium but now of Shecum as well. Shecum sensed his fear, and it gave him an overwhelming feeling of power—unthinking, unholy power.

* * *

So far, Antium had done nothing more to Lariah than frighten her since she had awakened in her shelter following her father's death. Shecum's foolish entrance onto the scene, although it had enraged Antium, gave her a welcome reprieve. For over an hour, Antium had stalked about the blossom-scented meadow, cursing and cracking his whip. He had said nothing more about Lariah fixing his breakfast, so she stayed quietly in the shelter and awaited his next order.

Lariah shifted her tender body to relieve her cramped muscles as well as her injured thigh. Her leg was in pain, and she tugged at her skirt, pulling it up to reveal her injured thigh. An angry red welt marred her smooth white skin. Even as she fingered the injury, testing its tenderness, she knew it could have been much worse. Only the double folds of her wrap-around skirt had limited the whip-mark to just a painful welt.

She considered making a run for freedom as she had dozens of times since Antium had taken her captive. But Antium had her father's bow and had discovered how to use it. She knew that even if she did manage to get away, he would eventually track her down, and then he would be doubly dangerous.

She still had her knife, and as she thought of it she flexed her right hand. It was feeling a little better, but she doubted she could handle her knife with it yet.

Lariah did not want to think about her father, for it made her heart ache, but she could not look at her welt without vividly recalling the deep, bloody gashes Antium's whip had left on Ontius' face. With a trembling hand, she pulled her skirt down over her injured thigh.

Distracted, Lariah had failed to hear the approach of Antium. "That is too bad, Lariah," he said mockingly. "Such an ugly welt on such soft and pretty skin. Let it be a lesson to you, woman. Never cross Antium the Younger!"

Lariah ducked her head to avoid having to look at Antium's disfigured face. Antium mistakenly interpreted it as an act of humility and contrition. "I see you are learning," he laughed. "You will get along with me just fine."

Her hands were clutched tight against her stomach, ready to reach inside her skirt if Antium came too close. He did not, however, enter the shelter as she was afraid he would do. Instead, he said, "I'm hungry."

Lariah stood up and left the shelter to prepare some food for him. As she passed, he extended a massive arm and pulled Lariah against his chest in a smothering, suffocating embrace. Lariah could feel the coiled whip in his hand pressing against her back. She screamed, the sound muffled by the filthy black hair of Antium's beard.

As she fought her rising panic, she remembered her knife! With all her strength, she struggled against Antium's iron grasp, but she was a tiny force against the brutal strength of Antium the Younger. His arms closed tighter as she twisted and writhed in his arms.

Antium apparently found her struggles humorous, for he began to laugh, an evil, raspy sound that blew across her hair with his hot, smelly breath. Instinctively, Lariah attacked with the only weapons at her disposal. First, she kicked a sandal-clad foot into one of Antium's hairy shins, which had about the same effect as throwing an overripe banana at a charging wild boar.

Antium lifted her clear off the ground, and her feet kicked wildly but with little effect. In desperation, Lariah swung her head back as hard as she could, connecting directly with Antium's nose. She heard a horrific crack, and instantly Antium's grip loosened. She slipped down until her feet again touched the ground.

When she pulled away from him, Lariah reached into her skirt with her uninjured hand for her knife. Antium shoved her violently to the ground, and she rolled onto her side, away from him, pulling the knife from its sheath as she did so. At any moment she expected to feel the terrible sting of his whip on her back.

She was not wrong. The blow came, and it hurt terribly, but Lariah was fighting for her life and she could not give up now. With strength borne of desperation, she rolled back toward Antium, rose swiftly to her feet, and charged as he drew the whip back for another blow.

Using her left hand, she finally managed to free her knife from the tangles of her skirt, and without hesitating, she plunged it with all her power into Antium's belly. He bellowed and she pulled it out, striking again. This time, the sharp blade sunk to its hilt in the flesh of his hip, and her hand lost its grip as he twisted away, screaming in rage.

Lariah had no way of knowing how much damage she had inflicted on Antium with her knife, but she prayed that it was at least enough to slow him down. She ducked beneath his swinging left arm and fled. Looking over her shoulder, she caught a glimpse of his whip lying on the ground. It was almost as though she had cut off one of Antium's limbs, the whip had seemed so much a part of him.

She thought of her blow-tube as she spun away from Antium, but she did not dare to stop for it. She only had time to do one thing now: run! And run she did.

* * *

Shecum was also running. What little fear of Antium he had not been able to shed had evaporated as he watched Lariah fight like a cornered animal. He had yelled Antium's name as he ran toward him, sword in hand. But he was too far away to get there quickly, having entered the meadow at the far end. His shouts were drowned out by Antium's screams of rage.

Shecum had planned to strike Antium dead with his sword when he reached him, freeing Lariah from his grasp, but he was still almost a hundred paces away when Lariah fled. Antium stumbled and collapsed, but Shecum did not pause to finish him off, for he did not want to lose Lariah again.

"Watch him!" he shouted to Zermanah as he ran past their fallen leader. He assumed that Antium was badly wounded or even dead, or he would not have fallen on his face on the ground. And there was blood all over the big man.

Shecum ran with confidence, for Lariah was not carrying her blow-tube, and the knife she had used, she did not have, for he saw it dripping with blood in Antium's outstretched left hand.

For several minutes, Shecum pursued Lariah, surprised at the speed of her flight. All at once she stumbled and fell in a heap on the ground. She lay with her head down, crying softly.

Shecum quit running and walked toward her where he stood looking down with a grin of triumph on his narrow face. He had won! Antium was dead or badly wounded, and Lariah was in his power. Totally in his power. As he gazed at her, he again felt the hatred he had harbored for the past few days against Antium, for her skirt was pulled up just enough to reveal the bright red welt on her smooth thigh, marring her perfect beauty!

That Antium would hit her with his whip and mar her in this manner was outrageous. And he had done it twice! Shecum suddenly hoped that Antium was yet alive, for his revenge was not complete. Antium must feel the sting of his own whip!

"I have come for you, Lariah," Shecum said.

She reacted instantly and violently. Screaming Antium's name, she lunged to her feet and dove at Shecum, clawing at his face and kicking his knees. He pushed her and backed away, but she came at him again.

"Stop it!" he yelled. "I'm not Antium. I am Shecum!"

She hesitated only a moment to identify his face. She dove at him again. "You . . . you would have killed Jath!" she yelled. "I hate you, too."

The name of Jath, the young man she professed to love, enraged Shecum immeasurably, and he struck her across the face, knocking her to the ground. Her head struck a rock, and she lay still.

For a moment, Shecum feared that he had killed her, but when he knelt and held his cheek near her mouth, he felt her warm breath. Relieved, he sat beside her and rested as he watched her. She awoke after a few minutes, but the fight was gone from her.

"Come, Lariah. Let's go back to your meadow. I must finish what you started with Antium," he said in a mocking voice. Then he added, "Behave yourself, and I won't have to slap you again. All you have to do is obey me, and you will never be hurt again."

She did not answer, and he interpreted her lowered eyes as resignation.

"Get up," he ordered brusquely, pleased that she was giving in to him so easily.

He reached for her arm and jerked her roughly to her feet. In doing so, he noticed how swollen her right hand was. "Did Antium do that to you, too?" he asked indignantly.

"No," she replied curtly.

He did not press her for an answer, but he firmly took her left hand in his and dragged her back toward where Antium lay, awaiting his punishment. Holding Lariah's hand in his, Shecum reveled in the thought of his new possession.

* * *

However, Lariah had not been defeated. For now, she must let Shecum think she had given in to him, but inwardly she was prayerfully scheming. She brushed the hair from her face with her swollen hand and glanced at Shecum.

Compared to Antium, he could almost be called handsome. Compared to Jath, he was very ugly. What mattered most though, was not his appearance; it was what was in his heart, and she had already had more than one glimpse into Shecum's heart. It was nearly as black as Antium's.

He glanced over at her, and despite the grin on his red-bearded face, he could not disguise the evil that lurked in his hard blue eyes. "I'm glad you don't have your knife anymore, or your poison darts," he said with a sneer as their eyes met briefly. "You're quite fierce even without your weapons."

"I thought you were Antium," she said, partly because it was true but mostly to gain his trust.

He seemed to accept her explanation. "I wouldn't blame anyone for trying to scratch out Antium's eyes." He laughed. "He certainly deserves it."

She forced herself to smile at him, then let it fade as she said, "He is the most horrible man I have ever seen."

Shecum nodded in agreement, and Lariah wondered why he couldn't see how much like Antium he was. He did not fill her with fear in the same way that Antium did, but she knew that he would resort to violence with the slightest provocation. She vowed not to provide that provocation. She smoothed her skirt over her stomach and felt a measure of reassurance, for she still had her poison darts, and she vowed that she would use them at the first opportunity Shecum gave her. Then she revised her vow: she would use them at the first opportunity he gave her after he had done to Antium whatever it was he planned to do.

* * *

Shecum expected to find Zermanah waiting beside Antium. He was shocked to find Antium on his feet, waiting beside the dead body of Zermanah. An evil leer stretched across Antium's face.

"So, you brought Lariah back to me!" he said with a glint of triumph in his beady eye. In his left hand, Antium held the dreaded whip of braided leather. His right arm hung limp, blood-stained, and useless at his side. A piece of cloth, obviously torn from Zermanah's clothes, was bound tightly around it, covering the wound Lariah had inflicted.

Antium's mutilated face was caked with blood. The wound on his stomach still oozed blood, and his clothing was drenched in red. His dark eye flamed with hatred.

Shecum still held tightly to Lariah's hand, but at the sight of Antium the Younger, she gasped and fainted. Shecum allowed her to fall to the ground beside her shelter. "It's just as well, Lariah," he muttered softly. "This way you won't get away or get in the way while I repay Antium for his mistreatment of me."

Antium snorted contemptuously as Shecum approached him. "Mistreatment, you say? You got only what you deserved. I was very patient with you. I should have killed you. Zermanah told me everything before he died, the poor weak fool."

"You . . . you . . ." Shecum began as his hatred, untainted now with the fear he had known, drove him on.

"Silence!" Antium bellowed. "You were the only one in the whole lot I thought I could depend on. Now, even you have betrayed me, and all because of that . . . that girl!" Antium shouted, his eyes drawn to Lariah's motionless form. "First I will deal with you, Shecum, and then with her. Lariah will beg me to slay her before I have finished with her."

"You tried to take what was mine," Shecum retorted fiercely. "And you whipped me. You should never have done that, Antium."

Shecum had never seen Antium use his whip with his left hand, but the body of Zermanah was more than sufficient proof that he could do it. Warily, Shecum drew his sword and began to circle Antium. The whip cracked, but Shecum just smiled.

"I will get you, Antium," he threatened. "You are in my power now, and I will make you pay."

"You fool yourself, Shecum. Zermanah thought that he could tie my hands while he waited for you to return. Look at how wrong he was," Antium laughed crudely.

"But I am not Zermanah," Shecum said softly. "He was a coward, Antium, but I am not. You will regret the day you used your whip against me."

As he talked, he continued to circle, and Antium turned, careful to keep Shecum from getting behind him. Shecum was in no hurry. The advantage was his, for Lariah's knife had inflicted several terrible wounds on Antium, and the longer he circled, the more blood Antium would lose and the weaker he would become.

Neither of the wicked invaders noticed Lariah as she awoke. She spotted the knife, bloody and repulsive, but she picked it up anyway and put it back in her sheath after wiping it on the grass. Only when she tried to sneak away did Antium yell, "There goes Lariah!"

Shecum whirled and charged after her, striking her harshly. Again she fell, and unconsciousness came quickly.

Antium lunged at Shecum, and the whip tore a gash in his back, but before he could inflict more damage, Shecum was facing him again. "Oh, Antium," he hissed. "You will live just long enough to regret that. And then you will die, you crazy fool."

CHAPTER 20

Amoz flew from the east and landed lightly on Jath's shoulder. "Still no sign of Lariah?" Jath asked, discouragement evident in his voice.

"Lariah," Amoz said.

"Go that direction now, Amoz," Jath commanded, pointing south.

Amoz departed instantly, a bright splash of color against the dark green of the forest. "Is he searching for Lariah, or is he just up there looking at the scenery?" Uri asked Jath.

"He's searching, and he'll find her," Jath said emphatically.

Deep inside, he was not so confident. He hoped, he prayed, and he worried, while they all waited along the banks of a clear, gurgling mountain stream that wound out of sight in the forest to the south.

They were constantly alert for the three invaders but saw no sign of anyone. Uri, however, was nervous, and he finally admitted that he kept hearing sounds that bothered him. "I think we're being followed," he said.

That made the other young men worry more. As they all thought back over the past two days, they could each identify times when the hair raised on their necks for no identifiable reason. "We're tired and a little frightened," Kib suggested.

"That's true enough, but I still think we're being watched," Uri insisted.

Before the discussion could continue, Amoz returned. Instead of flying directly to Jath and perching on his shoulder as he had done each previous time he was sent out, Amoz circled over their heads.

"Lariah! Lariah!" he chanted.

"He's seen her! Let's go!" Jath shouted, jumping to his feet. "Okay, Amoz. Take us to her."

The bright colors of Amoz flitted through the trees and disappeared. Then he returned calling, "Lariah." The young men hurried, but the forest was dense and their progress was much slower than they would have liked.

Uri brought up the rear, and despite the excitement of following Amoz to what they all hoped would be a reunion with Lariah and Ontius, he kept glancing over his shoulder. Someone was back there. He was sure of it.

The stream was always close at hand as they followed Amoz. With that in mind, knowing he would not get lost or disoriented, Uri suddenly made a bold move. He spun around, drawing his sword, and rushed back in the direction he had just come from. He almost ran right into . . .

Migroni!

"What are you doing here?" Uri challenged as he waved his sword at Migroni's chest.

"I'm . . . I'm . . . following you," Migroni stuttered. "I was hoping I could help you again."

Uri studied the young Lamanite's face. Then he put his sword back in its sheath. Extending a hand, he said, "If you want to help us, then come on."

Migroni hesitated. Then he took Uri's hand and the two young men shook. "You're sure?" he asked.

"After what you've done for us, Migroni, how can I not be sure? Anyway, Jath says you're not like the others at all. Hurry, let's catch up before they get worried. We're following Lariah's parrot. We think he has spotted her."

Three worried young Nephites met Uri and Migroni on their way back. Uri grinned broadly as he said, "I told you we were being followed. We have some help now, men."

Jath rushed forward and slapped Migroni on the back. "Welcome!" he said enthusiastically. "Thanks for all your help. Why didn't you join us sooner?"

"I wasn't sure you would trust me. I heard some of your men talking, and they surely don't want me around."

"I trust you, Migroni. You saved my life. And in time, the other men will. These already do," he said, waving his hand toward his companions.

"Lariah!" Amoz called impatiently from overhead.

"What are we waiting for?" Migroni asked cheerfully. "That parrot acts like he has something to show us."

The young men chuckled as they surged forward again with renewed vigor and enthusiasm. For several minutes, they followed Amoz down the stream. Amoz continued to fly forward and then return, calling, "Lariah," with great fervor.

Then, after flying off one time, he failed to return when they expected him. The four Nephites and their new Lamanite ally stopped in confusion. "Where could he have gone?" Uri asked in frustration.

"Maybe he went to Lariah," Jath suggested. "After all, he's her pet, not mine."

"Probably," Kib agreed. "At any rate, she must be close by."

As they moved southward again, they were more subdued, speaking only in whispers. Then, after several more minutes, Amoz came speeding through the trees, but instead of turning in flight and leading them as he had before, he perched on Jath's shoulder.

"Where is Lariah?" Jath asked in sudden concern. "Did you lose track of her?"

"Lariah," Amoz squawked, and it sounded like there was sadness in his voice.

The strange behavior of Amoz brought new and fearful concerns to the five young searchers. "Lariah would never hide from Amoz if she knew he was around. Something is wrong, very, very wrong," Jath said in a frightened whisper as the five of them huddled.

"Ontius was getting strange. You said so yourself," Uri reminded Jath. "Perhaps he has gone mad and has hidden Lariah from Amoz."

"Maybe," Migroni agreed doubtfully. The four young Nephites turned their heads to him in unison.

"Maybe what?" Jath asked.

"Maybe Antium has found her," he said. "I'm sorry, Jath," he added quickly, "but we better be ready for that."

"Then we also better get a move on. I'd say we continue right down this stream the way Amoz was leading us," Kib suggested.

"If Antium or Shecum has captured Lariah and Ontius, it will mean they may have that bow you've been talking about, Jath," Kim added.

"And even her poison darts," Uri contributed.

"Remember one thing, men," Migroni said in a more positive tone. "Antium is overconfident. That is his greatest weakness. Next to that is his natural cowardice."

The five of them agreed to spread out and move in one sweeping front down the gentle slope. The march lasted close to half an hour before they burst into a beautiful, fragrant meadow at the same time the sun burned the message of mid-day on their backs.

All five stopped and stared, their eyes focused on a sprawling, blossom-filled tree that stood alone near the center of the flowering meadow. Hanging from a stout limb only about seven feet from the ground was a ghastly, ghostly figure that was swinging gently back and forth.

In morbid fascination, the young men moved toward the tree and its horrid decoration. Not a word was spoken as they closed in. It was soon apparent that the dangling form was the badly disfigured and mutilated body of a man!

Jath's first thought was that it was Ontius. He quickened his step, then stopped abruptly and gaped in horror at a single protruding eye that glared from the apparently dead body of . . .

"Antium the Younger!" Migroni gasped, breaking the silence.

The men looked at each other in horror. "The whip!" Migroni exclaimed as their eyes returned to the horrid figure. Then he added in softer tones, "Hanged with his own whip! There's a certain justice to that."

"Who could have done this to him?" Uri asked in a voice choked with dread.

"Maybe it was Ontius," Kim suggested.

"It's hard to tell, but whoever it was, he, or they, did not spare Antium the torture of his own whip," Migroni said. "Look at the marks on his body."

The men looked, but not for long. They turned away from the gruesome sight, leaving Antium hanging by the whip that was looped loosely about his neck.

"Look!" Kib shouted. "There's a shelter over there." He was pointing across the clearing at the west edge of the trees.

All five young men rushed over, glad to leave behind the horrible sight that dangled from a tree branch by a strip of braided leather. Jath was the first to spot the next body. It lay bloated and purple in the center of a bed of red and blue flowers near the front of the shelter.

"Zermanah," Migroni announced at Jath's inquiring look.

"That leaves only Shecum," Jath concluded grimly as he approached the open front of the shelter. "Maybe Lariah and Ontius were never here."

Maybe Antium . . ." He stopped without completing his thought as he spotted something.

"Lariah!" he cried as he dove into the shelter, emerging with her blow-tube in his hand. "She was here! Amoz did find her. She must be with Shecum. That explains why Amoz became confused," he cried. "She and Ontius must both be with Shecum."

Uri took Jath by both shoulders and said sternly, "Calm down, Jath. We'll find her, but we've got to be very cautious. We've got to think this thing out carefully."

"Okay, but first, Amoz has got to search again. He found her once. I know he did. And he can find her again. She can't be too far," Jath insisted.

Amoz had landed on a branch that protruded from the front of the shelter's roof. Jath reached up and coaxed the parrot onto his forearm. Then he said in pleading, pathetic tones, "Go, Amoz. Go find Lariah."

"Lariah," Amoz echoed, and he flew away.

A search of the area around the shelter soon produced Ontius' empty sack in a bed of yellow flowers. "Everything he had in the sack is broken," Jath said. "Destroyed."

"His quiver is here, but his bow and his arrows are gone," Migroni noted.

"And so is Lariah's sack," Jath said as he rose to his feet clutching a small gold coin. "I wonder what Ontius needed this for," he mused. Then he flung it violently into the trees.

"Calm down, Jath," Uri reminded him again.

"Calm down? I can't calm down! Not until I find Ontius. This is all his fault! If only he weren't so stubborn and . . . crazy! Lariah would have been safe with the rest of us."

* * *

"You are safe now, Lariah, so quit bawling!" Shecum ordered in frustration. Ever since she had regained consciousness just as he was finishing the arduous task of hoisting Antium into the tree with his own whip, Lariah had not stopped crying.

He couldn't understand why. She was unconscious during the fight in which he had finally overpowered Antium. She had not witnessed him turn on Antium with his own whip and inflict the punishment he so much deserved. Nevertheless, when he left Antium swinging from the tree with the whip tied around his neck, she had told him, "You can't do that, Shecum!"

"Antium got only what he deserved, Lariah. Why, he even struck you with the whip," he had reasoned. "He lived a brutal life. It is only fitting that he die a brutal death."

Even after so carefully explaining all that to her, she still cried, and it made him very angry. He was also nervous, wondering if one or more of Samuel's people were prowling about this part of the island in search of Lariah. Twice, he would have sworn that he heard someone calling Lariah's name.

She had picked up her sack of woven grass before following him. That angered him, for it slowed them down as he led her south toward the falls. He had headed that way, for he knew he could easily find his way from there back to the waiting canoe by following the rim of the mountain, then descending to the jungle below using the same route he and Zermanah had taken.

When they reached the rocky ledge where the stream plunged over the edge of the mountain, he stopped to rest, for he was very tired after the fight with Antium. When he was ready to go on, he turned to Lariah. "Leave the sack!" he ordered. "It is slowing you down."

"No," she said stubbornly.

He snatched it away from her. "We don't need it," he said, dumping its contents onto the rock. A brightly painted gourd clattered to the ground, and Shecum stomped on it. "Junk!" he grumbled. As the gourd cracked open, gleaming gold and silver jewelry scattered across the rock.

"You're rich!" Shecum exclaimed in greedy delight as he dropped to his knees and began to scoop the precious items into a pile. "I'm rich," he corrected himself a moment later.

"It belonged to my mother, Shecum. It is of no value to anyone but me," she protested.

"This is gold and silver, Lariah. And there are precious jewels here. They are worth a great deal. We are rich, I tell you! Is there more in these other gourds?" he demanded.

"No," she said flatly.

He did not believe her and stomped another gourd until it broke, spilling a variety of seeds among the pieces of jewelry. He cursed. "Seeds? Why would you carry seeds, Lariah?"

His answer called out from above him. "Lariah."

"Amoz," Lariah squealed, bursting to her feet. Amoz perched on her shoulder and began to rub his head fondly against her cheek.

"I should have known. That stupid bird," Shecum said in disgust. "Let me get my hands on him, and I'll wring his pretty neck."

Shecum advanced menacingly toward her, and Lariah backed toward the trees that lined the rocky ledge. "Give me that bird. We can't be packing food for him. We must travel quickly."

"Fly, Amoz," she commanded sharply, and Amoz left his perch and rose gracefully into the air above them.

"I ought to choke you for that, Lariah," Shecum threatened. But instead, he swung his bow off his shoulder. "I'll shoot him right out of the air," he said smugly as he bent over his quiver which still lay on the ground.

Lariah reached inside her skirt while Shecum was selecting an arrow. Glancing over at her, he let out a startled gasp, for in her left hand she held a bloodstained knife. He recognized it instantly as the one with which she had fought Antium.

"Put down the bow, Shecum," she said in a voice trembling with emotion. "I will not let you hurt Amoz."

"You're crazy, woman!" he exclaimed, dropping his bow and arrow.

"That's better," she said.

Shecum was very angry now, and he yanked his sword from its sheath.

Lariah looked at him and knew she could not fight him. "I'll throw the knife down if you'll put your sword back," she offered. "I just didn't want Amoz hurt."

Shecum laughed again. "Throw it down, then."

She reluctantly dropped her knife, and he put his sword back. "Now, kick it over to me."

She obeyed, and Shecum bent and picked up her knife. "So, you hid it beneath your skirt," he said. "Poor old Antium. He really let you outsmart him. I think I'll just keep this," he said as he thrust it beneath his belt. "It's made of quality steel."

Amoz landed and perched on Lariah's shoulder again. Shecum eyed him for a moment, then said, "I really don't like that bird." He bent and picked up his bow and arrow again. "Hold still, or I might accidentally hit you," he said menacingly as he fitted the arrow and pulled the string back.

"No!" she screamed.

"Lariah!" someone called out, and Shecum knew it was not the parrot, for he was looking straight at Amoz, and the bird had not called her name.

"Lariah, help me!" the voice called again. It was weak and barely discernable, but it was a human voice.

"Who was that?" Shecum demanded, relaxing the string on his bow and looking at Lariah for an answer.

"It came from over there," she said calmly and pointed toward the edge of the cliff.

"Impossible!" he said. But Shecum knew it was possible, for he had heard the voice above the roar of the plunging falls. He dropped to his knees, and dragging his bow and arrow, he began to crawl forward.

Lariah's heart was pounding. She was almost overwhelmed with joy! The voice she had heard was not only real, but it was the voice of . . . no, that couldn't be. But it was. It could only be the voice of . . . Ontius!

Shecum peered over the edge of the cliff. "There's someone down there," he said in disbelief.

To Lariah's absolute horror, Shecum slid his bow forward and prepared to reverse the incredible miracle that was happening to her. He was going to shoot a man she had believed was dead and had grieved for as dead, but a man who was very much alive. Her father.

The darts, she thought, and tore at the folds of her skirt. Shecum was too busy to notice what she was doing as he attempted, in his awkward position, to get his bow ready to shoot again. She selected a dart and let her skirt fall shut. Then she approached Shecum.

"Stay back," he shouted.

"That is my father down there," she pleaded with Shecum.

"No it's not. Antium said that he . . ." Shecum began as Lariah inched closer.

"Antium lied!" she said fiercely.

"Get away!" Shecum screamed, but it was too late.

Lariah hurled the poison dart at his naked back where it stuck. Shecum dropped his bow and arrow over the cliff in his haste to pull the dart out. But Lariah had intentionally thrown it in that one area in the center of the back below the shoulder blades where it was the most difficult to reach. He roared in rage, and then he slowly relaxed as the poison began to do its work.

As soon as Shecum was unconscious, Lariah pulled him back from the edge of the rock and crawled out there herself. "Father, are you really down there?" she called.

"I'm here, Lariah." As he spoke his head appeared. He was sitting on a small shelf that was almost entirely hidden from above. On one side of it, a small tree grew. Its roots were anchored in a deep crack.

"But you fell, Father. I thought that—" she began.

"The tree broke my fall, and I was able to drag myself to this little spot. I guess God is teaching me a lesson for being so mean and rebellious. I hope I've learned it now, because I'm terribly hungry and ready to get up there with you," he said.

"You must be thirsty, too," she suggested.

"No, there is water here. It seeps through a crack in the rock. You will need someone to help me up from here, Lariah."

"We'll help," a voice called out from behind her. She knew that voice! The sound of it thrilled her to the core.

"Father, it is Jath," she said happily. "We'll save you now." As soon as she had delivered her message of hope to Ontius, she backed away from the edge, leaped to her feet, and flew into Jath's waiting arms.

"I found her!" Jath called loudly a few moments later as she stood with her head against his chest, letting the tears flow.

"Who are you calling to?" she asked.

"Uri, Kim, Kib, and Migroni."

"Migroni!" she said in alarm, jerking her head back and staring at Jath in disbelief.

"Yes, Migroni. He is one of us now."

Just then, Uri appeared from the forest. "Who is this?" he asked, pointing to the figure on the ground.

"Shecum," Jath said.

"What's the matter with him?"

"I think Lariah must still have her darts," he said with a grin.

"But we found the blow-tube."

"That's only for long distances," Lariah explained. "I can do just fine without it when I need to."

"Why, will you look at that!" Migroni exclaimed as he followed Kim and Kib onto the rocky ledge. "If it isn't Shecum himself."

"Tie him up with something," Jath said. "This poison of Lariah's is a little weak, and he'll be coming out of it before too long."

"Jath, my father is down there," she said, pointing to the edge of the cliff. "He needs help getting back up."

"I guessed he must be, but what's he doing over the edge?" he asked curiously. "That could be very dangerous."

"It was Antium," Lariah explained breathlessly. "He tried to kill him. In fact, until just a few minutes ago, I believed he was dead. But a tree broke his fall, and he is alive!"

"Let me have a look," Jath said, and he crawled to the edge. "Ontius," he called down.

"I'm right here, Jath."

"We'll find a way to get you up from there," he promised. "Kim, Kib, Uri, and Migroni are all here."

"Migroni!"

"That's exactly what Lariah said," Jath chuckled. "He's on our side now. Would you like us to drop some food down to you? Then you'll be strong enough for the climb up."

"Please do," Ontius said gratefully.

Jath pulled back from the edge and stood up. He whispered to Lariah, "He seems different, like he's okay."

Lariah smiled. "He is. He is fine now. He even told Antium that I had chosen you and that we had his blessing."

Jath blushed, and Lariah reached up and brushed her lips against his. "I hope it's still okay with you," she said with a grin.

"Of course it is," he said brusquely.

She could tell she had embarrassed him. "I'm sorry," she said apologetically. "I've just missed you so much. Anyway, enough of that. Let's get Father some food, and then we need to figure out how to get him up from there."

"We can use the whip," Migroni said in his low, soft voice.

"The whip?" Jath asked in surprise.

"Yes, if he's not too far down, we can lower the whip and pull him back up. You know, Antium's whip."

Jath remembered where it was. Overcoming his revulsion, he said, "Of course. I'll go and get it. Will you help me? We'll have to lower his—"

"Jath," Uri interrupted. "Maybe I should go after Samuel and Gadoni and the others. The danger is over now, you know. They could join us here, and then we can all return to the other side of the island together."

"Yes," Jath sighed, "the invasion is over. We have no more enemies. While you go after them, Migroni and I will get Antium's whip. Kim? Kib? Help Lariah gather some food and drop it down to her father. Then let's get back to the others."

CHAPTER 21

Jath was in a rush to get the whip and return to Lariah. She had fared well on her own, but now he wanted to do something for her that she could not do for herself. Getting her father safely up from his precarious little perch was one thing she could not do.

He chatted with Migroni as they walked, thinking how much like Samuel and Gadoni they must appear. He smiled at the thought. His father and Gadoni had been best of friends for many years. He hoped he and this young Lamanite could be friends, too.

Jath could smell the fragrance of the clearing before he ever got there. What a beautiful place it was. He had also been impressed with the magnificence of the falls and the jungle and ocean view the ledge provided. He had said nothing to Lariah about it, for it must be a place of unspeakable horror to her. Maybe someday the nightmare would die away, and together they could enjoy coming here.

He entered the meadow a step behind Migroni. The young Lamanite yelped as if he'd been shot with an arrow. Jath's heart lurched and he leaped beside Migroni, who was staring in horror, pointing at the flowering tree where Antium had been left hanging. There was no one there!

Antium's body was gone!

Jath remembered with a jolt what his father and Gadoni had so often called the first Antium, the one he and Gadoni had been forced to battle for many years back in the area in and around Zarahemla. They laughed about it now, but Jath found no humor in it as he looked in horror at the whip hanging empty in the flowering tree.

Ghost!

That was what they called Antium the Elder. "That old ghost Antium," Samuel liked to say when he was telling stories of the old days.

"He is a ghost!" Migroni said with a voice that cracked with terror.

"I was just thinking that same thing," Jath said. "Maybe there is a logical explanation. There has to be one! We better go see. The whip probably broke, and Antium's body is lying in the grass below the tree where we can't see it."

"That whip would never break," Migroni said, refusing to take another step forward. "It was braided from the finest leather that could be found on Hagoth's island."

"Come on, we'll see for ourselves," Jath said with bravado that he did not feel.

Reluctantly Migroni followed as Jath led the way slowly across the meadow. Jath's eyes searched the ground below the tree, expecting at any moment to be close enough to see Antium's mutilated body lying in a heap in the tall grass and colorful flowers.

There was no such thing as close enough. Antium the Younger simply was not there!

"He was dead!" Migroni exclaimed as he turned back toward the forest.

Jath grabbed the young Lamanite by the arm to keep him from bolting. "Wait, Migroni. Think about it for a moment. We never did get very close to the tree, only close enough to see who it was hanging there. And I do remember noticing that the noose looked very loose. And that one eye, the one that was not swollen shut, it seemed almost like it was watching me the whole time we were there," he reasoned.

"You mean he was not dead? Shecum left him hanging there alive?" Migroni asked doubtfully.

"That's exactly what I mean. He must be close by, for he was hurt badly, that much was very clear." As Jath spoke, he approached the hanging tree. He stopped beside the dangling whip. He reached out and took hold of it. "Look, Migroni. It has been cut!"

"Zermanah?" Migroni asked.

"No. He's dead, Migroni. I got a good look at him," Jath said, trying his very best to speak with calmness as his heart raced and his hands shook in fright.

"Then who cut him down?" Migroni demanded. "Don't tell me he did it himself."

"I don't think he could have done that," Jath said as he looked closer at the noose. Shecum had tied the narrow end of the whip around Antium's neck. He had looped the handle over the tree limb, and then, after pulling Antium up, he had wound it around the limb so it would not slip. There was, however, no knot.

Jath examined the cuts. "This is strange. It is not a clean cut. This has only been cut part of the way through the leather. It tore loose the rest of the way. Look, Migroni, and you can see what I mean."

Migroni reluctantly inspected the whip. He looked about them nervously as he did so, as if he expected Antium to suddenly appear. Gradually he relaxed. "You're right," he acknowledged at last. He studied the whip thoughtfully for a moment more before letting go and turning to Jath.

"You know, Antium had a habit of snaking the end of his whip around things. He could pull a sword from a man's hand if he tried. Didn't I hear Lariah telling you that he had done that to Ontius, and that he had flung his sword over the edge?"

"Yes, she did say that," Jath recalled. He and Lariah had not had much time to talk, but she had explained briefly to him what had happened to her father. Now it made sense.

Except for one thing.

"How could anyone, even someone as mean and tough as Antium, live through the injuries he had received and the torture that Shecum must have put him through?" Jath asked Migroni.

"It seems impossible to me," Migroni said as he tensed again and began looking fearfully about them.

"Here, help me get this whip down, then we'll see if we can spot Antium before we go back and help Ontius," Jath suggested.

It only took them a few moments to uncoil the whip from the tree branch. Jath coiled it neatly before letting his eyes sweep the ground below the tree. The grass and flowers were bent, creating a clear trail. Antium had dragged himself across the meadow to the stream. The bank was muddy and bloody where Antium had entered, but Jath could not see where he had gotten himself out on the other side.

They walked upstream for a few paces but did not find either Antium or any place where he might have left the stream. They looked downstream but again they could see no place where he had crawled out of the cool water. The vegetation soon became too thick for them to proceed farther without a lot of work, and they did not have time for that if they were going to get Ontius back on the ledge.

Although Jath was anxious to get back to Lariah, Migroni was equally anxious to find Antium. Finally, Jath said, "Migroni, Antium may not have been dead in the tree, but he probably is now. If not, he soon will be. He was injured too badly to ever survive. We can look for his body later. Ontius is alive and needs our help."

Migroni slowly nodded in agreement, but Jath could sense that he was far from convinced that Antium was dead. But they gave up the hunt and returned quickly to the rocky point where Lariah was waiting anxiously with Kim and Kib.

"Was it difficult getting Antium's body down?" she asked as Jath laid the whip on the rock. "You must have taken time to bury him. You were surely gone a long time."

Jath looked at Migroni, who was still shook up. Jath didn't know what to say, but Lariah expected an answer. "Well, was it just awful?" she pressed.

Finally, Jath took a deep breath and spoke the truth. "He wasn't there, Lariah."

Gasps from Kim and Kib were almost as loud as the one from Lariah. Quickly, he explained what they had found, even showing them the cuts on the whip. "He did jerk the sword from Father's hand," Lariah said. "That might have cut it."

"And he jerked mine away, too," Shecum retorted.

Jath spun toward him. He had temporarily forgotten that they had a captive. Shecum was bound and lying on his side near the trees. His face was a perfect picture of terror. "He'll kill us all!" Shecum whined. "He will find us and kill us!"

"He will do no such thing," Jath said bravely. "You left him in rather bad shape."

"I thought I left him dead!" Shecum hissed. "That was what I intended and what Antium deserved. Did you look for him?"

"Yes, but we couldn't find him." Jath turned back to Lariah and the twins.

"Right now, we have a task to accomplish," he said. "Let's see if what is left of the whip will reach Ontius," he suggested calmly.

It reached, but barely. "Ontius, can you hold onto this whip while we pull you up?" Jath called down.

"I'm sorry. I am too weak," he called back up. "You will have to find some other way."

Jath pulled the whip up and tied the small end around his waist. "Jath, what are you doing?" Lariah demanded with wide eyes.

"Kim, Kib, and Migroni can lower me down there, and I can tie this to Ontius' waist. Then maybe I can give him a boost while they pull him up," he explained.

"But what if you fall?" she asked as her green eyes misted with tears.

"Me fall? And leave you again? Not a chance, Lariah," he said in a feeble attempt at humor.

After the whip was secure, he stepped near the edge of the gigantic drop-off and looked down. If Lariah were not here watching him, he knew he would never have the courage to go through with it. But she was and he would.

"It's not long enough, Jath," Migroni observed.

"It is if you lean out over the edge about the time I get down there," Jath said uncertainly.

"I don't think that's wise. In fact, I don't believe it's possible," Migroni argued.

"Let's add something to it," Kim suggested.

Kib was eyeing Lariah's sack. "Lariah," he said. "When we helped you put your things back in that sack of yours, there were several dresses. Would you be too upset if we cut one of them up and used it to add length to the whip? I think it would only take one."

She quickly grabbed the sack. "Not if it means saving my father and making it more safe for Jath," she said. "Anyway, I have plenty more at home, now that we will be going back there."

"If Antium doesn't get you first!" Shecum called out with a frightening shrill.

"Be quiet," Jath ordered, advancing toward the captive invader. "If you don't, I might be tempted to try this whip out on you."

Shecum must have decided that Jath was serious, for his mouth shut with a snap. It was good he did, for the look of terror he had just brought back into Lariah's eyes made Jath angry enough that he was quite sure he could do it if necessary.

The skirt they selected, when torn in wide strips and twisted tightly, made a stout rope. When they were tied together and added to the whip, Jath was ready for the descent.

Well, not quite ready, he admitted to himself, but he was willing. "Let's try it," he said.

"I will help hold the rope," Lariah volunteered.

"We can handle it," Kib said gently.

"I'm sure you can, but I just want to make sure Jath and Father have every advantage we can give them," she said with resolve.

Jath went down without incident. To his surprise, Ontius shed great tears of gratitude as he stepped beside him on the narrow shelf. They sat as far back as they could while Jath secured the whip around Ontius' waist.

"Okay, hold on to the whip while they pull from up above. It will only take a minute," Jath assured him.

With his own back against the vertical wall of the ledge, Jath supported Ontius as the older man stood and grabbed the whip with a weak hand. "Are you ready, Ontius?" he asked.

"I'm ready."

"Pull!" Jath called out.

Slowly and painfully, Ontius ascended, but he did not complain. Jath discovered that he could be of no help. If he had tried to step out to where he could push, he would almost certainly plunge to a horrible death, so he let the others do the work.

He was relieved when Lariah called down. "We got him up, Jath. Thank you. You have saved his life. Oh Jath, I love you!"

Jath felt a large smile cover his face. It was all worth it. "And I love you, too," he called up to her. "Now, get me up from here!"

In a few moments, the whip descended again. Jath tied it around his waist and said, "Pull."

They pulled. Going up was going to be much slower than coming down had been. "Hurry," he called up. "This is spooky."

"We are," Lariah answered him.

After he had only gone a short distance, his upward progress stopped.

"What's the matter?" he called up at them.

"The rope is snagged," Kib shouted. "Just give us a minute and we'll get it loose."

The minute became several. Jath began to panic. "Please hurry, I am not a bird."

"I can't reach it, Jath," Kib answered.

"Then pull harder. It will probably come loose."

It broke!

Jath's heart leaped to his throat as he fell. He heard Lariah scream just as his back hit the same tree that had arrested Ontius' fall, and his arms flailed about for something to grasp onto. It appeared unlikely that he would find anything in time, for he was slowly slipping from the trunk. Even though his feet reached the ledge and rested there, he expected at any moment to plunge down the gigantic drop-off that awaited him.

When he had almost given up hope of saving himself, Jath's hand struck a limb, and he gripped it with all his strength. For a moment, he hung suspended with his feet barely touching the edge of the ledge and his arm stretched above him, holding onto the limb. He inched his feet over until his back was again touching the leaning trunk of the tree, then he twisted violently, flopping onto the trunk with his belly down. From there, it was just a matter of easing his way along the tree until he was safely on the tiny ledge.

"Jath?" several frightened voices called down over the cliff.

"I'm all right," he answered. The truth was, he had managed to get to safety on the ledge, but he was still scared to death.

"Oh, thank goodness," Lariah said with a sigh of relief. "I have never prayed so hard and so fast in my life."

"I'm glad God was listening," Jath said humorously.

"Jath." It was Kib this time. "We'll fix the rope and try again. It got caught on a sharp piece of rock that nearly cut it in two. We'll try it a little to the west next time. Now, you'll have to throw up your end of the rope . . . uh . . . of the whip."

Jath untied the whip from around his waist and tossed it up. Kib caught it on the first grab. "Good. We'll hurry," he said cheerfully.

The next attempt was better, despite Jath's wildly beating heart and sweating palms. When he was safely stretched out on the rock on his belly, tempted to kiss it in relief, Lariah dropped beside him and buried her face in his neck.

Ontius recovered slowly, but by nightfall, he was feeling better, and Jath was relieved to see that his mind and attitude remained good. "We'll spend the night right here," Lariah announced. "Father needs plenty of rest before he tries to go anywhere."

No one argued, and they made a modest camp a few feet into the trees. Thoughts of Antium were on Jath's mind, but he said nothing, and they rested quite well that night. The next morning, they decided to await the arrival of Samuel and the others right where they were.

"This is as good a place as any to wait for them," Jath said after Lariah expressed a horror of the meadow where the body of Zermanah lay and near where, most likely, the body of Antium also lay.

* * *

As the time of the likely arrival of at least some of the islanders neared, Migroni became increasingly nervous. He was fearful of their response to him, although Jath continually assured him that everything would be fine. Nevertheless, at the sound of cheerful voices approaching through the trees, Migroni turned to Jath and said, "I'll just slip out of sight until you call for me. If I am not welcome, I'll disappear. If I am, I'll come and meet the others."

He hoped he would be welcomed, for it was still his desire to meet Gadoni and learn from him why he had accepted the Nephite ways and the Nephite God. He wanted to believe as Gadoni did, and maybe, if he spent some time with him, he could learn to do so.

After hiding himself in the bushes and trees, he listened as Samuel and Gadoni greeted Jath and the others. He heard Ontius' plea to them for forgiveness for his stubbornness. "I almost paid with my life and the life of my lovely daughter, as well," he said to them. "I have learned a very hard lesson, and I thank God that I have been given an opportunity to make amends."

Not only did Samuel and Gadoni quickly forgive him, but so did most of the others who had come with them. Then he heard the voice of Uri ask, "Jath, where is Migroni? I told the others how he helped us. Gadoni and Samuel are anxious to meet him."

"He was not sure he would be welcome," Jath said.

"Of course he is welcome!" Samuel thundered enthusiastically.

"I want to meet him," a little girl's voice cried.

"You will, Maribel," Samuel answered affectionately.

"Find Migroni, Jath," another voice spoke up. "I am anxious to meet him."

Migroni recognized the voice of Gadoni and marveled at the sincerity in his voice.

Maybe it was time to join them, he thought, and took a deep breath. But then another voice, the one that had spoken against him before, said, "I'm still not so sure it is a good idea to befriend one of the invaders. I think, if we are to preserve peace on this island, we must hang both Shecum and Migroni. Then our families will be safe."

Migroni's heart sank as that one dissenting voice dashed his hopes for forgiveness and complete acceptance. He was aware of the argument that followed Jarium's remarks, but he had heard enough. Slowly, quietly, he slipped from the bushes that he had been hiding in, and moved quietly away, determined to find a canoe and leave the island, taking his chances on the open sea.

He had not gone far when he became aware of footsteps behind him. He dove behind a large shrub and crawled beneath it, curling his legs under him to hide himself completely. Then he peered out between the leaves. First Jath appeared, studying the ground beneath him. Then Uri came into sight.

"We've got to find him," Jath said urgently. "I'm sure he heard what Jarium said and left, but Jarium is the only one that feels any reservation at all. And Father will take care of that in time. Jarium is really a good man, just a little hot-headed."

"Jath," another voice called from somewhere out of Migroni's limited vision.

"We're right here, Limre."

"Have you found Migroni?" the one called Limre asked, and Migroni thought he had never heard such a pretty voice. He wondered who she was.

He did not wonder for long, for she said, "Father is concerned, and so is Samuel, that Antium may still be alive."

"You tell Father and Gadoni that Antium can't possibly hurt anyone. If he is still alive, and I doubt it, he is certainly in no condition to do anything to anyone," Jath assured her.

"All right, but they are worried about you two," she scolded mildly.

"Quit worrying about us," Uri said. "We'll find Migroni and persuade him to come back with us. Then we'll return and look for Antium's body. By the way, do they know that you are out here alone?"

"I don't think so," the sweet voice said. "I'll go right back. Please, don't be long."

"We won't be," Jath assured her. "Migroni is somewhere near."

It became quiet as Jath and Uri studied the ground. "I can't see his tracks anywhere," Jath complained, "but I know he came this way."

"The trees here are so thick overhead and it is so shady and dark that we may be missing something," Uri reasoned.

"Migroni! It is Jath," Jath suddenly called out. "If you can hear me, come here. We need to talk."

He was almost persuaded to leave the protecting cover of his shrub, but before he could move, the one called Limre stepped into view beside Jath. Migroni's heart stopped. Her skin was dark, like his own, and without a doubt, she was the most beautiful creature he had ever seen. He knew she would be the daughter of Gadoni!

"Call him again," Limre said earnestly. "We can't leave him alone. He is a Lamanite, like Father, and—"

"And like you," Jath broke in with a grin.

"Yes, and like me," she agreed.

"Migroni!" Uri called out.

Migroni was too stunned to answer. With his heart in his throat, he could not take his eyes off Limre as she stood in the deep shade of the jungle and looked anxiously about her.

"Let's go back to where we lost his tracks," Jath said. "We can't let him get away. We just can't."

The two young men moved out of view together, but Limre did not move. "Are you coming, Limre?" Uri called.

"In a moment. I'll call for Migroni myself. Maybe he will hear me," she said.

"You think you can shout louder than me or Jath?" Uri asked with a laugh. "I don't think so, but try if you must. Then catch up with us. We'll be right over there."

"My voice is not as deep as yours," she said with a chuckle that made Migroni's spine tingle with excitement. "Maybe it will carry a little farther."

Then she turned and shouted, "Migroni!"

He was still so astonished at seeing a Lamanite girl, and one so pretty at that, that he simply could not find the strength or the courage to make his presence known.

Then she really shocked him as she faced the very bush under which he was hiding and said softly, "You can come out now, Migroni. I won't bite you."

He hesitated. She could not possibly know where he was.

"Please, Migroni. I know you are in there," she pleaded.

Then Migroni began to laugh. He could not help himself. And Limre, as she parted the heavy, broad leaves and took his hand, also laughed. As he stumbled to his feet, their eyes met.

Then, with a move as natural as life itself, their lips met, their hearts welded together, and a wave of unspeakable happiness swept over the two young Lamanites like the sea as it rolled over the sands of the beaches of this island paradise.

Migroni and Limre were in love.

CHAPTER 22

Jath looked at Limre and Migroni with surprise as the young couple approached him, bringing the search to an end. Her face was aglow, and her teeth sparkled when she smiled. "Well, well. It looks like it took a girl's charm to find you, Migroni," Jath chuckled.

Migroni grinned, and Jath studied him for a moment. Then he turned to Uri. "He couldn't have been far from where we left her, Uri. I wonder how she did it."

As Jath spoke, Migroni's arm encircled Limre's slim waist. "She promised to protect me if Jarium decides I am worthy of a noose."

"You can count on her," Uri promised.

"And once you saw her, even the threat of a hanging was not enough to keep you hidden," Jath said with a chuckle.

Migroni gazed at Limre, and she laid her head against his shoulder. "Once I saw him," she said boldly, "I would not let him leave."

"Well, we better get back and break the news to Gadoni," Uri joked. "He can be one stern Lamanite when it comes to his daughter."

Over half of the islanders had followed Uri back from their hiding place on the mountain that day. With the single exception of Jarium, they all welcomed Migroni warmly. All Jarium needed was a little time.

Laishita fussed over Migroni like he was her own son. Gadoni shook his hand somberly and stood back to assess both Migroni and his daughter, Limre.

Only a blind man could miss the affection that bound the young Lamanites together. Gadoni was not blind, but he was pleased. Jath was sure of that, although the sturdy Lamanite said nothing to that effect.

Ophera, who was standing beside Samuel, was close enough to Jath and Lariah that they overheard her say, "Samuel, I worried over nothing, I see. Limre has found herself a young man."

"I believe he is a good one, Ophera. Oh, he was misguided at first, but we must forgive him of that. What he used to be like is not important. What matters is what he is like now and what he will become."

"Samuel, I believe that God led him here for a purpose," Ophera said softly. "Do you?"

Samuel smiled at his lovely wife. "I do believe that. God knows the hearts of all men, and he certainly knows the heart of Migroni. Yes, something special will come from the uniting of those two, something very special," he said with a faraway look in his eyes.

If Samuel knew what that something special was, Jath was sure he would not say. He knew his father well, and some things he kept to himself. One thing was certain, though, and that was that God approved of the love that had so instantly blossomed between Limre and Migroni. Jath could only hope and believe that the Lord also approved of the love that he and Lariah shared.

A sudden shrill cry of terror split the air. Maribel, Jath's little sister, had been standing beside Samuel and Ophera. But now she was gone!

"Maribel!" Samuel cried at the very instant of his daughter's scream.

"Father!" she called from somewhere near the head of the falls.

Jath bolted as quickly as his father did. Together they left the trees and dashed onto the ledge. The sight that met them there sent ice through Jath's veins. Shecum had been left unattended but securely bound when Limre had announced Migroni's return. Now he lay beside the falls, still bound, but dangerously near the edge of the drop-off. Beside him, with his one good arm holding Maribel tightly, was Antium the Younger!

"Stop right there, Samuel!" he rasped. "And you, too, Jath."

"Let go of her!" Samuel commanded.

"On one condition," Antium said with a sneer that did nothing to improve his hideous, mutilated face.

"And what is that?"

"You and Gadoni must atone for the death of my father. You killed him! I have waited my whole life for this day, and I will not be denied my revenge."

"Atone?" Samuel asked. "But we didn't kill your father. He was strangled by a snake."

"But you *were* there!" Antium said hoarsely. "And in some way you led him to his death! Now you must die."

Gadoni stepped forward to stand beside Samuel. "We are both here. And you have come all this way for nothing. It is as Samuel said. Your father did not die at our hands, although he tried enough times to take our lives."

Gadoni's words only enraged Antium further. "You lie! My father was a great man," Antium howled.

"Father," cried Maribel. "Help me. I'm afraid."

"Do something, Jath!" Shecum cried out at that moment.

Antium's attention was momentarily distracted by his disloyal follower. He turned an ominous gaze toward Shecum. "You beat me and left me for dead," he said slowly, "but I did not die."

Indeed, although Antium was badly crippled, he was very much alive. With the life of little Maribel in his hands, Samuel thought Antium had never been more dangerous than he was at that moment.

But it was Shecum's life that was now threatened. "My whip!" Antium called. "Give me my whip!"

No one moved. Casting a dark look at them, Antium grinned evilly and then suddenly swung Maribel until she was almost at the edge of the cliff. "The whip, or she goes over!"

They gave Antium the whip.

He held it in his fist and glared at Shecum. The combination of his glare, the whip, and the very fact that he had survived Shecum's punishment were more than Shecum could stand. While Antium paused to secure Maribel between his knees, freeing his hand to use the whip, Shecum's anxious attempts to free himself brought him to the very edge of the drop-off.

"Be careful, Shecum!" Samuel warned.

But his warning went unheeded as Shecum twisted to avoid the whip. He did not live to cheer about it, however. He slipped over the edge of the drop-off, and no chance tree or small outcropping of rock broke his fall.

Antium laughed. "Now, Samuel. It is your turn. No one ever crosses Antium the Younger and avoids the sting of the whip. You are first, and Gadoni is next. Then I will decide what to do about your little girl."

Samuel tried to reason with him. "Antium, this is insane. No matter what you do to me or Gadoni, you cannot win."

"I will win when you and your Lamanite friend are dead," Antium said calmly.

"I will gladly die," Samuel said, "if you will spare my daughter."

Antium shook his head and opened his mouth to say something. It did not get said, for at that moment his terrible eye grew wide and he began to sway dangerously. A small dart was embedded in the very center of his forehead.

"Jath! Get Maribel!" Lariah cried.

But Jath was too slow.

Motivated by a parent's love, Samuel was halfway there by the time his son had even started to move. A moment later, Samuel held the trembling child in his arms. Still another moment later, he passed her to her mother. Ophera, tears streaming down her face, soothed Maribel. "It is all right now, Maribel. You are safe. Antium cannot ever touch you again."

Seeing that his sister was safe and Antium was unconscious from the effects of the poison dart, Jath pushed through the crowd just as Lariah walked into the trees. She carried her blow-tube in her right hand. Though her hand was still badly bruised and swollen, she was able to hold the bamboo rod.

"How did you do it with your hand so swollen, Lariah? Your shot was perfect."

"Migroni held the blow-tube for me," she said softly.

"Well . . . ah . . . thank you," Jath said, unable to find words that would more fully express the gratitude he felt.

He was ashamed, for once more Lariah had done something he had been unable to do himself. His own act to save her father could have well been accomplished by someone else. Lariah had done so much and he had done so little!

It doesn't matter, Jath told himself firmly. *What does matter is that God is watching over us all.* The Lord had restored peace to this little island. Jath, Lariah, and all the others were only tools in His hands.

Seeing a strange look on Jath's face, Lariah paused uncomfortably. But when he suddenly smiled at her and held out his arms, she happily stepped into them.

"Now we can all live in peace," she said, smiling deeply into Jath's eyes.

That was what life was all about on this island: love and peace.

* * *

Antium did not regain consciousness. He died late that afternoon, and they buried him alongside Zermanah in a single grave beside the meadow. The next morning, when Jath awoke, Samuel, Migroni, and Gadoni were gone from the camp near the falls. "They said to tell you that they went to the flowering meadow," his mother said.

"They wanted you to come, but I would not let them awaken you. You needed your rest after all you have been through."

"Oh, Mother," he said and kissed her lightly on the cheek.

"Go now," she said. "I think they will need your help."

Jath found them a few minutes later. They were busy piling big rocks on the grave of Antium and Zermanah. "Why are you doing that?" he asked.

"Because we want to make sure Antium stays in there," Gadoni answered without cracking a smile.

Jath got the feeling that Gadoni really meant it, and he pitched in and helped until the grave was a huge mound of the largest rocks the four of them could carry.

Antium the Younger had obtained his piece of the island, but what a terrible price he had paid for a very, very small portion.

* * *

After Gadoni baptized Migroni in the sea, Samuel performed the wedding of Limre and Migroni. A great celebration was held, and thanks were given to God for delivering the peace-loving islanders from the clutches of an evil and conspiring band of men. A warm, glowing sun shone down upon them, and little Maribel made a very significant statement.

"Father," she said to Samuel as she ate a plateful of baked breadfruit and yams, "there is no thunder today. I am not afraid anymore."

Indeed, there was no thunder in Samuel's island paradise that day, and no one had any fear anymore.

Baronihah recovered completely in the warm days that followed. The men of the island constructed a new house for him and his family. It was even bigger and better than the old one that had burned. They also built a new house for Ontius and Lariah, placing it very near the one where young Jath lived with his family. It made courting the girl he loved a very convenient thing for them both.

Ontius became a contributing member of their society, putting his ingenious, inventive mind to good use. Under his direction, they constructed tools that made raising crops easier, built traps that caught game humanely but effectively, and even built boats with designs that were much more advanced.

* * *

One year after the invasion, Samuel performed another wedding. The men of the island pitched in and constructed another house. Jath and Lariah moved into it. Not long after that, Ontius, who had been single for so many lonely years, married the island's only widow, and he devoted his energies to raising her children, and before too long, another daughter of his own.

The first child of Migroni and Limre was a daughter. A year later, Limre bore Migroni a son. He was a sturdy child with a quick mind, and was named Samuel after the best friend of his grandfather, Gadoni. Whenever the older Samuel spoke to Ophera of the little brown child, he called him Samuel the Lamanite, and he spoke of a great work the Lord had in mind for the child. And each time, after he had finished speaking to her of little Samuel the Lamanite, he always stood and silently gazed in the direction of the far distant Nephite city of Zarahemla.

ABOUT THE AUTHOR

Writing is something Clair does because he loves it. He has always been an avid reader, and writing was a natural outgrowth of his interest in books. When his children were young, he used to enjoy telling them "make-up stories" before they went to bed. Now he enjoys the same activity with his grandchildren. He values the helpful ideas that his children and their spouses give him on each new book he writes.

If you would like to be updated on Clair's newest releases or correspond with him, please send an e-mail to info@covenant-lds.com. You may also write to him in care of Covenant Communications, P.O. Box 416, American Fork, UT 84003-0416.